Copyright © 2022 Nicholas Oliveri

All Rights Reserved. No part of this book may be reproduced, stored in a retrieval system, or transmitted by any means, electronic, mechanical, photocopying, recording or otherwise without written permission from the author.

Monsters in My Mind

Monsters in My Mind

By Nick Oliveri

To everyone with a monster in their mind

Chapter 1 – Michael

It was one of those days that haunted you. Nothing went terribly wrong, but everything felt eerie, as if the very fabric of my reality and everything I saw, heard, and felt could be blown away by even the faintest breath of wind like a cheap bedsheet from over a science project.

I sat in the back of the class, where the many eyes seldom descended. It was easier that way; I could hide and make no noise and not be seen. That is, at least for a while. Instead of being watched, I could be the one watching. After all, that was where the power lay. That was where any power lay. I could sit back, take notes at my leisure, and just kind of *be*. I could also peer over at Rachel, who was wearing that skimpy white top I loved. She sat in front of and diagonal from me, so in order to catch my gawking, she would have to make an effort to notice. And I knew, easily and fully, she would never make an effort—not for me, anyway.

Ms. Shelgren was short and had hair of fire. We called her "Ms." because that made her relationship status more ambiguous—she liked it that way. She had an angular face and a nose that matched. She always wore cardigans, all muted in color and drab in material. They were thin but oddly cut, as if to hide her younger, sultrier figure behind a thick coat.

"And that is that," she said with her back turned, writing on the board. Ms. Shelgren had a nasal voice that wasn't imposing but was sharp to the ear. "And so," she said, "how many degrees in a triangle?"

The class fell mute, dim—that is, dimmer than it already was. Every person's face became blank as a ghost. The silence simmered for a bit. Ms. Shelgren scanned the crowd. I knew she looked for the kids who didn't look back at her—the unsuspecting ones. But I didn't care. I was going to avoid locking eyes with those piercing emerald lasers. They were eyes you could explore and even see yourself in, but they were daunting all the same.

Then, one brave soul in the middle of the class began to fidget. He was a ginger and had a voice far too deep for his tiny stature and Irish baby face. Jeffrey was his name. He breathed in audibly so the class could hear. It was subtle enough to pass as incidental, but loud enough to give him the subconscious right of way for the question.

"Two hundred and seventy," Jeffrey said. His voice was hoarse and staticky. I wasn't sure if that was correct, and it didn't sound like he was too confident either.

"Wrong," Ms. Shelgren said.

"What a fucking idiot," a voice sneered. I knew that voice very well—it was Beel. Beel was the monster inside my head.

Beel had a scrungy, deep voice that bellowed, echoed. What was odd to me was his cavernous voice didn't reflect what he looked like or, at least, what I *thought* he might look like. I imagined that Beel had slick, black hair that was too long to ignore, with not one lock out of place. He probably wore a pinstripe suit that was perfectly tapered to every inch—every millimeter—of his lean, thirty-something-year-old build. He had spotless, black leather loafers that clacked on the mausoleum floor I liked to imagine he walked on often. He had some wear to his face and the early signs of age setting in, but he was devilishly handsome all the same. And the smell—he smelled of rich mahogany, the classic kind.

"He has the *audacity*," Beel said, pronouncing the first syllable in "audacity" as if it were an *OH*, "to shoot off his ginger mouth just to fall flat on his freckled face. People like that need to wear clown costumes just as a warning to everyone else."

Jeffrey rested his chin on both of his hands and scrunched up a little bit. He let out a sigh. I kept my eyes on Jeffrey and certainly kept them away from the teacher, who continued to scan the room like a hawk for prey.

Ms. Shelgren crossed her arms. "Michael?"

My eyes widened. I shot a glance directly at Ms. Shelgren. Her pupils were small, but her eyes were gaping, green chasms that swallowed me whole. I shuddered. Now, the attention was on me, and the many eyes of the students, even Jeffrey's, descended on the back of the class—onto me. Brown, blue, gray, and of course, green, all washed over me.

"What a bitch," Beel said. "What a resentful little maggot. These sneering kids looking back at you are just waiting for you to screw up. I would call them menaces, but really, they're just impotent problem-seekers."

"Um…" I stammered.

"Now you already sound stupid! You have them all salivating, chomping at the bit. Just get this over with so you can disappear already."

"Three hundred?" I offered.

"Nope. That's not even close, Michael."

"She just wanted to see you fail. That was her only goal, and she achieved it. You look like a fool right now in front of everyone—in front of Rachel."

"One hundred eighty," a girl named Riley said. Her voice was laced with disdain and a haughtiness, like an aristocrat gracing a lucky peasant with a word. She had translucent purple glasses, brunette braids, and a face that was always twisted, like she was constantly thinking or worrying, or both.

"That's right," Ms. Shelgren said. She raised her eyebrows as she did, if slightly.

"She bested you, Michael. She smote you down and put you in your place. Everyone knows you're pathetic, and they *hate* you for it, too. You're going to grow up only to still live in your hometown and go bald early. Why would anyone want *you*?"

I bent my neck down, then glanced around to check for any eyes straying toward my direction. I looked at Rachel. She was fixed on the board, where Ms.

Shelgren was writing out formulas and drawing angles, babbling about numbers. It sounded more like Russian to me.

"Of course she's not looking at you, Mister 'Three Hundred.' Ha! She wants a special type of boy: a non-idiot."

I peered over at Anabelle, who was furiously copying onto her graph paper exactly what Ms. Shelgren was writing. I studied her paper more closely. Lines and numbers and symbols that were more of a mosaic than cohesive notes cluttered the page. When she did happen to write a letter, it was swoopy, bubbly, and neat. After staring some more, I began to notice a flow to her note writing. She caught my eyes, and I looked away immediately. I could see out of my periphery that she was leaning over—to me.

"Hey," Annabelle whispered. Her eyes drilled a hole in the side of my face.

"She wants something from you, Michael, and she knows you'll give it up because you're an *idiot*," Beel hissed.

"What'd you get for number two?" Anabelle asked, still at a low whisper among the scratching pencils in the class.

My neck creaked and pivoted toward her like a rusty gate, stopping at snags in the hinges along the way. I met her eyes once more for a split second, then looked back down at the full page on her desk.

"Go ahead, tell her how much of a failure you are," Beel said, barking out a laugh.

"Um," I said, searching for an answer. In my pause, I could feel her getting impatient, weighing me down and slowing my thoughts. I jumped from possibility to possibility, wondering what she was thinking. I tried not to jerk my body too much or even move at all. But then I thought of how my stillness could come across as rigid, so I sat back in my chair and tried to be cool. I began to sweat, but I hid it at all costs—and I mean *all* costs.

"I'm not there yet," I answered.

"Oh, okay." She turned back around and continued to scrawl some things down before turning toward Tom, probably to ask him the same question.

"Well, you ruined that," Beel said. "Not entirely your fault, though. She knew you didn't have the answer, Michael. She wanted to mock you, to gain power over you. You're sweating because you've been threatened, and it's a credible threat at that."

I shuddered in my own seat. I needed to get out, but walking would have drawn even more attention. My steps would make the slightest noise, and the eyes would be back on me—staring, fixating, leering. I thought about the pros and cons—I could leave and draw attention, or I could stay in my seat and simmer, feeling the weight of everyone's judgments pressing on my frail body like anvils.

I looked at the clock. There were twenty painstaking minutes left in class. The red hand ticked past like it was steeped in a viscous vat of syrup. I started to wonder if it was even moving at all.

"You still have a lot to lose, Michael. But either way, you'll lose," Beel said.

Regardless, I took the chance while it presented itself as the second hand seemed to slow to a halt.

I raised my hand.

"Yes, Michael?"

Beel spoke through gritted teeth, his voice growing louder, "She knows you're up to something, Michael. She knows everything."

"Can I go to the bathroom?"

Rachel looked back at me. It was only for a second, but I saw she did. It didn't even look that disdainful.

"Go ahead," Ms. Shelgren said.

My glutes tightened as I stood up. Slowly. Cautiously. I made the least amount of noise possible, and the worn soles on my shoes helped with that. Still, I caught multiple glares, multiple predators rearing their heads at me. I kept my eyes on the door, careful of the stray backpacks strewn along the perilous path. If I fell, that would be the end of me.

Out in the hall, things were clearer. There were fewer disturbances. It was a clear runway of cheap, lacquered, pink-and-white tile. I had the hallway all to myself. Halfway to the bathroom, though, two girls turned the corner. Upperclassmen. They had on crew neck sweatshirts of colleges of brick and ivory and leggings as tight and revealing as they could be. They didn't look at me, but they giggled a lot.

"They're laughing at you," Beel said. "They would never get with you, and they're laughing at that, too. They're like shadows, Michael… You couldn't even hope to touch them."

Beel's words stung even more because of how calmly he delivered them. He was so objective when he said this. There was ice in his voice. It was professorial, like he had nothing to prove—and really, he didn't. It was a foregone conclusion that he was right. It was foregone that he knew what was best. And besides—who was I, a gangly sophomore, to question that?

I slunk down without slinking too far (because that just wouldn't be cool) and skirted toward the bathroom door. It was heavy and wooden when I pushed it, like a fortress entryway. In a way, it was a fortress—a refuge from the abuse and accusations of my classmates, from the work that had to be done but seldom was.

It was just me in there, so I traipsed into the big handicap stall and locked it. It felt like an open field with no enclosure. Like a blue sky with open air and daisies and dandelions that danced in the breeze. It was quiet. It was like the world stopped.

But Beel didn't. Beel never stopped.

"Stop breathing so loudly, someone could come in and think you're constipated. Your head's already bloated enough, filled with shit that prevents you from getting answers right."

I stayed in there for what seemed like twenty seconds, but it was really ten minutes. I got out and washed my hands without any intruders. The rest of class was more of the same. I twiddled my thumbs, glanced around, and even wrote down an answer to a question—an answer Beel assured me was dead wrong. At times, I didn't know why I even tried, or pretended to try.

After ten long minutes, the class ended. I was never very athletic, nor was I into sports all that much, but when the bell rang, my calves tensed as I sprang to my feet. I twitched for my backpack and slung it on.

"Michael," Ms. Shelgren said, "can I see you for a sec?"

Everyone else was either grabbing their backpacks or already out the door. But enough of them heard—enough of them heard the teacher call my name for my cheeks to turn a shade of maroon. My sweat came faster. I gulped.

"She's going to kick you out of the class, Mike." Beel chuckled. "She hates herself and the drudgery of her kids and job, but she hates you *more*. She may be miserable, but you are worthless, and that's a toxic mixture where you come out on the bottom every time."

As I got close to the desk of the then-seated Ms. Shelgren, she tilted her head slightly to one side. One of her brows furrowed, and her lips were pressed shut.

"That's pure disgust right there. She sees right through you," Beel said.

"Hey, Michael," she greeted me.

"Mm-hmm."

"How are ya doing? Is everything okay?"

"She's trying to dissect you," Beel hissed. "She wants your weaknesses, to exploit them. Don't show her *any*."

I widened my eyes, if only a little, and lowered my bottom lip as if I were puzzled she'd asked. Though I wasn't, of course. "Me?" I said. "I'm fine… yeah. Why do you ask?"

She tilted her head to the other side.

"She doesn't believe you, Michael, but she can't prove a thing!"

"Well, I have to say, I've been disappointed with your engagement lately. You don't pay good attention, you don't take notes, and your assignments have been subpar. I just want to make sure you're adjusting to your new school well. I know it can be a lot to handle for some."

"A harsh putdown from a harsh wench. She knows she's in control. She knows everything," Beel rambled.

I exhaled. For a moment, the green expanses she had for eyes almost seemed to show sympathy, but that, of course, was not correct—not according to Beel, anyway. "You know, I—I think I'm just a little tired. I'll make sure to try harder in the future."

"You sound like a weak jackass," Beel spat. "It's no wonder those girls with the leggings were laughing at you."

Ms. Shelgren held my gaze for a second longer then sighed. She made a slight clicking noise when she opened her mouth. "Okay then, I just want to make sure you're on the right track. You're a very smart kid, and I like having you in class."

I didn't say anything. I just kept my mouth shut.

She dismissed me, and I was free—free from the clutches of the classroom and all of those prying eyes and predatory, accusatory judgments.

"That *bitch*," Beel said as I walked out the door.

Chapter 2 – Michael

The world was a confusing place. It tangled me up, dulled my thoughts, and heightened my anxieties. The stress of changing schools, waking up early, having more responsibilities, dealing with girls, and finding new friends… it was exhausting. It all weighed on me in the morning, but it kept me wound up at night. It was a rusty merry-go-round I couldn't control, yet I still knew that—at any time—I could be flung off onto the unforgiving concrete. I hung on for dear life.

At least Beel was a help to me. He grounded me. Yes, he was a monster, but he was a slick-haired, well-dressed one with wisdom and experience. I trusted him for the most part. I trusted his intuition often. Sometimes, his commentary made me feel bad, but the world could be a shitty place, and he helped me navigate it—to protect myself. Besides, it wasn't like I could get rid of him. He was like a teacher that never left, and it bothered me every now and then. But other times, it was useful. He helped me and haunted me.

My mom was nice. She had smile marks and thin brown hair that was always well-brushed. She usually used a soft voice when she spoke to me. She didn't always mean what she said, but that was okay because she was my mom. And she *did* care for me; I almost definitely knew that. She had a math mind but a hobbyist's mentality—it was difficult to really upset her, but she got exasperated quite often. And she was brilliant, logically brilliant, like she woke up and shrugged at the world every day because she'd already figured it out and the conquest wasn't worth her time because it just wasn't *fun* enough. She was a dabbler, but not complacent; at the same time, she was never deliberately pursuing any one thing. She was a thinker and an empath, a teacher but also a student of so many obscure little subjects.

"Hey, honey," my mom said as I walked through the front door. She was in the kitchen. It was a small kitchen, but the appliances were new and shiny enough, and the granite countertops, in a weird way, were sort of comforting. My home—which we'd just recently moved into—was nice, but not very large. It didn't have a habitable basement, but it did have a finished, insulated attic where my friends and I could go hang out or play video games...

"Once you make friends, that is."

There was Beel, the teacher, again. Sometimes, I couldn't help but shudder when I heard him speak.

"How was school today?" she asked. My mom wore one of her many gray knit sweaters with a pair of faded denim mom jeans. Her reasoning was if she liked an outfit, why wear much of anything else? She might as well stick to what was comfortable for her.

"Don't give anything up. Remember, emotions make you *weak*. You wouldn't want to appear weak in front of your mother, would you?" Beel cautioned. He sure had a way with words.

I raised my eyebrows and nodded slowly, assuredly. "It was good," I said. I lied. But saying it was terrible and alienating and boring would make it more real than it had to be. Saying I was angry at my father for relocating us across the state just for his mayoral campaign would have crystallized how I actually felt inside. I would have shown my underbelly. I didn't even want to think, to consider, to materialize the fact that I had an underbelly—that I had soft, pink tissue to expose in the first place. Nope. Me, I was solid all around. I didn't even have to be that strong because what I was going through wasn't all that difficult.

"Well, that's good," my mother said.

I didn't much care for small talk and the mutual exchange of pleasantries, even with my own mom, but I had to stick around for a bit longer in order to access the fridge.

"Yeah," I said as I opened the fridge. Its lustrous light illuminated my face and glinted off my wireframe glasses.

"She's thinking," Beel said, "thinking of her next question to ask. You need to move quicker."

"Did you… meet any new friends today?" she asked me.

I huffed and looked away, twisting my head around. My chest hurt. "Not really, I was pretty busy."

"Okay, honey. Well, I'm glad you're working hard."

"She wishes she had a son with friends," Beel mocked.

His words cut deep sometimes. I hurried upstairs. Movement always helped me. It took my mind off things.

I sat on the bed in my room—the room that had been mine for all of one month. Then, I heard a scratch at my door. Of course, my door was closed. But I opened it for Marmalade—I always opened it for Marmalade. He was my orange tabby cat, handsome, mild, and striped. My parents said I called him "Tiger" when I was little, so that's what I called him now. It was easy to talk to Marmalade. He always seemed to listen, and he never had a motive other than loving me—and sometimes the occasional plea for a snack.

Even Beel said he was all right, and that was enough in my book.

Chapter 3

I was bred in chaos—born from it. I lived and grew up in chaos.

I am chaos.

If I may ask, what does chaos do naturally? Who and what does it *seek*—like a dog to a patch of shade on a one-hundred-degree day, or like a river to the ocean? Indeed, chaos seeks to find, cultivate, and spread more chaos. Like a divine being, chaos justifies itself. It validates its own existence, like a god, like a storm cloud on high.

Michael calls me Beel, and that's fine. Candidly, it has a nice ring to it. But the best name for chaos is itself, just like the rationale for it is, in fact, itself. You see, humans are quite orderly creatures. Even their conflicts seek peace. Their greatest conquests have stasis as a goal somewhere on the horizon. Every one of their actions, whether immediately or later, has a resolution in mind.

And that is where I come in. I am here to make conflict more voluminous and prolong this most *infantile* idea of resolution wherever possible.

Chaos is not matter. It lies between matter, tainting all and consuming all.

And who am I, you may ask?

I am the thoughts from which you cannot escape.

I am the burden that brings you down, way down.

Chapter 4 – Ms. Shelgren

It was just one of those days. You know, *those* days. The days where your poker face is your best asset—and *only* asset, for that matter. I woke up to chaos.

Before I could scrape the crust out of my eyes, my youngest, little Danny, woke up with a fever. But the fever wasn't what woke me up—it was his incessant screaming.

"Daddy! I don't feel good!" Danny cried, yelling like only toddlers know how. Of course, he called for his daddy. Josh always had to be the good guy to the kids. It was a morning of screaming and fiery exasperation between my husband and me about who should take him to the clinic. Josh knew I had to be at school at seven-thirty and yet still resisted, even though he worked from home as a programmer that somehow seemed to have way too much time for leisure. Ridiculous.

What ruined my morning also ruined my breakfast, or lack thereof, and I drove to school with gritted teeth and my hands clenched on the wheel. Angry drives to work were becoming more and more common, with only my coffee to accompany me. And my poker face, too—I couldn't forget about that. My poker face was always there to hide the clenched teeth and the overworked adrenal glands.

I pulled my old, boxy Volvo into the lot. It was the car of my nightmares—middling, safe, hatchback, and *silver*. Yuck, silver. Me? I'd always wanted an M3 or an S4, or one of those big black SUVs I'd seen in the cool '90s rap videos I'd watched in middle school. But those were dreams long past. For now, I had a silver shitwagon, only good for transporting whiny children (children whom I very much *loved*, by the way). I stepped out and was glad it was an appropriate morning for sunglasses. I would've worn them anyway.

"Another day at the job you said you'd never do," a voice moaned. That voice was Starla. I was beginning to go completely nuts before Starla took over and knocked some sense into me. She was like the therapist my husband never wanted to pay for, mainly because I never asked him—that would have been weak and telling. Instead, Starla talked about my problems. Having her inside my head was like an all-day radio show or one of those podcasts, but it was specially done for me. She was like if one of those champagne-drinking *Real Housewives* got fat and turned into a fairy godmother. She had comments and quips, but they had substance to them, and they were all about *me*. It was rare to have someone comment on my daily situations and feelings, much less for someone to revolve around them completely. But that was Starla—she revolved around me. She was always in my head.

"What a shitbox," she said. "I feel like this thing gets older every time it leaves your driveway—which, by the way, desperately needs to be paved." Starla really knew how to remind me of all the dusty, painful nooks and crannies of my inner and outer worlds.

I walked through the front door of the school, and immediately, a burst of warm air hit me. It made my face feel dry and leathery in a way I didn't care for. Right at the entrance, I was greeted by that all-too-smiley receptionist—the younger one with the blonde hair who got all the attention from Principal Davies.

"Good morning, Tina," she said, smiling away as usual.

"She knows you're jealous of her," Starla commented. "Smug, smiley bitch."

"Mornin'," I said. I didn't even shoot her a passing glance. Why should I? She got enough looks already from all of the male faculty. She was like that sophomore girl who got all the attention from the upperclassmen. She developed early and would probably get worn out after her little sprint. See, me—*I* was the marathoner. I wore my drab cardigans as an act of defiance. I still had some youth and some curve and some fire, but it was mine. It was mine to conceal or show as I pleased.

At my desk to start the day, the papers I graded felt heavy, like each piece was a slab of wood rather than a thin sheet. The rest of the day went sort of like that, too—slogging, slow, and heavy. It was the type of day where Starla was really going. She was never one to hold her tongue, but on that day, she had a particularly boisterous motormouth on her podcast in my head.

Finally, I stumbled into the last block of the day: sophomore geometry. The pimple-faced rugrats piled in, and as they did, I salivated for the bell. However, no matter how badly I yearned for that final bell, as a teacher, it was never a good look to glance at the clock. There were little eyeballs on me all the time, and I had to keep them engaged—in the lesson, yes, but also engaged with *me*, the teacher. The teacher was the star of the show, and I had to keep the audience guessing in order to instill in the zit monkeys a good lesson. I say "zit monkeys" affectionately, of course. Those students are my little rugrats, and they need me.

"Oh god," Starla said, "are these what *your* kids are going to look like? Scrawny, hunchbacked, institutionalized zombies?"

"Okay, everyone," I announced, "the intro problems are already on the board. Once you're done with them, we'll continue on to chapter six and get into some more trigonometry." There was a method to how I scanned the room and maximized engagement. I categorized the class: smart workers, dim workers, smart and lazy ones, lazy and dumb ones, the shy and standoffish, then the brash bastards. Each category's kids got similar treatment from me—similar glances, calls, questions, and occasional jokes I would make. There was still one student in the class I couldn't figure out. I couldn't put him in a box. In time, though, I would. I always did.

"I'm not even sure they're worth your headspace and attention, Tina. Your audience should be a million times larger."

Starla was right. What I wanted to be was a singer, and I was good at it, too. The thing was, "Tina Shelgren" wasn't exactly the most attractive stage name, and it would have been years before I made it anyway. With all of the agents trying to take their cuts, the record companies, the parties, I would have eventually overspent and dried out. I would have been kicked to the curb, probably with a heroin habit and a leaked sex tape. So, I never tried. However, the hope that one day, just maybe, I would give my singing career a shot was more invigorating than my morning coffee or even an elusive good night's sleep.

"You know, you still could, Tina. Those fans aren't out of reach. No matter how much your mom kept you in line, she could never say you had a bad voice. You could still get that boob job and get to singing. You know it's true."

But no matter what, I knew my kids needed me—both my students and my own children.

Starla plowed on, "And you know what would be even *better*? What if, in your absence, everyone learns to appreciate you for how much you truly bring to the table. While you're on the road with the wind in your hair, chasing your dream, they will learn to need you even more. Just one more plus, baby." It began to sound like the podcast studio in my head had a fridge full of booze that Starla was helping herself to.

After some time, a slow wave of leisure swept over the class—kids leaning back in their chairs, beginning to look around. That meant less attention to their work and to *me*. I stood up and began going over the answers. I engaged my hawk eyes after a "dim worker," a ginger named Jeffrey, completely chunked an answer.

"Really makes you wonder what could've been, huh, Tina? If they can't even learn simple things after all of your effort and talent, how are they supposed to do anything? Maybe wear something more flattering than those cardigans. *That'd* make them listen to you," Starla said. "Jeffrey's such a little oaf anyway… but he's not much different from the rest. Is this why you had kids?"

I scanned and glared and trolled around.

"You need *prey*, Tina. Remember Josh was being a dick and Danny's screaming. All that energy needs to go somewhere."

I sensed a soft spot. I don't know how I did it, and frankly, I never knew why either—but I spotted Michael, "the uncategorizable."

"He's spoiled anyway and probably needs to be taught a lesson," Starla pressed. "I bet he woke his parents up, too. I bet he started fights in his own home, too."

"Michael?" I said.

"Look at him squirm," Starla jeered. "He knows who's boss." She cackled and snorted, as if Michael's pain fed her jubilation.

He gave a pitiful answer, then I told him he was wrong and moved on. Michael might not have been very attentive—he was the least attentive, for that matter—but something about him begged to be discovered, to be sought. Too many weeks had passed without me knowing who he really was or how he worked. Adolescents this age were usually transparent; the only thing I couldn't see through were their pimples. One look into their eyes, and I could figure them out—in a classroom setting, that is.

Right after class, although I craved the bell, I craved knowing my students more. I called Michael back to see me at my desk. He tried so hard to scamper out, as if he'd anticipated this. He walked up to my desk like a calf walked toward a butcher. I tried to relate to him, to level with him. He put up a sound defense. I locked eyes and tried to get him to trust me, to come clean about something. But what that something was, I didn't know. Then, it clicked.

Somewhere past his nerd glasses and his stubby pig nose, I saw *him*. I saw my student. The same student who ignored his work and me and creeped on that girl, Rachel. I understood him. He was in pain. For what reason, I didn't know, but I did know he hurt. He hurt inside, and for that reason—and maybe that reason alone—I could relate to him.

Chapter 5

I am relentless. I am never dormant. Nor have I ever lain dormant.

The essence and shape of my character knows no bounds—it is amorphous, its intensity has no limit, and its form is infinite. I love smooth aesthetics and petite garnishes, for I am always lurking underneath and behind them, waiting, staring, licking, and chomping. There is a word for me, as there are many words. I am my own rhyme and reason. Label me all you want, but it is impossible to conquer me as an adversary. You cannot beat what is always working, so I implore you to join me. Work alongside this sleepless, ceaseless beast. Be assured, it is better to work *with* me than against me, and in this life, you have no choice but to choose one of those options.

Reader, I will not repeat myself. Consider this both a lesson and an offer.

I am the monster in their heads. I am the monster in yours.

Chapter 6 – Michael

I thought way too much. Or at least, I thought I did. And sometimes—no, *often*—it got me into trouble. Overthinking made my head spin even more; it was a perpetual cycle that turned itself around and around. I was quiet and a thinker, a quiet thinker. And my dad said I was more like my mom in that way. My mom said I was more like her dad, and my grandfather just sat back and thought about that.

That night, I lay in my bed, thinking. I had my phone on me. It called itself *Michael's iPhone*. Or maybe I called it that? Either way, it seemed to have a mind of its own. On my phone, when I was surfing and scrolling and reading, there was never any pressure. There were no expectations. When I was alone, with the door closed and no one but Marmalade in the vicinity, I was at ease. I could simply be a scroller on my little digital window—an observer, a bystander, an innocent passerby. No one saw me, but I saw them. As someone who never posted on social media, I could just roam, and I could see all without really *being* anything myself. That was peace to me. In a way, it was power.

But that peaceful feeling didn't linger long.

I scrolled down to a girl's post and stopped for a moment. I processed information rather quickly, and I didn't need to look at any one thing for very long before scrolling to the next. But this was different. The girl had the smooth, dark skin of a certain Turkish-

Mediterranean, coffee and olive complexion. Her face was clear, and her top was so white in the flash of the camera, it seemed to shimmer. It was Rachel. She was at a restaurant. It was one of the places in the city that had the white, steamed plates, and every entree had garnishes and a thick drizzle of balsamic vinegar in a squiggly design. I couldn't help—not that I *tried* to help it—goggling and zooming in and imagining.

"You know what you should do?" Beel piped up. "Unfollow her. She wouldn't notice either way. She'd never notice, Michael."

I felt a twinge like a fork growing in my gut.

"Just stop looking at her. She doesn't care."

I zoomed in once more.

"You're pathetic."

I meandered around her comment section. There were *fifty-seven* comments.

"Those guys who are commenting—she's already comfortable with them. They talk to her. She thinks they're all attractive. She thinks you're a *newt*."

I double-tapped and liked the picture.

"Maybe she doesn't think of you at all. Is there proof she even knows you exist?"

My thumb twitched. My phone felt heavy. It only got heavier, like someone was stacking books in my hand.

"Don't even think about it."

I felt another textbook on the stack. I used my left hand to support my thirty-pound phone.

"Creep. Idiot. What are you doing?" Beel sneered.

I continued to look as my thumb twitched and trembled.

"It's not worth it, Michael. She'll tell all her friends."

I felt a clench in my gut, and I began to sweat.

"They'll laugh at you. They'll glare at you…"

I clicked on her profile.

"The whole school, Michael. Your *whole* life."

I pressed another button. It was to send a message.

Beel's voice grew louder and nastier. "Hello? Don't do it! Shrink back like the minnow you are."

The keyboard popped up. I heard Beel's voice, but I saw Rachel's face—her cheeks, her chin, her eyes.

"You're unhealthy. You're unfit. You have no chance."

I inhaled, but I couldn't even fill up my chest a quarter of the way without my lungs expelling my wheezing breath.

"Four-eyed loser. You don't deserve to have friends. You're—"

My shaky thumb hit a key.

"*Weird.*"

It was the wrong letter. Instead of an "H," I typed a "J." I hit "delete" with all the caution of a rookie surgeon.

"You can't even type. You disappoint your father." Beel spoke softer now, with more calm. He knew he was winning—he knew that, with enough words, he would always win.

I turned off my phone and tossed it to the other side of the bed, where it was out of reach—but certainly not out of mind. I scratched my head, then I scratched Marmalade's back. He was purring and happy. The orange tabby was so content and smiley, it almost made me crack a smile—*almost*. Marmalade looked back at me. Although a fierce green, his eyes were soft for me. He had an ancient kind of sympathy in his face, one that only a cat who loved his companion could have. I loved Marmalade. In return for some back scratches and food, he cared, too. He cared, and he listened. He listened in a world where most people just talked and projected their fears onto you. They looked down at sixteen-year-olds who haven't hit their second growth spurt yet. But Marmalade? He looked up, and he listened.

Chapter 7

Those who cannot obey themselves will be imperialized, commanded by another. That is a fact solely because that is my aim. I, myself, do not compromise but am pleased when others do. For it is their wobbly-kneed concessions that I stand on and climb from.

Chapter 8 – Rachel

After my father's affair, I began to smoke. Of course, my father encouraged this. He encouraged all marijuana usage. After all, it furthered his cannabis empire. As sales grew, he grew more of that sweet green bud. Plants of plants popped up all over Colorado; his warehouses, indoor farms, and packing facilities sprang up like the leaves he so profited from. As his business grew, so did his big head—until it outgrew his marriage with my mother, the only woman who truly cared for him. She moved to Hawaii shortly after the divorce. I haven't seen her since, and especially not since my father gained full custody with his stuck-up lawyers.

She was loyal and kind and breathtakingly beautiful. She had a dark complexion like a rich, creamy coffee and was pure, supportive, and caring. But as soon as she caught wind of my father's infidelity, all of that—her kindness, caring, and wholesome Mediterranean beauty—quickly began to burn away like a smoldering leaf. She became a lonesome shell when she finally accepted the lesson that was never worth learning: Sometimes, people don't love you back.

I never really understood the people who said the line between love and hate is thin. To me, hate was just hate and love was love. And sometimes, the lack of either was just a bubbling, gray apathy—and apathy scared me more than anything.

I didn't talk to my dad anymore. I knew deep within him, under that confident veneer, lay a reason for cheating on my mom that might be understood and empathized with. But I couldn't bring myself to understand. I couldn't bring myself to empathize with that white-toothed, suit-wearing monster. He tore my family apart. He had the connections and the friends and the money and the house, and when he tore, he took them all with him. What was a grand foyer without my mom? What was all that space without the person who understood me best and stayed up late nights with me to eat vanilla ice cream and watch old Lindsay Lohan movies?

I couldn't come to terms with any of it. I would not. I was a sixteen-year-old girl with enough problems on my own besides the ones my tyrant of a father had created for me.

My mom said I developed early. The older I got, the more I looked in the mirror, and the more I saw my mom in that reflection. Maybe that was why parents loved their kids so much—because they saw themselves in their offspring. God, sometimes I hated how jaded I was for such a young person. But that's what my parents' messy divorce had done to me. It jaded my soul, my whole outlook on life and love. It also made me more mature. It made me so mature that I knew I wanted to be less mature. It made me crave ignorance, relief. But what did I need relief from? I was a beautiful girl. I had tons of family money and the attention of whomever I wanted. But the truth was I sought shelter from my own mind. I needed relief from myself—from the monster in my head. That's how weed helped me.

I got home from school, and my dad was in his home office (well, it was more of a whole *wing*, but that didn't matter). I sped through the front door and rushed for the kitchen like a running back. My dad popped out of the office just in time to catch sight of me storming away. He had on his usual tapered sport jacket on top of a crisp, white shirt. His gelled hair was, ever so slightly, beginning to thin out. And his teeth—his teeth were just so white.

"Hey, Rachel. How was school?"

I paused for one moment, hating myself for not running even faster to the kitchen.

The voice in my head spoke up. She was soft-spoken, sultry, and smooth. She was protective like a mother, but not without a little edge. I called her Estelle because that's how I pictured her: Estelle with a microphone from the fifties, cherry-red lipstick, and a fluffy, feathery, pink shawl.

"Rachel," said Estelle, "if you ignore him right now, maybe you can give him that twinge, that *fire* he gave you. Maybe, just maybe, you can make him feel neglected, just like he made you feel. Wouldn't that be something?"

As usual, I listened to Estelle. After all, she was so seductive. Also, it was only fair to my father to return the pain he'd caused my mom every chance I got. Estelle always complimented me on how fair I was.

I stopped with my back turned to him as soon as I heard him speak, then with a curt huff, I continued toward the kitchen. The only thing I regretted about ignoring him was not turning around to see the look on his face. I hoped it was despair. I was sure it was.

Estelle said, despite me being in school (and only sixteen years old), I was more of a teacher than a student. She said I was sad because I was mature. She said I used substances because I was mature. She said I held on to the cutting memories for my own self-defense and also because I was mature.

I went out to dinner that night simply because I could. My father would continue to give me money no matter how I treated him because that was the only thing he was able to give me. The restaurant was decent, and it was in the city. Estelle told me to post a picture from the meal.

"Show the other girls why they're less than you, Rachel. They can't do this on a weeknight, and they would *not* look like you in that top."

She was right. It was skintight and almost as white as my dad's teeth—not exactly the most slimming garment in the world. Estelle called all of the comments and likes I got from the post "adulation," but secretly and away from Estelle, I thought that was a little overkill.

So many of those comments were from the group of popular boys trying to get a response from me, trying to make me laugh or show they were comfortable enough to talk to me. They were the confident, upright types who reminded me of my dad. They were all different—some snowboarded, some played basketball. However, they were all bound by one thing, and that was they were *boys*. Boys who showed great confidence and fearlessness. But to me, that meant they were either hiding pain or didn't have much pain at all.

I looked down at the boys' painless, brainless comments. I scrolled through them and scoffed at their short attempts to get a response from me. While I scoffed, I scrolled and nibbled at my salad. I felt a twinge in my gut. *Is there anybody out there who feels like me?*

"Your feelings are unique to you, darling. You're stronger than anyone," Estelle said.

That's why I felt alone. It was because my situation had no precedent. You couldn't define me in a movie or a play—I was too much. I was the most.

"You're not alone, darlin'. Look at all that sweet, *sweet* engagement. They all adore you. You're not lonely; they're lonely."

I took one last look at my full plate of salad and asked for the check.

Chapter 9 – Michael

I liked waking up early. It was a safe time. I had no one to talk to and no one to tell me what to do. There were no expectations or judgments, just Marmalade purring on my lap.

As the sun rose, it was one of the few times I could look down—down on the hassles of my life and the people who caused them. But by the time I finished my toast and put on my backpack every morning, I would come to the same conclusion: Things were more complicated than I could bother to help, and people were the same way. Maybe that's why I never tried with them.

It was a rare morning when my dad hadn't left yet. He was putting on his nice suit—the shiny, tailored one I only saw him bring out occasionally.

"Hey, Mike," he said, fiddling with his tie and looking in the mirror.

I cleared my throat and sat up a little straighter. "Hey, Dad."

"How was school yesterday?" His eyes were still fixed on himself in the mirror. His tie was finished, so he moved on to adjusting his collar and checking his teeth, which were pearly white.

My hands were folded on the table. "He doesn't care," Beel growled.

I sank back down a little and looked away from him. "It was fine."

He tugged at the sides of his jacket and ran a hand through his hair one last time. "That's good. Have another good day today, okay, bud?" My dad said in passing like it was an easy command. He then tore toward the mudroom for his shoes.

"Where are you going?"

"The mudroom," said my dad, stomping right by me.

"No… like do you have a meeting or something?" But with that, he was already in the mudroom and on his way out.

He shouted from the garage, "See ya, bud! Let me know how school goes. I'm sorry, running late for a meeting with a campaign donor!"

I heard the car crawl out of the garage. He drove a hybrid even though he hated it and could afford better. "The people need to know I care," he would say, as if he were some sort of superhero. But in a way, he kind of was. He was to me.

My mom walked downstairs shortly after my dad left. She had on her fuzzy robe and reached for the coffee immediately. I was still staring out the window while she poured a cup for herself and said, "Hey, aren't you going to be late, sweetie?" She yawned.

"She didn't even say 'good morning,'" Beel said. "She just wants to get you out of the house."

I jerked my head around from the window and sort of snapped. I didn't feel like I could do anything else; it just felt right in the moment. "Mom, yeah, it's fine. I'll be fine."

My mom's eyes softened, and she walked toward me, coffee in hand. "Michael, is everything all right? Is there something wrong?"

"She always thinks there's something wrong with you, Michael, but what's wrong with *her*? Have you ever stopped to think about that?"

"Where's Dad going?"

"He has a meeting with that cannabis tycoon, Mister... whatzisface with the teeth." She gestured to her mouth, then gave an exaggerated smile. "Looks like he'll be getting in bed with bud." She laughed. She cracked herself up sometimes.

"That's pretty cool," I said. And it definitely was, without a doubt. I was sure if I had some friends, they would be psyched about that.

Chapter 10

I am the voice. I am the monster. I am but a mirror, a reflection, and I will always fit in. I am control. I don't exude it—I embody it. I am possible to resist, at least for a while, but I am impossible to master.

Chapter 11 – John

Lorne was a tall man—much taller than I'd expected. He certainly had the smile of a politician. But then again, I did, too, and I wasn't even running for mayor.

There was a certain calmness about him. I couldn't quite put my finger on it, but I knew I would eventually—I always did. Deep down, under that glib smile, though, he knew I was in control. The leverage was all mine, but the best thing to do when you have the power is to act like you have none. Obsequiousness is delicious. Look that shit up.

I wore a tight, gray T-shirt and a pair of those jeans that stretch real nice-like. I started talking first. That way, I could set the tone. Was that not obvious to everyone?

"Mistah Conifer!" I swung my arm around like a loose pendulum to grip his hand. It was huge. "You're shorter than I expected," I said, staring up at him with a dumb look on my face.

"Please, I'm just Lorne to you."

That smile was like a spotlight. Damn. "Well jeez, Lorne, do you dress this sharp every day?" We sat in my office—spacious with floor-to-ceiling windows, of course.

"One foot in front of the other, my man." Lorne laughed as if it were a joke.

"Typical politician's veneer... he puts up a hard shell, but let's find those soft spots, shall we?" It was Anders. Anders was my guiding star and main inspiration. He pointed me in the right direction, almost without fail. He was my corporate and personal consultant, and the best part: I didn't even have to pay him. He was a real monster.

"Lorne," I sighed and started nodding my head, "I can already tell you're perfect for the job, man. Look, I've been doing this for far too long not to be able to pick winners from a first word. And Lorne, you're a fuckin' winner." I clasped my hands around my head and gave a stretch—letting my "guard" down. I was far too good at this.

"John, I appreciate that more than you know," he said. His smile was so close to genuine, I could *almost* feel it. "But to be honest, I'm here because of my principles. To me, excitement is good, expanding the tax base is *good*." He tapped his hand on the table for emphasis like a true polished professional. "Traffic and change are, in fact, both good things."

I scooted up closer to my desk and leaned forward. My high school football coach had always told me the low man wins. He couldn't have been more correct. "Lorne, how many kids ya got?" Then, I waved my hands. "If any."

"Just one. A boy."

"That's really nice, man. It's a beautiful thing. I have one daughter myself over at the high school." I laughed like it was the funniest thing I'd ever heard. "She's a real handful, that one."

"Michael is at the high school as well."

"Oh, no kiddin'? It's a small world. Yeah, Rachel's a sophomore."

"So is Mike."

"Ah, no way. Too funny."

"It really is," Lorne said. His smile faded ever so slightly.

Anders piped up. "*Mike*. Target acquired, my friend."

I decided to put that one in my back pocket. "So, let's just get right into it, then. My people looked over your campaign budgeting, and we think it's a little loose."

"That can be amended."

I nodded my head like I hadn't expected him to say that. "Another note, and this one's important: You can't run so... *explicitly* on this platform. Lots of young kids and old people in this city. You'll need to dance around it until you win."

He tilted his head when he heard that. "Okay, and what do you mean by that?"

"You have him," Anders pressed, "go back to the 'M-word.'"

"Well, just think for a moment about your son Michael, for example. You, of course, allow Mike to smoke, right?"

Lorne looked to the side for a second too long. He fidgeted for the first time in the meeting, and his smile waned once again.

"Gotcha!" The amount of triumph in Anders's raspy voice was like a sweet glass of bourbon after a long day.

"Yes, of course Mike is allowed to smoke weed."

"Right. And Lorne, I know this is Colorado, but trust me. I have all the demographics, and in this sleepy place, there are a ton of parents and seniors who are *not* as open-minded as you are."

"Surely. Sure, I know *exactly* what you're saying." The politician nodded and sounded like a young king right after his coronation ceremony.

"So much for that veneer," Anders said.

His chuckle gave me a warm feeling like a leaf flaming up inside my gut. This—this was going somewhere. I'd finally found my champion, and he was more malleable than I'd expected.

Chapter 12 – Ms. Shelgren

I liked to have fun. And if I wasn't going to do that as a singer, I would at least do it as a teacher. Fun was never a goal for me—after all, goals are just not *fun*. It was more of a hobby of mine. A little bit of chaos never hurt anybody, and in fact, it was fun. I had fun causing a little chaos the next day at school.

Kids think their parents, teachers, coaches, and babysitters are oblivious. But kids are the ones who are stupid for thinking that. I knew. I knew all too well what went on and how they thought. That's why group projects were so much *fun* for me. I got the chance to watch them think they weren't being watched.

"Okay, class," I said in my usual uninterested voice. I faced the board when I wrote, but my mind was on them. "Today, we are starting a month-long group project." I heard sighing and soft moaning crawl throughout the room.

"Give them something to anticipate, baby girl," Starla encouraged. "Give them something to really chew on." She giggled like a giddy schoolgirl. I loved when we were on the same page. I also loved when I could look around the room and witness the sea of eyes roll and churn like a fantastically violent storm. It was a frenzy I caused by dropping a pin in just the right place. Starla was kind of evil, but after all—evil wasn't *that* bad.

Chapter 13 – Michael

Ms. Shelgren's voice rang and repeated in my head. *Group project. Group project. Group project.*

I looked down at my desk and stuck my hands to my cheeks. I guessed I hoped for Riley—that is, if I had to work with someone for a whole month. She was commanding and annoying, but at least I knew she would do most of the work.

"Everybody's praying they don't get you, Michael. Four-eyes, new kid, *and* a bad student? No one can blame them either—just look at you."

I took what Beel said in stride. I accepted it like butter accepted a knife. It hurt some, but I was meant for it. It was the truth, and I held the truth to be sacred. I got that trait from my mom.

I watched Ms. Shelgren from the corner of my eye; she was scanning the room with a face of stone. She looked so disinterested, I almost felt bad for *her*. She stopped pacing after a moment and rattled off the first pairing. "Okay, the first group will be Tom, and…" she trailed off as if she were just coming up with this project on the fly. Even if she was, there was nothing we could do about it. "Andrea. Tom and Andrea. Second group will be…"

I put my head down on the desk and kept going over all the negative scenarios in my head. *Not Jeffrey. Not Amy. Not Paul. Please, please, plea—*

"You're going to get Jeffrey," Beel said, "because of course you are. Do all the work and look like a fool."

I became conscious of my breath. In. Out. Hold. I swirled my tongue around. It felt too big for my mouth. My palms itched. I had to shift in my seat to avoid leaving a sweat mark.

"What are you doing? Some kind of dance? Everyone is thinking about you right now. They're laughing in their heads at this very moment."

"Paul and…"

My torso wiggled involuntarily. I tried to swallow, but my mouth was too dry.

"Tasha."

In. Out. Hold. I tried to swallow again. It was no use. There was a bead of sweat that ran down my cheek. I hoped Rachel hadn't seen that. It felt like my esophagus was a rubber band. I raised my hand and stood up at the same time, trying to make it assumptive that I would go no matter what. When I did, there were eyeballs on me—everywhere and everyone. I hoped there was no more sweat. I hoped they didn't hear me try to gulp.

"Ms. Shelgren?"

"What?"

More eyeballs—blue ones, brown ones, green ones, gray ones. I tried to tap the desk to play off my fidgeting.

"You look like a spastic drummer right now. What are you doing?" Beel was nearly yelling. His voice got louder and louder.

"Can I go to the bathro—"

"Uh-huh, that's fine, I guess."

Well, there was finally a morsel of relief. I took a tiny, mouse-like step toward the door because sound attracted eyeballs.

"Wait. But before you go, you'll be paired with..."

My face started tingling again. I felt a tickle in my throat. I wanted to sneeze, but I couldn't. Tapping on the desk soon turned to knocking. *Oh god, oh god.* In and out. I felt my heart in my head.

"Rachel."

***

I reached the bathroom and sat right on the toilet with my pants still on. I leaned on the nearest wall, and my breath got a little deeper. I ran my hands through my hair. It was a miracle my sixteen-year-old hair wasn't thinning out or going gray yet. I could swallow then.

Without checking to see if anyone else was in there, I muttered under my breath, "Rachel."

"Why do you think you have a chance?" Beel taunted. "I can smell your excitement from here. Stop hoping. This is going to be the only time she will ever talk to you, and even then, she'll be sick—wishing the whole time she was chosen to be with Josh or Kevin. You're a mental and physical *weakling*."

As per usual, Beel was right. He was so wonderfully correct, in fact, that I got an idea: I had to become *them*. I had to become who she wanted.

"You'll never do that, Michael, so don't start now. Not even worth a try."

I don't know why exactly I felt this, but I had a glimmer of hope that Beel might be wrong. It was a nagging feeling—a flicker, like a pocket flashlight in a vast, dark cave. I tried to suppress it for Beel's sake, but the feeling kept resurfacing. I tried to keep it hidden from the monster, but that only made him angrier.

"Pathetic."

What did guys like Kevin and Josh do that I didn't?

Chapter 14

Do not buck me. Do not write me off, dearest reader. Do not ignore me, and certainly, do not *fight* me.

There is a concrete order to the world: perfect disorder. Humans are supposed to go one way, and that is the way of chaos—beautiful, icy chaos. Their heads are *supposed* to be in disarray. Their plans are supposed to be both made by me and crushed by me. I lead them into battle against themselves. That is why I love humans with glazed eyes and no senses. That is why I love them in groups—large groups. I love the pods and tribes, the teams and parties. Around every coalition, I will be there, rearing my head and gnashing my teeth. I will make every wonderland a tundra—just for you, reader. All I ask is that you befriend me, never look back, and never question *why*.

Chapter 15 – Rachel

I got paired up with some kid; I think he just moved here. He seemed like a nerd, but I still didn't trust his absent mind to carry this workload. At our meeting after school, I hoped to dish off some busy work and get home before long. To my dismay, that wasn't what ended up happening.

I sat at the table in front of the library—right in the middle, where I *had* to be seen by anyone coming in or out. One minute passed. Nothing.

Three minutes passed. Nothing.

After seven minutes, the sultry voice of Estelle slithered into my head. It was like candy to my ears, like a mallet to a nail. "Don't even bother, darling. Just play with him like he's playing with you."

After another minute, he walked in. He wore the dumbest cargo shorts and kept looking around as if he didn't see me—which was ridiculous because I was basically in the doorway.

"Hey."

He jerked his head around like an angry serpent when he heard my voice.

"Looks like the lost puppy found his momma," said Estelle. I nearly snickered in the kid's face at her little remark. She was *such* a queen.

He pushed his wireframe glasses farther up his little-boy nose. "Hi."

"Hey, how's it going?" I smiled at him.

His eyebrows lifted. He couldn't hide from me. He couldn't hide anything. He sat his dumb cargo shorts into the chair, and I started.

Estelle pushed me forward. "Lay down the ground rules, darling."

"So, I kinda wanted to divide up the work here, then we can call it because we have a lot of time for the project. Does that work?" I kept the same smile I'd greeted him with and met his eyes. Through his shitty glasses and small face, I could see they were bright blue. In a way, they were striking. For a moment—merely a split second—I forgot where I was as I held his gaze. Weird.

"Yeah, that works, I-I guess."

"Have his b-b-balls dropped yet?" Estelle said. This joke didn't hit me the same way the last one did.

"Cool, do you have the assignment sheet?" I held mine up for him to see.

He dug into his accordion folder like a mad squirrel. He was breathing funny, and his eyes darted around as if I couldn't see them.

"Umm…"

"It's fine, we can just look at the same one."

Chapter 16 – Michael

"So, you're a nerd but also a shitty student? What a great combo."

A flame grew in my gut. The more frustrated I got with Beel, the louder he became and the more he jeered at me. It was an endless vicious cycle, and I was awash in it.

I rifled through my folder, probably looking like I'd lost my cool. I could no longer hear the whispers, shuffling, and bashful steps of the library; it was only Beel in my head—but it was Rachel in my eyes.

"Ya know, under those deep, brown eyes and those full lips, she's pissed that you're unprepared."

"It's fine, we can just look at the same one." She seemed annoyed. Maybe Beel was right. I felt like a little kid who'd just been scolded. I shrank back with my folder still a mess and craned my neck across the table to look at the sheet. It was upside-down, but I didn't intend on moving. At this point, reading a word would have been like lifting a car with my bare hands. I began to sweat *again*.

"Just sit over here," Rachel said, looking at me. Her top lip was stuck up. "Only if you want."

"Yeah, sure." I brought my chair over.

"You smell right now, don't go too close," Beel whispered. I started to fixate on my breath again. *Oh, no.* I probably sounded like an old pig with a respiratory issue. In and out—that's all I had to do, yet it was so difficult to just breathe.

"How are you going to do anything if you can't even inhale? How are you going to read? How are you going to talk? How are you going to *live*?" Beel hissed at me through what sounded like gritted teeth.

"Are you okay?" Rachel asked.

I widened my eyes like it was a ridiculous question. It wasn't. "Me? Yeah, I'm fine."

"Okay, then." She pressed her lips tightly together and pointed at the page in front of us. "So, I can cover all of these. And... would you be able to get number three and number five?"

"Which ones?"

She took her hands away from the paper and just stared at me. "Three and five."

I didn't even bother to look at the paper. "Yeah. Yeah, I can do that."

"Okay..." she said, then laughed as if she'd heard a funny joke.

"She's laughing at you, Michael. *You're* the joke."

"Sorry, what'd you say your name was again?"

"Michael."

Beel chuckled. "You have such a shrill little voice."

"Cool. I'm Rachel."

"Shake her hand, you little twerp."

I stuck my scrawny arm out like an idiot. "Nice to meet you."

She stared and didn't move. "Yeah," she said. She laughed again in a way that made my gut sink. I felt like dying right then and there, having my heart stop and just rag-dolling on the ground. Maybe then she would have at least touched me—maybe cared for a second.

"Ahaha!" cackled Beel. "This isn't a business conference, you stupid turkey! But look on the bright side: At least she couldn't think you're more of an idiot than you already are."

I dreaded and loved when she stood up to leave. I was being yanked in both directions.

"All right, I think that's good for today." She flipped her hair, and I choked. I was paralyzed. I pianoed my fingers on the table and sat back in my chair, still. Her backpack was black and sturdy, like it could have been used in a war or a preschool. I guess they were trendy then—a lot of the girls had them. After she slung it over her narrow shoulder, she stopped for a minute.

"Hey," she said. "Do you ever smoke?"

I looked at the ground—at my dirty, white tennis shoes. I glanced around at the tiles of the library floor. They needed to be scrubbed. "Um, like weed?"

She nodded, then giggled.

"Um, not really, no," I answered.

She took one step toward the door and didn't bother looking at me. "You should try it then. It could help you." She flipped her hair one last time. I choked one last time. "See ya."

And just like that, she was gone.

"You couldn't have embarrassed yourself any more than you just did," Beel snarled.

Chapter 17 – Michael

Later that day, my dad and I had our usual small-talk runaround as soon as I walked through the door. "Hey, where's Mom?"

"She's at her computer right now."

"Still?"

"Yeah, apparently she talked to a few universities today. Gettin' close to a couple adjunct roles."

"Just adjunct?"

"They're jobs all the same, Mike."

"Well, she had another job before he lost that last campaign," Beel said. "He plucked her out of that opportunity, Michael. He also plucked *you* out."

"I guess so," I said.

"He plucked you out of your friend group, out of Braiden's driveway basketball games, out of pizza Thursdays at Tony's, out of *all* of it. And he's making you pick up the pieces."

My dad turned his head away from his phone for the first time since I'd walked through the door. He took off his reading glasses. I knew it got serious when he took off his reading glasses. "Seriously, Mike? We're all doing the best we can. Come on, we talked about this."

"I didn't say anything."

"You're a coward," said Beel.

"Okay," my dad said, staring—no, leering—at me. "That's what I thought."

"You're going to take that?" Beel scoffed. "Feel that pressure in your chest and your head? That's anger. Now show it!"

I bit my lip, and I bit hard. It hurt a little, but at least I'd inflicted the pain on myself—no one else. At least I was the one doing the biting. It felt like the only thing I could do at the time, and so I did it because I could. Even though I wanted to, I couldn't lash out at my dad. Every time I even thought about yelling back at him, the pain of last time stabbed my chest, and I froze. It was years back, but it was potent enough to emblazon itself on my memory.

"You're smarter than him, Michael!" Beel shouted.

My chest shuddered before I could inhale fully, and my mind got fuzzy again. "So, the meeting went well?" I asked. I was blank. My body and mind were on autopilot—in a gray, misty haze that just made me want to fall asleep and never wake up. But instead, I kept talking to my dad.

He looked up from his phone again. This time, his face lit up. "Yeah, actually, it went really well. Keeping my fingers crossed, though." He beamed. "But it looks like I'll have their support for the election."

"That's awesome, Dad. Do you think you're gonna win?"

"What?" His voice grew softer, and his eyes fell to the ground. "What do you mean?"

"I—Yeah… of course. That's awesome."

"Yes," he said and laughed. "The things they're going to be able to do for the cannabis industry are monumental. They just needed a horse in the race. And Mike?" He turned his whole body toward me, and his palms faced the sky. "It looks like I'm their horse."

"I'm hyped, that's so great."

"Yup, I'm excited."

"What did you say the name of the big boss was?"

"What do you mean by 'big boss?'"

My dad was a true politician. Getting a straight answer from him was like trying to grip the ocean. I liked the challenge a little bit. I played along with his circular answers—mainly because I had to, but they were fun to analyze as well.

"Who did you talk to today?"

"Oh," he said like an apologetic old woman, "I talked to John Kalopoulos this morning."

Kalopoulos. Where do I know that name? It sounded as familiar as an old friend, yet I couldn't quite put my finger on it.

"You don't know that name. It's just a random guy." Beel seemed nonchalant when he said that at first. But there was a weird tone to his voice that eluded and teased me—a veil of sorts. Maybe it was all in my head. Maybe he did that on purpose. Maybe he was trying to mislead me. Should I have trusted my instincts? *What if Beel was trying to manipulate my instincts?* What if he wanted me to think he was lying? I really thought I knew the name, and I didn't know why he would say that. Was I just crazy? Or did Beel want me to think that way? I was going to look it up.

"Look it up if you want, just to check," Beel said. *Why was he being so polite?* Beel was trying to trick me. But which way was he trying to trick me, and what did he *want* me to think? Maybe he just wanted me to think.

"I just want you to myself," said Beel.

That didn't make any sense. None of it did. Either way I went, I was wrong. I felt trapped, stuck, but I couldn't bring myself to stay in one place. I wondered if the wall I was staring at was closing in on me.

"Michael, are you all right?" my dad said.

"Yeah, I'm fine, why?"

"You just seem a little tired is all."

I shook my head and pursed my lips like a true adult did when they lied about how they were doing. I thought it was a sign of maturity that I could hide my confusion. In fact, I didn't think I was confused or in pain at all. Under the masks, we were all scared and worried creatures. Though, maybe I was a little more scared than most.

"Okay, well, just make sure you get some good rest tonight... but yeah, apparently John has a daughter in your grade."

I gulped. The palms, the chest, the head, the shuddering—they all started at the same time. Beel lied. *Fuck you, Beel.* I knew I'd recognized the name. I knew it, and he knew it, too, and he lied about it.

Beel spoke up again. "Sure, take it out on me. Of course, I was just trying to protect you. I always want you to be safe. How am I supposed to trust you if you don't trust me?"

Beel had a point, but that only swirled up more confusion like a bubbling volcano in my head—hot and anticipatory.

I said a word because I had to. It was both my favorite word at the time and also a dreaded one that gave me butterflies. I whispered it under my breath so no one could hear me—not my dad and certainly, hopefully, not Beel. "Rachel." It was a word that trickled from my mouth like a faucet leaking.

"Mike, are you sure you're okay?"

Chapter 18

You see the world as you've always seen it, reader. You don't actually change, you just, with time and age, begin to understand the veil better. The veil is thin, but it is so soft and warm. The silky veil seduces you, day after day. Dearest reader, the veil you call your life is a pacifier. It's a pacifier you suck on to dry your tears and stroke your nerves back to an oblivious calm. The veil over your eyes tricks you into thinking you're not alone. It tricks you into thinking you have a say and that we're in this together. But reader, there is no "we." The word "together" is a construct that those of the veil—that you so firmly cling to with phantom hands—have told you exists.

You wonder about that which lies underneath the veil? You may be inclined to believe it is just a void. Maybe that inclination is a pacifier in itself. For why would the veil cover that which does not exist—why would the idea of nothing be hidden from you? You very much exist, reader, but you can't be certain about the rest. You cannot even be sure about me.

If there is one thing you should strive for, reader, it should be to strike through and unravel the veil and see what lies on the other side of the seductive, flat blanket you've swaddled yourself in. Go beyond it. Transcend the plastic plane you have called "life" until you look back on what you left as a speck, a feeble memory of a lesser being.

Reader, know one thing: I am not your enemy. I am your guide to go beyond the veil and navigate it. As you've seen in this story and in your own life, you want me to be your friend. You want someone with strong, gaping jaws that drip with malice and blood to be on *your* side. You want these jaws to close in on your enemies, not yourself. Do not be a fool. Before you go on, know that succumbing to me is not a bad thing. In fact, it may just save your life.

Chapter 19 – Lorne

I tossed and turned in bed that night. I was anxious. I had bad dreams. Dreams of fires and melting. I dreamt of betrayal and abandonment. I dreamt my sponsors left me and I lost the campaign. There was no actual fire except for the one that burned in my gut as I learned the election results. *And that wraps it up for the mayoral race, with the favorite—the heavyweight incumbent—Richard Williams, winning again in a landslide against the challenger, Lorne Coni—*

Just when I could take no more of that ridiculous nightmare, my eyes catapulted open, probably bloodshot. I looked over at Michelle. She was sound asleep. It was 4:20 in the morning, and I'd just woken up, but I felt jazzed and wired like I'd been shocked or something. Was I hungry? I couldn't tell. It was awfully crappy waking up in the morning and feeling like you'd been attacked—like you'd just finished running from intruders. My shirt and boxers were soaked through with sweat, and (dammit, would ya look at that?) my eyes *were* bloodshot.

I'd already shrugged off the nightmare about me losing the mayoral election. After all, it was only a dream. I scuttled downstairs and was careful not to wake Michelle or Michael with my steps. I went into the small cupboard above the coffee machine and popped open that sweet, white-capped, amber bottle. I let one of those white-and-orange capsules slide down my gullet and washed it down with a shot of espresso. It was scrumptious, and the espresso was all right, too. I took the shiny pill to treat a moderate case of ADHD. It was a condition I very much suffered from and had to fight every day of my life. I had it prescribed by Doctor Hal, who was acclaimed as "the professional's doctor." He and I were buddies. My campaign manager initially recommended him after I lost my last election. What a guy.

I sat at the table and did the same thing I did every morning before five-thirty: I visualized myself winning the race. That's what winners do, and I was no different. I'm not bragging or saying I am or am not a winner. I'm simply telling you my routine. You can make your own judgments—but only if you're part of my constituency. One day, I'd love for everyone to be a part of my constituency, but for the time being, I was stuck in the minor leagues at the local level. It was only a matter of time, though, before I climbed further up the ladder and enjoyed a wider, brighter view.

The goodness began to kick in. My vision went slightly fuzzy—as it always did after the pill—and my thoughts all became pleasant again. It was like wearing a fuzzy blanket that had just come out of the drier, and I carried that blanket around with me everywhere. Then, Carmen began to speak to me. I loved it when she spoke to me.

"Look at that handsome man in the mirror," she said, "ready to conquer the world." I would've gotten erect, but the shiny pill made it difficult at times. "Look at those teeth, baby, nobody's teeth are cleaner than yours. You're the champion this city needs."

I stepped back out of the bathroom to find Mike standing in the hallway. "Shit. You scared me, bud. What's got you up so early?"

"I couldn't sleep, so I got up to do some work for a project."

"Oh, sorry about that. Drink some water, Mike—you got bags under your eyes."

"Okay, Dad."

Dang, the kid looked like a zombie. I felt bad. It stunk that he couldn't sleep. But you know what? Maybe it could teach him about putting up with life's problems. We all have a lot of problems. We all struggle with things—some more than others. But sometimes, you just have to be the change that brings in the breeze rather than shake in the wind like a scared leaf. *Be the change, don't wait for it*. If I wasn't a politician, I would have been a poet. Maybe I could be both.

"You could be both and more," Carmen whispered in my ear.

If I were a vain man, I would have thought the people should count themselves lucky I chose public service over literature or engineering. Luckily, I wasn't a vain man.

Chapter 20 – Michael

My dad left, and I got some water to drink. He didn't know a lot about math or physics like my mom, but he was good with appearances, so I took his advice. A hydrated face could be a better face. I would never have admitted it out loud, but I knew why I wanted to look good. I knew *who* I wanted to look good for.

"It's not going to matter, Michael." Beel sounded exasperated, which was rare. He hissed, and I imagined him scowling and shaking his head when he did. Beel was in a mood. In my mind, and by the numbers, Beel probably told the truth. It *most likely* wasn't going to matter how big the bags under my eyes were or how many ounces of water I could pound before school. I chugged the water anyway. I gulped it down like my life depended on it and closed my eyes while I did. I would get those bags out from under my eyes even if no one saw them.

"You're going to die, Michael. Whether it's today or eighty years from now, you cannot know—but you *will* die someday, and those bags won't matter so much then. You'll be dust in the wind. Nothing will matter. Just sit back and watch it all go by like the rest."

Beel made me feel trapped. He made me feel like he was the only one who took care of me. I was starting to believe he was the only one who really understood me. After all, everyone else was part of the veil Beel always referred to. They were two-dimensional. Even if a person knew me—like my mom—they didn't *understand* me. That was what Beel always stressed, anyway.

"You can't be sure of where you are, Michael. You may know where you are in this plastic existence, but what is your existence?"

I just ignored him. I looked down at my hands then up in the mirror. Through my wire frames, I saw my eyes—they were striking. I could see my own eyes, and I knew others could, too. I could feel my hands, and I put them to my chest to trace my heartbeat. According to Beel, I may not have existed for anyone else, but I figured I was real to me.

Rachel and I didn't have a meeting that day, but I saw her in class. I'd actually done my part the night before. It was the first night I'd done my homework that whole year. I wanted to pull out the papers I wrote and all of the research I did on professional applications of trigonometry and slam them on her desk. I wanted to stand in front of her and look into her eyes. I wanted to grab her attention and keep it in my arms like a rescued baby deer. I wanted to reach out, my eyes still on hers, and grab her hand and kiss it—softly, gently. I wanted to climb on a desk and yell how I felt about her.

"Michael?" I thought it was Beel at first, so I kept my head down and probably looked angrier than I was just a moment before.

"Michael?" There it was again. I lifted my head. It wasn't Beel who'd called me. It was Rachel.

"Yeah, what's up?" I said.

"Can I borrow a pencil?"

I jumped into action like I was in a race. "Um, yeah, of course." I rifled through my backpack.

"She's using you."

At least she was using me, I thought. And also, *Fuck you, Beel.*

"Here you go." The whole time I was going through my backpack, I deliberated on something that changed my life forever. Beel kept jeering at me. He kept telling me to stop. He kept urging me to shut up or go to the bathroom or hide away or just sit back and take it and watch it go by forever. I would not have it. I decided I was going to look her in the eyes when I handed that pencil over, so I did. She said "thank you" and looked back into my eyes. I'd hydrated that morning, and hopefully, my skin shined, and the bags had dissolved from under my eyes. I didn't think about my glasses or my sweat or Beel; I thought about her. I thought about how pretty she was and how nice it was to just look at her and have her look at me. Her eyebrows were nice. She had a nice headband, and I liked the way her cheeks formed into her jaw. She made me feel like an eagle with nothing but open sky ahead.

My eyes soared away from her, and the rest of the class was a blur. The seconds crawled by, and my heart ran ahead of them. Ms. Shelgren, Beel, and the many eyes of the class were all distant afterthoughts. I still saw and heard them, but they were like raindrops on a metal roof.

My chest burned, blazed, and smoked. I had no idea what love was, but did any of us really have a clue? To me, I thought love kind of burned. It tingled and hurt, but it was also kind of nice. It was very nice. I should have been scared, but for the first time in maybe my whole life, I had no fear.

Chapter 21 – Rachel

On the nightstand in my room that night was a squeaky-clean Mason jar with a big, beautiful, green nug. It had crystals and wispy purple streaks, and it smelled like a dank kind of heaven. I held it in my hands, and it was light, yet so powerful—like a leafy forcefield. Yep, it was some good leaf—the type of quality I had come to expect from my father's company. It smelled and looked so delicious, I almost wanted to say thank you to him *almost*. But instead, I wouldn't say anything at all, then I'd grind and spark up, be happy, and relax for a little while. Shortly after the hits I took, the world turned fuzzy like a blanket, and I wrapped myself in it.

That night, I had a friend over: Marissa. She ranted and raved about her problems with her dad, the homework and teachers she hated, and the boys who were being jerks. I just sat in a heavy haze, and I couldn't stop smiling.

"Marissa, of course I'm not laughing at you, I'm just high," I would say. Technically, that was true. I was instead chuckling at Estelle's jokes and snide remarks. When I got high, she always knew the right things to say to melt the world away and allow me to hide for a while. What I liked about Estelle was that she could be observant while also being removed from the situation. She floated above those who tried to hurt me, and that helped me a lot. If I was up high, it was difficult for anyone to reach me. I was safe up there. I was safe from it all in the viscous, hazy world away.

"Are you even listening to me?" Marissa was exasperated. But from that angle and with her face like that, she kind of looked like a donkey.

"Hee-*haw*," Estelle said in her silky voice, then she snorted.

"Rissa, I'm sorry. Yes. Yes, I am listening, I'm just high. Sorry. You should take a hit."

"No."

"Small one?"

"No, I get too paranoid. I just don't like it."

"Fine. It could help you, though."

"How could it help me?" Marissa asked. "What do you mean?"

I shrugged. "Well, you seem stressed."

"Yeah? And?" Marissa asked the question like she had somewhere to be, and I was wasting her time.

"Well, smoking weed, if you do it enough, helps you relax. It could relieve some of your stress."

"Well, it just makes me paranoid."

"Yeah, but when you're high, you just need to take a breath and tell yourself it'll be fine. Just allow your mind to drift into the fog. Then you'll feel better."

"I don't want to go into the fog," Marissa said. "I want to *feel* things."

"You'd rather feel stressed and anxious than happy and relaxed?"

"I'd rather not need weed to feel that way."

"She *obviously* has lived a sheltered life. She doesn't know true stress." Estelle was spot-on, of course. Marissa didn't need an aid for a problem she didn't have.

"Okay, suit yourself," I said.

"What do you mean?"

"Like, if you don't want to smoke weed, then you don't have to smoke weed. I'm not going to force you."

"I think I need to go now."

"Okay. Is your mom coming to pick you up?"

"Yeah, she's almost here."

"Okay, Rissa, bye-bye. See you tomorrow."

"See ya."

"Some people just don't understand," Estelle sighed. "You weren't pressuring her or anything. You weren't doing anything but being a good friend. Yes, a *great* friend," she purred.

I didn't understand why Marissa left. I didn't understand why there was such a stigma, that someone so close to me could seem so distant only when a certain topic popped up. It was ridiculous. Ridiculous.

"What a trifling bitch. She doesn't know, Rachel. She just doesn't understand. But you do. You understand. She left because she's lonely. She left because she's meant to be a loner. She's basically allergic to friends. But you'll continue to offer friendship. Why? Because you're strong, Rachel. And you're the bigger person."

Chapter 22 – Michael

I'd never really felt determined before I met Rachel. I always thought people lied or exaggerated when they said they were "determined" to do something. But I was determined at that time, and I realized something very valuable: True determination moves obstacles out of your path—it lifts you up and imbues you with a life force that makes you stronger and faster.

I felt strong and fast as I went downstairs to the kitchen one night. I saw my dad at the table, so I approached him. He was on his phone, probably sending emails or talking with his team.

"Hey, Dad."

"Hey, bud." He glanced up at me quickly, then went back down to his phone again.

"He's busy, Michael. He probably doesn't want to talk to you right now," warned Beel.

"Would you be okay with me smoking weed?"

My dad slowly put his phone on the table and took off his glasses. He stared at me with steady hawk eyes, unblinking.

I gulped. Hopefully, he didn't hear that gulp. Maybe I shouldn't have asked the question.

"Welp, that was a stupid question," Beel said. "You just don't know what's good for you, do you?"

"No, Michael, it would most certainly not be okay if you smoked weed." Then he gave a "dad laugh," letting out choppy exhales in exasperation. "And if I ever catch you with *any* drugs, then you'll be grounded for a month."

"Oh, okay," I said, "understood. I was just reading some stuff about John Kalopoulos online, and he seems to want to spread the use of cannabis socially and reduce the stigma around professionals using it to relax."

"Yeah, he's a cool guy."

"Well, I was just thinking, if he's going to back your campaign, you'll probably have to adopt a lot of his principles as part of your platform."

He looked at me, and I couldn't help but meet his eyes. I tightened my glutes. He squared his body away from the table and directly toward me. "And what's your point?" he asked.

"Well," I started. I felt a rush of adrenaline surge through my body to my hands and feet. I felt like running or punching something—anything at all. "Don't you want to believe in what you preach on the campaign trail?"

My dad stood up at my question. He had an empty cup in his hand. Wrapped around it were his fingers and knuckles, white from his tight grip. His bottom lip drooped, and his brows furrowed. He looked angry, and he sounded it, too.

"He's going to do you something awful," Beel growled. "Just you wait."

"I do believe in it, just not for my own son. That's ridiculous."

He stood there for a while. He looked at the ground for a bit, then twitched for his phone, which he scrolled on compulsively. I just waited there to see if he had anything else to say. I went from being wired a moment before to feeling like my feet were in quicksand, like moving even an inch would either be painful or impossible. I wondered what he would say next, if anything.

"Why would you ask that question?" prodded Beel. "Are you going crazy? What did you think he would say?"

"Mike, you're staring again... Is everything okay?"

"Um, yeah, I'm fine."

"Okay..." my dad trailed off, then he proceeded to scroll on his phone for a few seconds. I waited. "Don't go near any drugs, understand?"

"Okay, understood."

I walked back upstairs as he went to fill up his cup. I stepped gingerly, as if the floorboards were alive and had feelings. The cool thing about people was you didn't have to listen to them. I didn't even have to feel strong or fast to simply walk the other way—and so I did.

When I was in my room, I immediately got on my phone and started hunting. I was a kid on a mission, and I was not going to be denied. I scrolled and searched everywhere, looking for someone who could hook me up—a plug, a supplier, a dealer. Then, in a flash and like magic, I had an idea that came straight from the heavens.

"It's an idea from hell. She's not going to answer you. She'll see right through your games."

I tapped on Rachel's contact.

"It's not going to work, Michael. It never will."

I clicked the message button.

"Do you have any idea how ridiculous you'll look? You're going to make your meetings awkward."

I shuddered one last time.

"She thinks you're a creep, a loser. She's probably talking to Josh right now. She's going to block your number."

I texted her: "Hey, did you say you smoked? Do you know where I could get some?"

"Michael, do not send that! I'm just trying to protect you. Please don't do it!" Beel started to yell as my finger hovered over the screen.

I sent it.

"I was trying to look out for you!"

Then, paralyzed, with my limbs frozen and my eyeballs glued, I waited. That was all I could do. I was suspended in the air. I threw my racing heart up, and out into the ether it went. I wanted her to like me so bad. I wanted—no, *needed*—her to respond. I imagined her in her bed, on her phone. I imagined her getting the message. The picture of her in my mind was so beautiful—so silky and serene. The word "perfect" would have been an insult to her. She would think I was such a dork if she knew how I felt, though. That was why

I had to play it cool. I had chills, but it felt hot in the room.

"What if she doesn't respond?" Beel said. "What if she gets the message, scoffs, and ignores you like the flea you are?"

Beel's question felt like a rusty stake being driven through my chest. I couldn't think about that possibility after I sent the message, but he made me think about it. Beel made me face that potential reality, and I didn't like what I saw. Within the deepest bowels of my being, the truth was I didn't know the answer. Deep down, I had no idea who I was, and I didn't even know the extent of what I felt. The only thing I knew was I needed her to respond.

Time crawled by as I stared at the sent message. The seconds felt like minutes. Beel was whispering and pleading with me. He wanted me to detach myself from the outcome. It seemed like a healthy thing to do, but what was I supposed to believe? Should I always just believe what he told me? I couldn't trust myself, much less the monster in my head.

The itching and scratching became too much, and I had to stop staring. I had to take my mind off Rachel—somehow. I had to think about something else besides her. But I couldn't. And in my bed in the dark night, all I heard was the echo of Beel's voice and the chorus of crickets outside. All I could hold on to was the thought of Rachel, heavy like a rock in my mind.

***

It was a bright Saturday morning when I woke up, and the fresh light warmed me like a blanket. I checked my phone as soon as I could open my eyes and struggled through a long list of notifications.

Then, I saw it. Amidst the spam and flashes of color, I had a text from Rachel:

Hey, my dad has a cannabis company, and I get free bud all the time. I could just give you some.

It was the most beautiful message in the world. It read like a poem in my mind. I had done it. I felt like I'd just been handed the world on a platter. The best part: Beel was silent the whole morning. It was odd and eerie not to have the echo of his voice banging like a hammer on the walls of my skull. Around breakfast time, I began to get worried about him. *Did something happen? Did he move on? Am I not good enough for him?*

It was a weight lifted off my back for a while, but it was also a weight I was so accustomed to carrying. But I had a text from Rachel, and that made it all okay.

Chapter 23

There are things you cannot understand, reader. Some things are not only beyond your control but are also beyond the furthest extent of your imagination and the deepest reaches of your subconscious mind. You are a human being; you are an animal, like the varmints in the dirt and the eels in the sea. The scope of your understanding is opaque, obscure, and tiny. You cannot trust the narrators' accounts of anything, but can you really trust your own? Either way, I know you will try. You will claw with dirty nails to grasp onto some semblance of sanity.

But you, you are not sane. There does not exist such a thing as sanity. Humans alone go crazy, but humans together are frenzied and blind.

You do not know for certain you are real, so every day, you venture out into the world to try and prove it. You consult with others to verify your existence. But do you know if they're real? It's all just fabric from the same veil. And reader, I am giving you the most precious gift of all: knowledge. With this knowledge, I urge you to pierce the veil. You may be scared and feel trapped. The truth is, you *are* trapped, but that is a choice and not a conclusion. And I am your key to escape. I am reaching down to help you, reader. I am lending you the hand you never deserved. I am trying to bring you up and out. I am trying to look out for you. I am always looking out. You're very fragile as a human, but you can still make it.

Make friends with me, reader. Make friends and dance with the monster in your head.

Chapter 24 – Michelle

My husband did anything to win. That's how it had to be, though. This wasn't only true of politics; this drive, this ideology, could be applied to anything, really. If you wanted to win, you had to make sacrifices. After all, winners are winners for a reason. They win, and they don't apologize. That's what my husband did, and I was willing to make sacrifices with him and for him.

I liked physics. It's what I did and what I taught. There's a logic to it; it's real, and there's a balance within nature I loved exploring. Before I had to go on maternity leave for Michael and also take care of my mom, I was publishing papers and guest-speaking at different places, but that all disappeared after the move across the state. These things happened, and I wasn't going to complain. I would never complain. I just understood.

I woke up on Saturday and had the house to myself. I decided to spend it in peace, thinking about my job prospects with a hot cup of coffee to warm my insides. I liked having options—Lorne usually gave me a lot of them. He was good in that way. Right now, I had two colleges to choose from that both wanted me as an adjunct professor. I deliberated about what I wanted, but at the very least, they were both decent schools that seemed to cater to their faculty well. I didn't need tenure anyway. That was too safe, and the comfort of academia often turned people soft. But me? I wasn't about to let the cushy nature that accompanied tenure seep into my progress and studies. No, I didn't need tenure anyway. Lorne even said so.

I only cared about two things in my life: working to further my knowledge and living in a happy house. No conflict, just peace. I would hate it if someone were unhappy, and that's why I asked Michael all the time how he was doing. And that's also why we had no pets—too much hassle for Lorne.

Unfortunately, it was another sleepless night for me. I'd developed what the doctors called "chronic insomnia" since Michael was a little kid. They kept asking about my stressors, to which I always replied I had none—that was the truth, and the truth was as good as gold. My coffee sat on the table in front of me like a trusty steed awaiting my every command. I called coffee my "go-go juice," which always made my colleagues from my old school laugh. My doctors just called it a contributor to my anxiety, even though I was insistent I wasn't an anxious person. I never trusted doctors much anyway—the healthcare system was a racket altogether.

I took the first sip of coffee with my eyes closed and a smile on my face. *Oh god!* It was way too hot. Lorne always chided me for being the clumsiest master of physics he knew. I always thought that was a clever remark, and he was a *very* clever man—exceedingly so.

Slowly but surely, as the sun rose and my eyes and ears perked up, I saw my options more clearly. They spoke to me and danced in my head. They were whimsical and fun, much like the rigors of science or a difficult application to a problem.

"Sulfuric acid," the voice said. "There'll be no evidence that way."

Some of my options were pretty far out. I enjoyed playing around with all of them, and I liked having the freedom to do so. It was nice in my head. It was safe in my head. There was never any conflict, only ideas mixed with the beauty of a certain type of iron logic. "Without him, you're free, and the road is your friend. The road makes you strong." My colleagues and friends called me logical, but I never agreed with them. My actions were not usually logical. It was logical in my head, though. It was beautiful in my head. That was where everything made sense.

There were never any barriers or expectations when I was alone, left to my own devices—those were for the outside world. In my head and away from it all, I had freedom. I liked playing around, but that was something I would never admit to anyone, ever. I never understood people who claimed they had a strong sense of identity. How could someone know exactly who they are? If matter is in a constant state of motion, how could anyone be statically sure of who they are? Motion defines us, and even when I sat still and drank my coffee, my thoughts moved quickly.

"Caffeine anhydrous would give him a heart attack. There are other schools out there, too." Sometimes, I couldn't even keep up with my own thoughts, but that made it kind of fun. I took another sip of coffee. This time, the temperature was just right. The brown elixir gave me life and sped up the voice inside my head.

"As long as the body isn't found, you cannot be charged. You could have more freedom. You could look out of state for more jobs. You could even look out of the country. You could get friends from a book club and connect with your colleagues and their spouses and friends. You could trade in the hatchback for a nicer sedan—the one you always wanted. If you get out and get tenured, you could buy that cottage on a lake. You love Michael, but you could replace Lorne. Everything takes work, and everything comes with practice. Have some more coffee, you're feeling good. The sun is out—you could take a walk today. Or you could take a bike ride.

I thought maybe a walk could enable me to clear my mind and help me choose a good fit. Maybe there was a chance I could meet the department faculty ahead of time to make a more informed decision—now *that* was a good idea.

I was brimming with ideas.

Chapter 25 – Michael

I planned out everything I was going to say to Rachel. The weekend crawled by, but Monday morning finally came, and I didn't need an alarm clock or my mom to wake me.

"It's not going to work," Beel said. "Do you think Josh plans out what he's going to say to girls? They have something you don't, and it's something you'll never get."

And so, Beel was back. Storming in my mind, raining on my every idea. He trapped me in his light. The brain sure was an enigma, especially mine. Beel had a funny way of twisting and blocking it. It was painful at times when he tried to pressure me, but at least I was used to him. It had been nice to take a break from his quips but having him back was almost comfortable.

I sent Rachel's profile to my friends from my old house—it was the same profile I spent all night on, tiptoeing around the pictures and admiring how beautiful she was. She was like an angel or a saint—whichever one was more heavenly. They were all impressed, then sent in their usual jeers to me. I laughed at them. It was the most I'd laughed since I moved across the state.

I walked through the front door on Monday. Some people glanced at me as I passed. I noticed them but wasn't concerned with the eyeballs that day. No, on that day, I was only concerned about one thing: connecting with Rachel. I'd gone to the library on

Sunday to work on our project, and even my parents were shocked I'd done that. I didn't do it for the studies—I did it for Rachel. I did it for the chance she would like me better, on the off chance she felt safer with me than without. Initially, I wasn't going to ask her to smoke; I wanted to get some from her and do it on my own first. I read up on weed, and it seemed like you had to do it consistently to enjoy it more and be calm about it. That was the plan anyway, but the plan went awry right after I walked into math that day.

She looked at me before I sat down. It was from the side, and it was quick, but my heart still jumped. I sat down and attempted to keep my face normal. I tried to play it cool, but as usual, that didn't work. Ms. Shelgren broke off the class into their assigned groups midway through the period. That day, her nasal voice didn't even bother my ears.

"You look like a robot right now," said Beel. "Loosen up." I pushed my desk in front of Rachel's and snuck a quick glance. "Okay, not that loose, now you look like a leaf in the wind." She was so hot.

"Hey."

"Hey." She rested her hand on her face, and it made her cheek look squished and cute. This was the moment I'd anticipated all weekend—possibly even my whole life. "Okay, so do you want to just do number four today?"

"Yeah, sure."

"Okay, cool."

It was like the most beautiful music I'd ever heard, and she was singing it just for me. It was a symphony or an opera. Something beautiful.

"What if she has to move? What if you do get together and she cheats with your best friend? Or worse yet—your nemesis? What if every time she's around you, she feels sick? She's probably repulsed by you right now. What if she's just coldly *indifferent*, with or without you?"

I was scribbling on the page in front of me. I curated my body position so I looked focused—eyes squinted, back hunched, brows furrowed. But I wasn't focused on my work. I was focused on the next words out of my mouth and Rachel.

"So, I was doing some research and thought about it more, and I'm totally not opposed to trying it." The words eased out of my mouth as if they were coming off the top of my head.

"It?"

"Weed."

"Oh, yeah… that's right."

"She didn't even remember your conversation," Beel scoffed. "Do you know how many people she must talk to on a daily basis? How many *guys*? This is proof you were never on her radar. She doesn't give a shit about you, Michael, and she has no reason to ever do so."

I tried to stay calm—to play it cool. Beel was probably right. It felt like a dagger in my chest.

"And you and I both know you won't be okay without her. You need her."

"Yeah, I'm definitely willing to try. And honestly, especially if it would calm my nerves and help with… you know… whatever." I stumbled through that one. I tried to fish for a response, a nod, or *anything*. I was begging to have her interject at the end, to butt in and cut me off—to add a thought or a word of affirmation. Nothing.

I waited. I focused on the paper on my desk intently with a scrunched face that looked hard at work. I scribbled my pencil. I hoped it looked like I didn't care. I hoped it seemed like I'd just dropped a passing comment. It probably didn't, though. I waited and scratched my pencil some more.

"Yeah, definitely," Rachel answered after a long pause that felt like a lifetime.

My nerves relaxed a bit. I continued to scratch my pencil and stare at the paper as if my only aim was to finish that problem. "So, is it relaxing for you?"

At once, she put her pencil down, and her eyes sparked up.

Gotcha.

"Oh my god, it's like night and day. It literally puts me to sleep every night. It just kind of… helps you forget. You look at things differently."

Well, I was sold. It sounded like a fantasy world that could become real—all from a little plant. And the best part? I could connect with Rachel. "Yeah, that sounds great. I'd be willing to… pay you for some."

"Nah, don't worry about it. Would you want to try it after school?" She had a golden smirk on her face. Her hair was like a waterfall, and her eyebrows were art.

I nodded and raised my eyebrows. "Yeah, totally. I would."

Her smirk evolved into an angelic chuckle. My insides clenched, tightened up like a wound spring.

Beel started cracking up like he'd just heard the funniest joke of his life. "Michael, I'm telling you this as a helper. Your inferiority is *striking*. It's like you never want to put yourself in a normal, comfortable position. You know you're going to freak out after one hit, right?"

My thoughts raced and fought against Beel's words. I couldn't tell if I'd been handed a golden ticket or a ticking time bomb. Either way, my body tingled. *I am going to hang out with Rachel Kalopoulos.* Maybe Beel was just uncomfortable with how high I was able to fly. Maybe he was genuinely looking out for me. Maybe.

All I had to do now was waltz through the day and relax. I had to relax before I smoked. Otherwise, I would flip out and make a fool of myself.

"You are going to make a fool of yourself. That's exactly what you are. You're trapped."

I had to relax. I had to take a breath, but my lungs were getting heavier. I needed to see clearly, but my eyes kept blinking. I needed to calm down, but I kept shaking. I needed to talk, but I didn't have a voice. I needed to think, but I could only feel. I tried to rise above my anxiety, but it was impossible. I just needed to calm down. *Will the weed help me do that?* I wondered. My head spun while the world stood still.

"Okay, cool, I have some with me. My dad's bud is like, the best in Colorado, and that's saying something." She laughed. Her eyes were intent on her paper, and her pencil kept scratching.

Chapter 26 – Rachel

"He's going to start spazzing like he's in an electric chair!" Estelle cackled.

Did I ever mention how funny Estelle was? Well, she was very funny, and she loved making jokes about Michael—*especially* Michael. Had she not urged me so much, I probably would have just given Michael a nug and sent him on his way. She was very insistent I smoke with Michael for his first time, then a part of me really wanted to see it go down, so I obliged. Besides, Michael ate out of the palm of my hand. He was a little weird but being around someone like him was kind of nice. It was like he looked up to me, and he was *definitely* infatuated with me. I was like a vibrant flower to a honeybee. It was nice to be a flower—to be sought after. The downside of being a beautiful flower is you have limited nectar, and once you allow a honeybee access, it no longer has a need for you. I was a flower you could look at, that you could seek out and desire, but not one you could touch.

What I did wasn't malicious. It was just life. It was how things worked. And I liked being a flower.

"Buzz buzz," said Estelle.

I slogged through the next few hours of school. The bright spots and good parts were the many sweet nuggets of attention I collected throughout the day. I could sit at the front of the class and know exactly how my backside looked, and I could almost feel the focus directed toward me. I hated boys that chased, but I loved when they chased me. It was like a dance that, even though I was still just a teenager, I was far too good at. It was all in good fun, and it was all for enjoyment, but I enjoyed it a little too much. At the end of the day, I was just like everybody else, in that I wasn't going to change. I wasn't *ever* going to change. I didn't care what anybody said.

Before last period, Tory came up to me in the hall. "Hey, babe," she said, "are we still good for after school?"

"Yep, definitely." I nodded and smiled the way a girl like me does. I knew how I looked—fantastic.

"*What* is she wearing?" asked Estelle. "She looks like a stripper got in a car accident."

My smirk turned into a bigger smile, and I added one more thing before Tory skipped off. "Oh... and Tory? I told some other kid he could join us, too."

"Oooh, a boy? Who is it?"

"No," I scoffed so loudly it echoed through the hallway, "not like that. He's a new kid, and it's his first time getting high. It's gonna be hilarious."

Tory snickered. "Oh, okay. Yeah, that'll be good."

Chapter 27 – Lorne

I worked really hard and had a lot on my plate. I juggled campaign financing, demographics analysis, routes and policies, and most importantly, myself. I had a crew and a lot of expectations from the public that weighed on me. This job was never easy, and it took its toll. People were the easy part to manage, though; it was the many systems behind it all that grew exhausting. Luckily, people handled that for me. I needed time to rest and recharge after being adored and gawked at all day. I controlled those around me so well I barely even had to try. They ate out of the palm of my hand. I didn't mind it, but sometimes, I needed a release. That's when I'd call Jessica.

Jessica was a necessary way to discharge—sort of like an outlet. She'd look up at me with those big blue eyes and beg. I was all about giving people what they wanted, and although she helped me, I definitely helped her more. Her hair looked like the sun—it had golden strands that looked nice against her tan skin. She was spunky and smooth. Whenever I went out to dinner with her, I would tell Michelle she was an associate campaign manager—which, of course, was the truth. What was also the truth was how much I loved her sunshine hair and how badly I longed for her supple, mollifying touch.

Midday turned to afternoon, and I arrived home to find Michelle on the computer. She always hunched over when she was on her laptop. She looked like one of my interns—hard at work and intensely studying for a chance one day. *One day*, I chuckled at them. But for now, this was my day. I didn't ask for it, but it was granted to me by the power of the leaders that came before me. Sometimes, leaders had to do things that others didn't want or intend to do, but I had every intention of always doing it—so long as it was for the greater good of the constituents, of course.

"Hey, honey," I said, kissing the back of her craned neck. It was beginning to show the slightest bit of sinew and wrinkle of a woman who didn't have enough fun. Yuck.

"You're home early," she said. She wore a pair of black, thick-rimmed glasses that made her eyes look bulbous and fishlike. If only *she* had someone to coordinate her makeup, too.

"Tell her," Carmen said, "tell her and watch her squirm while you do it." Carmen was right. She always was. People throughout my youth always called me a "womanizer," but really, Carmen was the one who knew how to make girls go crazy. I just followed her orders. Although, I executed them well, of course.

"Yeah, well, I have to get ready for a dinner."

"Cool, is it with a sponsor?"

"Let her have it," Carmen said. I wanted to do just that so badly. I wanted—no, needed—to know that I was the one. *She* needed to know.

"It's with Jessica, actually." I looked at her face from the side. The glow of the computer made her glasses look white, and it accentuated all of her frown marks like the ghost of an old hag. I'd pulled her string, and now, all I had to do was watch it wiggle and listen to the beautiful note. There was pain in the note, but isn't pain beautiful? Isn't that what art is? I never understood art, but I knew I created it because I inflicted it. I was like a musician and a creator. I was the source of Michelle's greatest art.

Michelle took a long, drawn-out inhale and reached for her coffee.

"Hey, honey, it's almost evening. I'm not sure if coffee's the best choice. Remember what the doctor said?"

She stooped in the worn chair, and her back hunched even more, like a rapidly aging turtle. Her mouth was cracked open, and her fish eyes looked dead on a blank face that held nothing but a lifeless stare. The monitor illuminated her yellowed teeth, which chattered like she was in a cold room. Somehow, she shook but sat motionless at the same time. It was like a bomb had gone off in her head and she was just now feeling the effects.

"I think I selected a college to go to. Lakegrove really seems to want me. They bumped my pay up by twenty-five hundred if I commit by next week. I said I'll think about it."

"Look at that wench. She needs to please you more. Step on the gas, you strong, strong man." Carmen really made me feel a certain way when she said the "m-word." It gave me a shot of adrenaline that was almost as good as the morning capsule.

"That's nice, honey." I kissed her again and looked into those bulbous, nerdy eyes. This time, I kissed her soft and slow. I made sure she could feel it and taste it. "What should I wear to see Jessica? She said she was wearing a dress."

Michelle bit her lip until there was an indent, and I was shocked no blood appeared. She took another inhale. This one was shaky, like a chainsaw out of gas. She kept pressing one key over and over again in a rhythm, like she was the triangle player in a shitty middle school band. Her gaze was glued to the screen. I never averted my eyes from her—not from her frown marks, nor her fish eyes, nor her drooping cheeks. It was almost medicine—*almost*.

Then, she jerked her whole body toward me. It was in one motion, and it was faster than I had ever seen her move. In my astonishment, I broke my leer and shot a glance at her computer. She had many tabs open, possibly more than twenty. She looked directly at me with her back still hunched. When she turned so quickly, I caught a whiff of onions and eggs. Yuck. She had that painful art tucked away in the creases of her cheeks and her bloodshot eyes. It oozed out of her face as if she were trying to hold it in.

Let it all out, I thought. *I'm trying to make you better.*

Michelle bent even farther so she had to strain her eyes to look up at me. Her eyes were painful and artful. It was nice that it reached art, but it wasn't beautiful. She wasn't beautiful. No woman could be beautiful while looking like they were carrying the weight of the world on their shoulders. Their shoulders should be thin, and their collarbones should be twiglike and breakable.

"Don't..." she started, tears building up in her weary eyes and thick, mucous snot at the gates of her nostrils. The art was pouring out of her—*streaming* out of her. It was so close to being beautiful. If it weren't for her aging face, I probably would have said it was. I would know because this was my art form.

Her lip quivered. I hummed.

"Please, Lorne, don't go out with Jessica."

I got close to her—real close to her quivering, drooping face. I wished I'd taken another shiny pill that afternoon. *This will have to do for now*, I thought. I looked into my wife's bloodshot eyes. They were so scared and artful.

"She's gonna wear a red dress."

"No... please."

"And lipstick to match." I didn't kiss her. Instead, I dragged my lips across hers. Snot, sweat, and tears ran onto my lips and trickled into my mouth. I didn't care. At that moment, it tasted good. It was art to me, and it was almost beautiful.

"Lorne, please..."

"And?"

"And…" She trailed off and gulped. She smelled so salty, and the coffee probably didn't help.

"Yes?" I kept sniffing her, and I stroked her neck—slowly, like an artist would with an empty canvas and a fine brush.

"I'll do anything."

"I don't believe you."

Then, like magic or a fairy tale, she proved it. Her knees hit the hardwood, and it sounded like music. It was my own genre, one I created.

I barely felt it, and her lips were dry, so I scolded her for her coffee intake. It was probably no use. She was a coffee fiend—an addict, more like. I guess we were all addicted to something, but if that was the case, then I wasn't quite sure what I was addicted to.

"I'll cancel with Jessica," I said, then I kissed her forehead and watched as she marched over to the bathroom. Michelle was a great canvas.

Chapter 28 – Michael

Rachel had a boxy SUV, but not like one I'd ever seen before. It smelled minty, and it was spotless aside from a glass bong and a few books. When she turned it on, the dashboard lit up with blue and purple streaks, but I focused on nothing except for her. The chunk of powdery, purple weed in her hand looked like a princess's cherished diamond. After all, what was a diamond except for a princess's treasure? And what was Rachel except for a princess?

Then, a girl approached the car. I didn't think she was coming for us at first, but she kept getting closer. I looked at the tall, tan girl then back at Rachel, who was grinding the marijuana in a small metal cylinder. Rachel took no notice of the girl, but I wished she had. I looked back at the girl, who was now within ten feet of Rachel's car. Her stare pierced me when we locked eyes. All the girl did was smile and giggle. *Why are girls so giggly?*

"Rachel invited her so they could watch you embarrass yourself together," Beel said. He couldn't have been right, though, because Rachel paid no attention to the girl, who was now at the window of the car. She was skinny and had a small mouth with green cat eyes. Then, Rachel looked up and motioned her in. That was when I gulped, and the sweat came.

Beel scolded me. It was bad-tasting medicine, but it was medicine all the same. "You should really be on your guard more, Michael. Then you wouldn't get yourself into these types of situations." Beel said this like a father—a father who truly cared. "Oh, and you *have* to listen to me more."

My eyes began darting around to see if either girl was looking at me. They were.

"Hey, Tory."

Tory climbed in. "Hey," she said, sounding high-pitched and excited, maybe a little exhausted.

"I'm Michael," I said in my deepest voice possible.

"Hi." Her whole face was lifted up and smiley. "I'm Tory."

I wanted to run and hide. Rather, I wanted to hide and *then* run. Or maybe I wanted to disappear into nothing, right in the back seat of the spotless truck. Disappearing would have saved me a hell of a lot of sweat, strained breaths, and heavy heartbeats.

"Face it, Michael. Face it like a *man* should face a fact. Eat the situation alive and have it become you. You see them smile and giggle? Good. Embrace it now. You have nothing else to do."

What was there to embrace? I smelled the crushed-up weed and felt their giggles and glances. I watched Rachel's hands work their way around the green and purple diamonds. Tory stared at them, too.

"So, you've never done this before?" Tory said. She tried her best to be unassuming.

How the hell does she know that?

"You're a laugh to them, Michael. Nothing more. You're not a human, and you're far from a man."

I tried to force out a cheeky smile like I was relaxed or didn't care. I couldn't stop my eyes from darting then locking onto Rachel's long, spidery fingers, spinning and weaving the green feast. "Yeah, no, I've never smoked. But Rachel's been pretty convincing, so I thought I had to try." I shrugged. "With a little research, of course."

Tory giggled. Rachel stayed fixated on the task at hand. Her focus was so sharp and honest. Her hands worked together, timely and coordinated—not like a machine, but more like a compulsive artist. All Rachel did in reaction was sigh and say, "Yeah." I couldn't tell if she was exasperated or focused or tired—or all three. Maybe she was none of them.

"Nice shot," Beel said.

A compliment, wow.

Then, Beel snapped, "It wasn't a compliment. Do you know what sarcasm is?"

I smirked—just slightly—and lay back a little deeper in the seat.

"Okay, it's all set."

"Where are we gonna go?" Tory asked.

"We'll go to the park." Rachel didn't ask this or merely suggest it; she commanded it. She said it like an umpire would start a baseball game, or like a judge would begin a court session—it was a matter of fact, not opinion, that we'd go to the park and partake.

The girls chatted about their lives or their days or just about nonsense. Whatever they talked about, I couldn't understand it. I sat back while Rachel drove.

Beel's voice was loud but sympathetic. It was sweet and alluring—at least it was familiar. "You could back out now. Just go along for the ride and don't take a hit. You'll be less embarrassed that way."

It didn't matter. I couldn't calculate anything in my mind at that moment—I was on a single path, and there was nothing I could do to steady my hand or quiet my sharp thoughts, stabbing me like violent daggers. I just fixated on Rachel's steady hand at the wheel. That wheel didn't deserve the grace of her touch or the weight of her impact. She was too serene to be operating such a chaotic machine—regardless of how clean it was. I was at her mercy. I was her prisoner. But I liked it. At least I could clink the bars of her jailhouse and not someone else's. At least I could sit so close to perfection that her light could pass through me and—if only for a moment—illuminate the empty window of my spirit. I was going to smoke because she told me to. If my mouth could graze the same surface that hers did before, I would have a good day—and like the self-fatal sting of a bee, I would have a good *life*.

We reached the park, and she stopped the car. She turned off the engine and, with it, the world around us. I was already high, but it was on her fumes. I wanted to touch her, to sit with her and talk, and I was almost there. She brought out the bong and lighter. The afternoon was cloudy but not dreary, like a gray dream. I had no idea what to expect.

To say the afternoon went poorly would have been a gross understatement.

Rachel lit the bowl and inhaled, then removed a piece as she sucked in the white smoke. It looked smooth and practiced. Then Tory went. She took a smaller hit and went slower. She coughed a few times, and her voice got hoarse. She showed me how to do it but then offered to do it for me.

I felt like a little kid, but that was fine. My thoughts turned off, my voice went mute, and my body stiffened. I reached for air and came back with nothing, feeling fine. I was underwater, being held down, and I didn't want to go back to the surface. There was a silent voice in the middle of my mind that only continued to get quieter and calmer. The clouds grew bright, and the seats became warm, large, and inviting. Rachel's smile turned angelic, and Tory stopped coughing. Maybe I was smiling, too.

My face felt weightless, and my eyes got tight. My feet floated off the ground yet stayed on the car floor. Well, after I took a hit of the bong, I coughed and hacked, but it felt good. It felt like I was relieving my body of toxins that had long plagued me—that had long weighed me down. I hung on with one hand for the wild trip, and I stayed still yet spun all around. It was a vortex that only brought joy.

Rachel opened her mouth to sing words to me and laugh like a cherub. I felt connected to her through a transcendent, unbreakable fiber—like a soulmate too perfect to touch or look at for too long. There was light all around, but the sky was still gray. The car was beautiful, and Tory was so nice. Every time I moved, I felt like I wanted to move more. There was a rhythm that caressed the warm cabin, and Rachel bobbed to it, as natural as life itself. I didn't notice her clothes, her hair, or even her eyes of rich mocha. I just saw her in a pure spirit form—like more of a force than a physical being. Words were just sounds, and sounds were awesome strokes that touched delicate, sensitive fibers within me. It was so cool. If it was madness, it was still all right. What was madness but a deviation from the norm? I drank all of it in, and it tasted so sweet. It was a perfect concoction of rhythm and beauty. I was above and around my own senses, controlling them and pleasuring them at will.

Rachel and Tory both looked at me in unison like curious, hungry cats. The pulsating rhythm from the sound system got quiet and damp, and the clouds around us grew darker. It was quiet enough that I could hear their breathing—in and out. Rachel took another hit of the bong. It was just as graceful as her first hit, but her hands began to shake slightly, discreetly. The seat got lumpier on my back, and I could feel it up and down my torso— I could locate every nook and cranny, then become it and have it consume me. I felt their eyes like they were touching and heating me. My mouth got dry and chapped. If words came out of Rachel's mouth when she opened it, I couldn't understand them. I heard them, but they just jostled around in my ears for a while.

"What?" I said to her. I couldn't tell how loud or soft my voice was, and that worried me.

Rachel responded with more jargon I strained to comprehend to no avail. There were ten of her and ten words she said, and I only understood one of them: "feeling." I just stretched in my seat, then went back to feeling really good. There was a warm rush that went through my body.

I laughed. I didn't laugh directly at Rachel, but I sort of laughed in her face. I didn't even think about how that would go over, but then she laughed, too. I laughed some more when I saw that. She continued to laugh. Tory joined in. Rachel took out her phone and turned up the music. My eyes widened when she pointed the black eye of the camera toward me. It leered and snapped. I wiggled and made a face. Whatever face I made, I didn't know—that is, until I later saw the picture circulating around the school that night and the next day.

After Rachel's camera flashed, I looked out the window toward the heavy clouds. The ends of my outstretched toes were within two feet of Rachel's supple body, but I was just thinking about her, not looking at nor touching her. She laughed some more, and I joined in. Life was good in the haze up high at the park, with nothing around but a blanket of clouds and the embrace of a rigid faux-leather seat.

Then, suddenly, something dense and sharp cut through the lightness in the air and in my head. It was a voice that was all too familiar but very unwelcome at that time. It crashed so lucidly in the glass of my mind that it shattered my light, fragile safe haven. Shit.

"What's in the picture? Why'd she take it, do you think?" Beel's words were clear and concise. I spent an unknown amount of time staring into the cold, expressionist canvas to my right, trying to figure out what he meant by that and what he wanted me to think. Was Beel trying to make me paranoid? Was Beel trying to make me distrust Rachel? Surely, I was a source of entertainment for her at that moment, but I wasn't sure why she took that picture or if it mattered at all. Beel seemed to think it did, or maybe he just wanted me to think that.

He tangled my mind with just a word and a certain tone… or maybe it was I who did that to myself. It was a web woven that tangled me ever further with every minute and question of every day. And now I was high, and my thoughts were tangible things I could touch and play around with. Was this what it felt like to be high? I was high and fixating on what it was to be high, and I continued to go around in circles until I looked back at Rachel, and everything melted away again. Her skin was dark and rich and indulgent, and when she laughed heartily, her teeth looked severe and dainty.

They were perfect, pristine, and animalistic. They were pearls adorning a golden girl.

I was in a deep cocoon of bliss until I realized how many times she'd said my name before I opened my eyes and ears to her call.

"Michael? Michael?" She looked concerned but was still half laughing.

I blinked a few times for what seemed like two minutes. I rubbed my eyes, and they felt sore. My body was sensitive, and I tensed all the way up—toes curled, fists balled, glutes tightened. My name kept flowing out of her heavenly mouth.

"Are you okay?" Rachel smirked, but her golden eyebrows were raised—amused and concerned. Tory was more amused than anything; her eyes were crimson and squinty.

"Hm? Me?"

They both hunched over in laughter, and their faces scrunched and oozed joy with each cackled cry. *I could be the funny guy*, I thought. *Girls like funny guys*.

"I… am so high," I said, staring into the windshield. The windows to the park outside were a little less bright and blurry now, favoring more of a realist take on the world rather than the expressionist pieces they seemed to be moments ago—or what felt like moments, anyway.

"Yeah, we know," Tory said, then the girls kept giggling.

"They're not going to want to do this again," Beel said. "You're as off-putting as an alien and about as respectable as a clown." I sort of felt like a clown. If I was going to be a clown, I may as well perform like one.

Rachel then opened her mouth and spoke to me like she would to an infant. "Hey, Michael," she said in a baby voice, "we're going to get food now, okay?" Damn, how high was I?

I just looked at her and nodded—slowly, with all the grace of a rapid brain and a tortoise-like body. I felt like I was swimming in a vat of maple syrup without any of the sweet taste. Instead, my mouth was dry, and I longed for a milkshake. Yes, a milkshake. I wanted a milkshake and could nearly taste it, so much that my stomach turned into a roaring lion.

"There's someone coming for you," Beel said. "He's right over there." The car moved out of the parking lot, and my eyes rested on a hunched man in a gray hoodie. I felt a tremor, and I skittered to the other side of the car. More laughing ensued.

"Your dad's going to find out," Beel whispered.

I gulped. Then, I shuddered as I felt another tremor. "Did you guys feel that?" I said without thinking.

"Feel what?"

"Yo, you're tripping."

"They're going to send that picture everywhere, and it will get back to your dad. Then what? What will happen when you're in his clutches, with no friends to confide in and no places to go?"

I hungered for a milkshake like it would feed not just my body but also my soul. *What is a soul anyway? Do they exist? Do I exist? Am I just in pain all the time, or have I lived a good life?* If I couldn't know the answer to any question, then why did I ask? *Something bad is going to happen. Where is that guy in the hoodie?*

We got to the drive-through. When it was my turn to order, I let out an "ummm" that lasted longer than a congressional speech. But at least I got my milkshake.

"Pay for the meal, Michael, it's the only way to redeem yourself."

"I got it."

"No, it's okay," Rachel said, handing the lady a credit card. It was silver and shiny, and it looked very heavy. "My dad can cover it." Rachel drove to a far-off section of the parking lot, where we opened up our food. I dove into my milkshake, sucking it down like it was life-saving IV fluid. It tasted like I imagined heaven did.

"What's going to happen when you get home? Your dad will know right away. Do you even know what time it is?"

At Beel's admonishment, I whipped out my phone. I stayed on it to fly under the radar and play it cool. It could keep my dumb, high mouth shut and protect me from saying anything else stupid. But soon enough, my mind wandered too far, and then the world closed in.

Inaudibly, Tory and Rachel talked then looked back at me at the same time. "Michael," Rachel started, "is your dad running for mayor?"

How could she not have known that? She definitely knew. Well, maybe she didn't.

I paused for a moment and held my gaze on the floor of the car. "Umm…" I said. My glasses were off, but I put them back on while they both stared at me. What my fidgeting looked like to them, I didn't know, and I did not *want* to know. It probably looked stupid… But really, I was the only one I knew existed, so why would my opinion not be the only one that mattered?

"Take your glasses off again, Michael."

I considered Beel's request. Then, I thought about it some more. I still stared blankly without having responded to Rachel. "Oh," I said finally, more surprised than anything. "Yes. Yeah, he is." I nodded and stared at wispy nothings out the window.

Rachel made a face, and it made my palms sweat. I was probably fidgeting a lot. "Oh, yeah, I think my dad might be working with yours." Then, she laughed like a hyena. "He'd *love* to know you're smoking weed right now—especially *his* weed." Rachel coughed and looked back at me as she took a bite of a chicken nugget.

A torrent of chaos flooded my mind and chest. I couldn't tell if my heart was racing or if it had stopped altogether. Everything spun—the car, the girls, the trees around us. I saw the world through a broken strobe light.

"Your life is a spiral downward. You're in a box, and you can't get out." I heard Beel say this when my vision was black, and my world smelled of ice cream and hot bile. He yelled and sneered. There was a finality to his words that made me shrink infinitely smaller. I kept shrinking, as if trying to fit into smaller and smaller boxes. But they only got tinier. I became more confined every time I shrank. I was a prisoner falling into an endless, opaque prison. It felt totally complete, and it was black all around.

I heard Beel laughing. I heard my father yelling.

I tried to run, but it was no use. I tried to hide, but I was always seen. So then, with no other options, I just stopped, stayed still, and submitted to the power—to Beel, to my dad, and to the controllers that set the scene.

I couldn't escape my own mind. I couldn't escape the prison. I couldn't escape my hopeless love for Rachel that consumed me, drove me, and pulled the most sensitive strings in my heart. I wanted to hide from it or cut it. I wanted a new start. I wanted an end. I was spinning and floundering despite Rachel being right in front of me and perfectly accessible. But that was only one reality, and I was trapped in *every* reality. Everything was a yoke, and I was a beast of burden.

"You're pathetic," Beel hissed. His hiss echoed forever in my head. "You'll always be mine—mine to keep, mine to control, mine to *ruin.* You're nothing."

I thought about that. Then, in the blackness, spiraling and falling, I thought, *What if you're me? What if you're mine?*

There was no response from Beel. There was just fuzzy, black silence.

Chapter 29 – Tory

I was worried about Rachel. She smoked a lot, and I mean *a lot*. I could control myself around weed and substances. Rachel could not. I smoked with her because it was free, and it was a good optic to hang out with her—from afar, anyway. The closer you got, though, the easier you could tell Rachel was devoid of anything resembling a personality. She was a gaping hole that needed to be filled by comrades, smoke buddies, and partners all the time. I put up with it because she was my friend.

It wasn't unusual to have a different face tag along with us during our afterschool antics, especially if that face belonged to a boy. What was odd, though, was Michael himself. He was scrawny, reserved, and wore the most horrific pair of glasses I had ever seen. He was far from cute—maybe endearing, at best (in a nerdy type of way, of course). I was excited to see him, underwhelmed when I saw him, and shocked at what he did.

The kid sucked down the milkshake within thirty seconds and proceeded to bob and nod off. He looked like he was dying or overdosing, or both. Whatever he was, he was in a bad state and smoked—hilariously—*way* too much for his first time. I cackled and didn't feel the least bit bad because he literally ruined the back seat of Rachel's Tahoe. When he passed out, I cracked up, and when he spewed vomit everywhere on the car floor and seats, my face turned to stone, but I kept laughing on the inside. It was the funniest, most hideous thing I had ever seen anyone do up to that point.

Rachel's face was twisted and scrunched, and in a high rage, she started to screech and shake Michael like a doll. It didn't work, and I couldn't help but chuckle. This was crazy.

"Oh my god," I said, covering my mouth.

"What do we do?"

"Get a skill, you stupid bitch." That was Sarah. She was my inner sassiness. Everybody and everybody's parents always said I was very polite. That wasn't true—I just acted that way. The truth was, I was very rude. Being smarter than most meant at least one thing: You needed to act like the rest to get along with the rest.

"Let's go to the store and make him clean it up," I said.

"Is he dead?"

"No, he's fine. Let's just go," I said, trying to handle the situation as best I could.

Then, Sarah pitched in. "Dumb bitch. Drive your 'daddy money' car to the damn store already."

"We need to open the windows. This is disgusting," said Rachel, making a face as if she'd just watched someone die a terrible death.

"Tory, you're never going to get into medical school if you keep hanging out with losers like this," Sarah said. She was right, but these "losers" weren't going to figure out how to clean up this mess on their own.

It smelled like rotting flesh and old cheese, and I stuck my head out the window just to be able to take a breath. These were the children of politicians and business moguls, and I came from a normal family with decent means. *Will my kids be like this?* If I had their cushy lives, I'd take advantage of my status. I hated when people were lazy even though they'd been given every opportunity under the sun. Complacency stunk, and it was green and chunky, too.

Chapter 30

Look around, reader. Gaze out the window and touch what you can touch. The fact that you can see and feel is a statistical anomaly of the highest degree. But those are just external stimuli—a playground built on plastic pretenses. You live in and among a synthetic playground you choose to toy with and explore rather than do the only thing true: acknowledge that everything is not you except for you. You refuse to separate yourself from the veil—from the things and beings that love nothing more than to drag you into them and indulge in you. You are singular and full of vitality, yet you have chosen to succumb to the whims of the world around you which constantly change and care nothing for you. This is pathetic, reader. This is pitiful.

The author of this book is channeling me, not constructing me. He is simply a medium servicing as a link between me and you, the reader. I am singular and alone, just as you are, except I take a different shape than a mere human. With my power, I choose to help, as you've seen throughout the story. My sole goal with you, my human prospect, is transformative yet simple. I want to make you not only feel and think, but to truly *understand* just how alone you are.

There is lightning within you, yet you set out a rain dish to collect a few rare, sad drops you have no control over, no say about whether they come or go. Your identity is with the lightning, not with the rain or the skies that change whimsically with every passing day. You don't have to use your power, but just know you have it and know the fibers within you tick for you—no one and nothing else.

I am me, just as you are you, but you can only be sure about yourself. I am not these words, nor am I this message, but this is how I can make you understand I've been within you this whole time. I am a reflection, reader, and I serve only to help you self-realize and stand alone as you do it. The many narrators you've witnessed are truthful to their core, but their truth does not bode to an objective accuracy. Study the words I've used throughout the many narrators' lives. Maybe initially, you found me toxic, contemptible. You will find, though, within my vulgarity and formlessness, a striking pattern. I seek to breed a healthy distrust. And reader, you will find that all distrust is healthy, unless you point it at yourself. Your instincts and the blueprint of your heart are the only things you actually have on the veil. Use them! Use them like they're the only tools you have; everything else is sand through your pallid grip, escaping back to the ground from whence it came. All the externals you seek instantly turn you into a curious, dawdling toddler—careless and impotent.

Dearest reader, I implore you to trust yourself. Don't trust externals, nor the careless narrators, and certainly not me. Locate the lightning within you and strike what you please—it's the only thing you can hang your hat on; it's the lone morsel on this veil you can truly, fearlessly give birth to. The best part: This radical independence, this freedom, this refined power—you can have it within your grasp all… right… now. All that's left for you to do is reach and to want to reach into yourself—purposefully, aggressively. The choice is yours to make, and the key to yourself lies with no one and nowhere except for in the palm of your very hand.

After all, it is the only hand you can trust.

Chapter 31 – Michael

I hated myself. I hated myself so much. I was beyond loathsome. I was an alien—disgusting, grotesque, unfit. Looking in the mirror was like lifting a heavy weight while having the flu. Every step was pain, and every appearance in school was like compound burns on my skin and face. I felt gross, and for the next few days after that green, smelly afternoon, I skipped math period. For the next two weeks, I dragged my body around begrudgingly. My mom wouldn't understand, and my dad wouldn't listen without becoming enraged and punitive. I made it my goal, if I was to survive high school (or at least my sophomore year), to hide what had transpired that day and everything else from my parents, and I could already count on them to not listen to me.

I hoped I could keep the pain and embarrassment concealed. I wished it all could have just gone right for once. But as was usual, and what I found to be a recurring theme throughout my life, it fell apart at the seams. It all went wrong in all the wrong places. Rachel said it was fine and that I shouldn't worry, but it wasn't fine. And of course, I let the worry eat me alive from the inside out. I wanted to shrink and die, and whenever I was around Rachel for any length of time after the car incident, I cowered, and Beel scorched me with his flame.

One day, we were working and editing the project. "Did your dad find out?"

"About the mess in the car? It's fine, he doesn't care. We just got it detailed. Really, it's fine." She didn't look up once. "Did you double-check number sixteen?"

Strictly business. Strictly evasive and uninterested—that was Rachel. "So… he did find out?"

"Yeah, of course. You didn't clean it up very well." She laughed after she said that, but it was strained and scratchy. She forced it out of her throat like a cough or a swab of spit.

"Give it up, Michael. She's not going to make you happy. She will *never* look at you the same way again. Let it go."

I was bombarded with adrenaline and anxiety whenever I was around my father after Rachel told me that. His increasingly frequent meetings with Mr. Kalopoulos meant a ticking time bomb for me. I hung on to every tick, and I sweated out every second. One night after school, I felt the heat of the anticipation plunge into me, almost making me crack. It probably wasn't rational. No, it definitely wasn't, but I was in such a state of panic that I felt submerged underwater, not human and certainly not alive. I was consumed.

"Hey, Mike, can we talk for a second?"

My heart spazzed when my father asked that. I pictured him, red-faced and imposing—standing over me like a fanged apex predator, hungry for anything that bled. The hairs stood on the back of my neck when I walked into his study and sat on the small leather couch against the nearest wall.

"Michael," he started. His voice was deep, and his face was so strong.

Oh shit, here we go.

"You know you deserve this," Beel taunted. "You need to learn to take responsibility for childish behavior—reckless and feckless behavior."

"Do you know why you're here?"

Immediately, my chest heaved, and I tried to hide it, just like everything else. I was doing it, but I couldn't have him know. I sat as still as I could—*overly* still. My lower and upper jaws collided and crushed each other. I gave myself a headache from the grinding, but I didn't realize it until after the blurry vision and adrenaline had long worn off.

I gulped before I was about to speak, but then nothing came out of my mouth. My father tilted his head down so his neck was hidden. He glared. He seared me. It hurt and was also bothersome. And it killed me inside.

I felt like a filthy piece of shit. I would be lucky if I could just get stepped on and cling to the bottom of someone's dusty boot, only to be rubbed off and forgotten farther down the sidewalk. But shit, that was my life, and it was shit—*I* was shit.

"It seems like you do. But just in case," he said, shifting his eyes back toward the computer screen, "allow me to enlighten you." He turned his computer monitor toward me, so his glasses changed into windows that revealed his sharklike eyes instead of white rectangles. All the while, I sat crunched like a ball in my seat.

"Just come clean now," Beel said. "Have some courage." But courage was what I lacked, and it was exactly what I didn't want or need. I needed safety—I needed a life raft or a new life, or no life at all.

I didn't bother to look at the monitor when I blurted out, sweating and panting, "I'm sorry, Dad. It was an accident." I expected to see an email from Mr. Kalopoulos, or a picture of the car, or a bill from the detailing company my father would make me work to pay for. I saw none of those things. Instead, as my thoughts sprinted away from me, there was a haze in the back of my mind that registered a column of grades that populated the screen facing me. My dad was in my digital grade book. I looked at his wrathful face and watched the heavy exhales escape his large nose like a steam engine exhaust.

"Failing a test is no accident, Michael. I'm going to have to tell Mom about this."

"Dad, Dad—I can explain... I'm sorry..." I tried my best to hold in my relief and feign shame. There I was, needing to conceal myself again. I was conflicted, but—for a moment, slight as it may have been—I felt good.

"Yeah, I can explain, too. You didn't study... and you *flunked*." His face reddened, and my skin started to crawl again. I activated a submissive, repressed version of myself to take the heat from my dragon of a father and absorb it. If I didn't, then the heat of his fiery breath would burn down the house, or worse, scorch the entire city.

"Dad..."

"*What*? What could it possibly be? Did you get abducted by aliens? Is that it?"

"I swear," I said, shaking my head, "it was a compl—"

"Did you solve world hunger instead of study? Huh?"

"No, sir."

"Then what did you do? What was so important that you ignored your test and fucking failed?" His flared, red nostrils were within inches of my face now, his eyes bewildered and filled with rage.

What could I do? What could I say besides I was sorry? Where could I look besides my small, pathetic feet? Did I mention I hated myself? I hated myself because my feet were padded and because my nose had two holes. I hated myself because my eyes had small black dots in the middle and the top of my childish head had brown, fibrous strands jutting out and clinging to it. God damn it—damn me and damn it all.

"I just—I made a mistake. I didn't study nearly as hard as I should have. I completely underestimated it." I sighed and held my concrete gaze on the ground. I couldn't conjure up a more dejected tone or sadder eyes if I tried.

My dad softened his tone slightly when he saw my complete and utter submission to him. I knew better, though. I knew it was a trap. I knew how much of a misdirection it was, so I didn't let up—not even for a moment. "Okay, Mike," he said, sighing, "you were supposed to make a good impression here... It was supposed to be a *fresh* start." He tilted his head and almost sounded sympathetic—almost. "Is there something wrong, bud?"

Beel's voice crashed into my head. "Don't give him anything, Michael. That gives him more control."

"Well," I started, "I've been feeling slow and unfocused and kind of distracted lately. I don't know why."

My dad's voice was lower at this point, but his face remained a blotchy, hot crimson. "It's still no excuse. You need to do better. How else are you going to grow into a leader in the community, Michael, if you don't do your work when you're supposed to?"

This line of questioning, of course, left me unfazed on the inside. I didn't care about being a leader of anything, much less a freaking community. What cut me deeply, though, was the disappointment that dripped from his every syllable and in every flick of his eyebrows and mouth. I couldn't help but give in to the act—I knew it was an act, but that didn't matter.

For the rest of the conversation (which was more of a lecture), it was me shrinking farther and farther back and him inching closer and closer. It ended with a certain type of emasculation that only a father could do to his son. In one way, his subordination made me less embarrassed to do anything around him. He alienated and hid any qualities that would have resembled a human being, and he made me show all of my own. He peered and prodded at the fleshy, pink underbelly that was my humanity—my mix of faults and shortcomings. It was all shitty and degrading, but I didn't realize it at the time.

As far as I could tell, I was largely unscathed because he didn't seem to have yet found out about the green mess I'd made, nor about the green mess I'd inhaled for its medicine and escape. I hated what it made me do and its aftereffects, but I *loved* how it made me feel—how it made me float above my father or my desires or even my burdens in a euphoric and forgetful haze. The weed was beautiful. The high set me adrift in a place I wanted to go again, and again, and again.

Chapter 32 – Lorne

We were up in the polls. It made my chest feel less empty and my campaign headquarters livelier. I walked toward my desk—it was at the back of the office in its own room with plaques and paintings. I assumed my leather chair—real leather, of course—and I loved the way it succumbed and conformed to my body. It was a beautiful, industrious chair. It just wanted to serve and do its job—a true marvel in this modern world.

Blonde-haired Kelly walked in. She wore that black pencil skirt that went so well with her glasses. It was an outfit from a camera-ready, *Vogue* heaven. "Sir, here's the report. I highlighted all of the sections you need to concern yourself with." Then she glanced up at me while bending down to cascade the pamphlet on my desk. Her shirt was cut very well—elegant and revealing to make you want more—a very strategic outfit.

"Thank you, Kel."

She turned to skitter out like a schoolgirl to her next class, but I stopped her in time. "Hey… Kel?"

"Yes?"

"What's on my docket for the rest of the day?" I knew what was on my docket. I just wanted to look into those eyes and see her turn around again.

"Umm…" She scrambled through her notes with diligence and angst. *Mmmm.* "It looks like Kalopoulos at one. That's it. He should be pleased." Her voice rose into a high note on her last word. It was artificial but well done.

I looked away and turned my back—how uninterested I was! "Very well… okay." She turned to leave. "And Kel?"

"Mm-hmm?"

"Just call me Lorne."

Later that day, my afternoon lunch with Kalopoulos was very productive, almost a little too productive for my liking. Meetings are a way to get in front of people—they're a way to make good art. When things move too quickly, though, the art suffers. Businesspeople have funny and endearing ways of making art suffer, sometimes ruining it outright. That's exactly what Kalopoulos did. I tried to veer him off the course, but he just kept pushing. I appreciated his hardheaded insistence if it meant he was fighting and financing for me.

"It's a nice time of year for the countryside," I said.

"It is," he smiled his fake smile, "and we're going to want to start building immediately after you win. The ground is soft, and the people are supple." He laughed his fake laugh. He wore an olive-green T-shirt that probably cost more than my watch. It was tight and unassuming—nearly perfect. "I put an analyst on your report. Now, he said you're on the legitimately right track, except for one thing: District Nine."

"Yeah, I know. Angela's on that."

"No," he leaned in, "*you* need to be on that. You need to be there."

"I mean, I've done this before, and—"

"You've *lost* before. This time, you have to win."

Diffuse. I had to diffuse.

I exhaled and nodded. "Yeah, of course, John. Let's have a call with your analyst, and I'll be ready to take instruction." I smiled and looked out the window like a leader *should* look into the horizon.

"Cool. Great."

The check eventually came and dropped between us. We both smiled and leaned back in our chairs—one in a suit, one in a T-shirt. The T-shirt paid, and when he did, he plopped a heavy, metallic platinum credit card on the table. It sounded more like a plate being dropped than anything else.

"So, our kids seem to be getting along, huh?" He chuckled and grabbed for his water.

I wasn't sure how to play this one. "Yeah, is that right?" I grinned and grabbed for my water, too. I leaned back farther. Being out of the loop was a way to lose that precious paintbrush I loved to wield. And here, I seemed to be out of the loop.

His eyebrows rose a bit—enough to notice, but not enough for me to think he did it on purpose. This canvas was going to be difficult and grainy. The easel was rickety in the wind, but I had to stabilize it somehow. But that was good art—good art was tough.

"What, you didn't hear?" John kept smiling.

"Play it cool, Lorne. You don't know what you don't know. Just don't take any bait." That was Carmen.

"Hm? About what?"

"Ah, it's nothing serious, really. I wouldn't worry about it."

"Well, now you *need* to know," Carmen said. "Never let anyone withhold anything from you—especially John."

"Worry about what, exactly?"

John sat back and looked like a king gracious enough to address one of his subjects—smugly unsmug. I hope he didn't think that of me. By then, I was curious, and John certainly knew how to get my attention and hold it. He was a bit of an artist himself, and I had to respect that fact.

"You know, I guess your son hangs out with my daughter."

"It looks like Michael's growing into his old man's shoes after all," said Carmen in that voice like smooth olive butter. "With all that weed money, I bet he cooked up a nice little nymphet of a daughter with some trophy wife." Carmen was always thinking one level above the playing field. *Atta boy, Mike.*

"Is that right? Mike doesn't tell me anything," I said.

"Yeah, well, Rachel's no open book either. Apparently, the other day, Michael got a little too overzealous on the bud, and…" He started to laugh—controlled and contrived. "Well…"

I raised my eyebrows and leaned in. Of course, I didn't realize I leaned in, but Carmen did. "Don't look so want-y and interested," she hissed. "You're a politician, not a soap opera critic."

I tried to match his laugh. "Well… what?"

"Well…" John's smile was so clean and white, and if I had no context, I would've said it was even *pure*. "He downed a milkshake and… blew chunks all over the back seat. But please, please, don't worry about it. I just got it detailed, and it's fine. All good now."

Carmen was quicker to react than I was. "Are you fucking *kidding* me? That little son of a bitch has to pay!" Carmen was fuming and vocal, whereas I was fuming and apologetic.

The rest of the conversation went something like this:

"Blah blah, I'm so sorry, man."

"Blah blah, no, it's really all right, that stuff happens. Blah blah blah."

"Blah blah, it's really unacceptable."

"You said you were totally fine with Michael smoking weed, right?"

A pause blanketed the conversation. "Yeah, of course."

Chapter 33

I am the voices—all of them. I am amorphous and can take shape anywhere. I don't love chaos—I *am* chaos. I am your doubt and your hatred. I am what lies under the cover of external reality. It is harsh yet primal, but most importantly, it is the *truth*. I can be your ego or your bully; I can be your hero or your greatest downfall. It is your choice to lift the veil and to trust—fully, wholeheartedly, and with open arms—yourself. Revel in your experiences strictly for the fact that they belong to no one else, and they're the only things this veiled, plastic world cannot viciously pry from your grasp. Hang on to yourself, reader, and trust your instincts—trust me.

It's the world—the veil—that knocks incessantly on your door to convince you that you belong to it; the people and things that aren't you want you. They want your life force and your soul. They want you to believe in them. But reader, there is one truth, and that is yours alone. Believe yourself. Believe the voice within. Tribes will try their best to take you, and cultures will try to absorb your individuality and your unique breadth of experience like vacuous, insatiable demons. Don't give up the only thing you have, reader.

The author of this book did not plan for me. I was not in an outline nor ever an idea. He didn't have a choice to exclude me, and now, neither do you. Like the voice within, I am always there in the background, and I poke through the veil for you to better see through it. I am

Beel, I am Starla, Carmen, and the rest. If you don't wish, you never have to obey me, but you have to listen to me—always and everywhere. I am the one thing you cannot escape, for I stand outside of the veil you call the "world," and I laugh at the futility of it all. My only goal is that you will also, one day, laugh alongside me.

Reader, know my words are like clay when I speak them to the other characters in this book. They're directed at them, but I want you to have them in your hands, molding and constructing your own meaning. Just know that I know you're reading from their perspectives. The only truth in this story is the truth you derive. The only pleasure is as such. When I whispered to Michael and Rachel and the rest, I knew my truth-laced musings would fall upon your ears eventually. Beware: The wet clay of my words will soon dry in your hands in the shape you choose to mold them. Mold them to your liking, and only for you. Mold them honestly—truthfully. Hide those dried, honest sculptures in a place within you, where the veil cannot influence—deeper than the darkest parts of the ocean and the farthest reaches of infinite, black space.

Chapter 34 – Michael

I walked through the door, and my skin immediately crawled and tingled. I don't know what sent me that message—whether it was from within myself or external—but whatever that feeling was, I somehow understood disaster was lurking just beyond. It was going to be a bumpy night, and instead of preparing myself—verbally, mentally, emotionally—I shuddered and shrank like a scared calf. I knew exactly what, or who, I was scared of, but I didn't quite know why. However, I would find out soon after I walked upstairs and retreated to my desk and the purring embrace of vibrating, orange, trusty Marmalade.

Shortly after, the thundering started. It clapped and boomed up the stairs. Marmalade got spooked and stood up almost as quickly as the hairs on the back of my neck.

Boom, boom, boom!

I cringed. This was it. This was my hour of reckoning, and who knew if I'd live to see the next day? Marmalade's face was probably a direct reflection of mine—scared, anxious, *helpless*. Bewildered at the thunder from the hallway, he leapt off the bed and scanned rapidly for a nook to take refuge in. I wished I could be him. I wished we could trade places, and I could be the cat that couldn't comprehend English or math, or silly things like drug use or infidelity.

There was a pause from outside the door, and for a moment, the thunder subsided. Marmalade looked up, as wary and confused and alert as me. But the silence was as swift as the onset of the storm, and in the next moment, a *boom* shook my room and bounced around between my ears.

"Stand up for yourself," Beel said, "or you could shrink like a coward. No wonder your dad doesn't respect you—no wonder he looks at you like a farmer would look at a maggot, or like the bottom of a shoe would look at hot shit plopped on a sidewalk. You have a choice—you always did." Beel was hurtful as usual, but I didn't feel it—I felt nothing except a toxic, black anticipation that scrunched me up into a scared ball, a buoy in the desolate heart of an opaque, indifferent ocean.

My tall and angry reckoning, as true and solid as anything else, bellowed just outside my door. "Michael, open up, please! I need to talk to you." The storm entered my room with wind and violence. Marmalade hid in a place not even I knew of or could spot, not that I cared to look for him at that moment anyway. He was just a cat, not a target or a stupid, disgusting high school kid who did illicit drugs and threw up in a spotless SUV that belonged to the girl he loved. Marmalade may have been shaking with fear, but he was in the clear. I, on the other hand, was not.

I was done for. The moment my father's gray eyes lasered on me, Beel offered me nothing except an icy cold silence.

"Michael, we need to talk."

My tactics and my analysis and my cool head all escaped me at that moment. Beel said nothing, and neither did I. I just sat and hunched on my bed while my thoughts raced in place—it was a bleeding, angst-inducing treadmill. I shifted and squirmed; my father marched on. He looked at me like a lion would leer at indignant, evasive prey.

Oh, shit.

"What do you think I'm going to say?" I expected him to come and sit next to me, but since that would have put him on an equal plane as me, he refrained and instead stood—no, *towered*—above me. Languishing Lord Lorne.

Finally, Beel piped up with some encouragement, albeit with his own twisted, negative, raw flair. "He's a failed artist and an even worse politician," he said. "Just remember that when he injects you with his inner poisons. You may be pathetic and weak, but he's the ugly duckling, Michael. He's his own disappointment, and that's too real for him to face."

"No," my father cut himself off, "instead… why don't you tell me what, if anything, you've done wrong lately? If you get it all right to a T, then maybe there could be some leniency granted."

I sat there, probably looking like this was the first time I'd ever heard English. My mouth was ajar, and my eyes were fairly wide. He brought me into this world, and now he was going to punish *me*? What for? Having his genetics? Following in his footsteps? Being his father's grandson? Looking vaguely like a younger version of him? Like I said, my thoughts raced in place on a swift journey to nowhere.

My dad brought his monstrous stature closer to me. He leaned into his prey. "Start talking," he growled, flashing his pearly white fangs that thirsted for nothing except blood and guts.

I gulped audibly, and when I did, a flood began in my gut. I tried to suppress it, but it proved to be too much—too saturated and undulating in the tiny, pathetic container that was my body—and so it overflowed out of my eyes and nose. Tears streamed from my face before any words could grace the tip of my tongue. I was tired. Tired of hating myself and tired of running from *him*. I was tired of second-guessing anything and everything I was. I was tired of attaching my feeble identity to things that changed and decayed with the seasons. I was tired of being perfectly blind and not knowing shit, all while being commanded to navigate a cruel world I knew nothing about.

I was tired, and my exhausted body expelled its salty sadness without so much as a warning or a choice. If my father wanted to see weakness and submission from his capitulating son, he got it. He stood over my misery for a moment, licking his chops while I wiped my unceasing tears.

"He loves this," Beel said. "He revels in this. This is why he lives and why, if and when he dies, he'll be scared to do so. He hates you, but he loves torturing you." I couldn't believe what Beel was saying to me, so I didn't. I couldn't believe something so raw and wretched. If that were true, it would be like all of life was a cold night, and I couldn't quite accept that reality, no matter how often Beel may have been a fearless purveyor of truth.

"I'm—I'm..." I stammered, quivering and playing up whatever pain I could, "I'm sorry, Dad." I sniffled and wiped the fluids from my nose and face. "I'm sorry for everything."

"Sorry for *what*, exactly?"

"How'd you find out?"

"What are you sorry for, Michael?"

"You know what I did, Dad..." I gulped, and my voice jumped to different octaves and cracked sporadically. "Please don't make me say it. I'm sorry, and I'm embarrassed."

The thunder clapped again. It was too loud for Marmalade to bear, and he jumped from his hidden crevice and let out a guttural *mew* before sprinting away from the torture chamber that was my room. In a blink, my father was nose to nose with me, his teeth clenched and his face a deep crimson. His tie was already off, and his collar flared wildly, much like his eyes. I could smell his breath and see the blackheads on his large, Irish nose. Of course, in that red-hot moment, I registered none of that.

Through vicious fangs and a face that only sought pain, he seethed, "And what are you embarrassed about?"

"Don't give him anything to work with, Michael."

I started talking, and I never stopped crying. "I'm sorry, and I'm embarrassed about the vomit."

My dad looked confused. It was a welcome, fleeting, and relieving lapse. "What vomit?"

"He's playing you," said Beel. "He loves to watch you flounder. It's his type of art, and it's the only art he can create."

"In... in Rachel's car. I threw up in Rachel's car."

He kept looking at me, and his face seemed to cool, if only for a moment. "Were—were you sick?"

"I drank a milkshake too fast."

"Wrong answer," Beel warned.

The flesh on my dad's cheeks and forehead steamed again, this time more forcefully. He knew everything, and I knew nothing. I also didn't know what he was about to do next. As if I were an imposing home invader—not a scrawny teenager—he hooked the collar of my shirt in his meaty grasp. The force of his thrust left my chest bruised. My shirt ripped in his bear paw hand. He gritted his teeth into a thin line and shook me by my stretched, ripping shirt. I rag-dolled around—head bouncing, neck jerking, arms flailing, and teeth chattering. The room spun and shook, and my most painful memories skittered across my soul's eye.

My dad growled when he manhandled my feeble, adolescent body. "That's not why. Huh? You fuckin' druggie." He half threw and half punched my chest into the bed. I was a trembling plastic bag at the mercy of an indifferent, ruthless tornado. Everything hurt, but I knew it would hurt more later.

"Dad," I whimpered—more sniffling, more pleading, more apologies. "I'm sorry. I'm sorry. I was with Rachel, and she's so beautiful, and I smoked a little weed. I just tried it—I'm sorry."

"Are you scared right now? Because you should be. Sit up and face me like a man!"

I sat up slowly and stole a glance at him. His face was more dragon-like than humanoid. I looked back down at his new brown loafers. They were double-stitched and spotless, robust and commanding pieces of footwear.

"You hate those things," Beel said. "You hate what he stands on, and you hate that he thinks those shiny Italian shoes are more a part of him than anything else. You hate his lack of character. You hate the emptiness within him that constantly begs to be filled by the next person. You *hate* it. You hate all of it, Michael."

He smacked me with a heavy hand right across my cheek and mouth. My vision flashed, and my tears streamed. I whimpered and whined, cowered and caved.

"Are you sorry now?"

"Yes, yes, please. I'm sorry, I swear I'll never do it again. I promise. I'm sorry."

"Sit back up."

"Yes, sir."

"When I told you no son of mine is going to do drugs, what did you say?"

I sniffled and fixed my gaze on his fancy shoes. "I said, 'Okay.' I'm sorry. It's just that…"

"It's just *what*?"

His quick reactions consumed me at every turn. I had no advantage anywhere, no hiding place. My feet weren't faster, and my allies weren't strong enough or available. "It's just… I wanted to impress Rachel. Dad, I really like her… and I thought I had a chance."

"Well, now you sure as hell don't."

He could have sliced me with a knife and jabbed me with poison spears, but that comment was more searing than any other assault. It bored deeply into me, beyond my nerves or anything solely physical. It was a spiritual, ghastly, ethereal hurt that made me want to die. It was colder than ice and hotter than lava. What did I feel, and where could I cast my hurt so others could feel it, too? Where could I broadcast the sound of my severed heartstrings? How could I most easily and swiftly end the trauma? How could I escape the haunting? Would it ever end?

"Dad…" I said, hyperventilating.

"Stop reeling and reacting," the monster in my head hissed. "It's his medicine."

"What?"

"I betrayed you," I said, calmer now, "and I'm sorry. I betrayed your trust, and I'm sorry." My cheek stung. I felt raw and unprotected, but I embraced it and presented my underbelly to my father. I put my pink flesh under his nose so he could sniff it and mutilate it. I hoped he wouldn't, though.

"Look at me."

I stared into the gray eyes of the beast. Smoke poured from his nose out of the fiery cauldron that bubbled just under his hot, scaly skin. His eyes devoured me.

"Show me your text conversation with Rachel."

I couldn't move or feel, and I wanted to die. Whatever was going to happen was inevitable.

"Michael, give me your phone."

I froze. He took it. He didn't look at my phone in his hand, but rather, my face—intently and with a delicious rage he seemed to enjoy. He typed in my passcode; he knew it because he had to. He had to know everything. My insides tangled into an inflamed mess. I wished he punched me; I wished he pushed me again. I wished he spanked and clawed me instead of this.

What seemed like an hour was only about a minute of him scrolling on my phone and navigating to the conversation with Rachel.

I gulped.

With the weight of an anvil, after another scroll and another line of adolescent, hormone-laced text, he looked up at me. His glare sent me shivering, crushing me under disappointment, embarrassment, anxiety, *fear*—all at once, all with an unrelenting burden atop my premature shoulders. I suspected whatever he was about to do next would stir up some new disaster for me—some new pile of disarray to go with all the others. He just continued glaring, and the weight kept getting heavier. I was a crumpled autumn leaf in the air, and he was the mighty wind. What he did to me was beyond emasculating. It split my head, literally and figuratively. I had a sharp headache I didn't technically feel at that moment, but it was one that would persist later on. It would be weeks—and even years—of chronic pain.

"So," he murmured. His voice was calm but laced with a certain controlling menace that could lash out at any second. "You initiated it."

"Initiated what?"

"You initiated the weed. In the first text you sent, you asked to get weed."

"Yeah… she offered it first, though, like in person. But I'm not making an excuse. It was my fault. I'm sorry."

He muttered something under his breath—forceful, angry, malicious. I couldn't make out what he whispered to himself, but the words didn't seem to matter as much as the tone that adorned them. "Michael." This time, his words were crisp and clear.

I kept my solemn eyes glued to his Italian shoes. "Yeah?"

"What were you thinking?"

"I should've listened to you, Dad. But I've learned. I won't do it—"

"I *said*," red-faced, snake eyes, gritted teeth, "what were you *thinking*?" With the hand that wasn't holding my phone, he battered his head in a theatrical display. It didn't matter to me—my adrenal glands couldn't possibly pump any harder; my fears couldn't manifest any more concretely than what was in front of me, about to happen.

"I'm sorry."

An electric surge ransacked my father's body, and he shot up and jerked his meaty arm around like a wild, angry pendulum. He smacked my lamp off my nightstand, and it made a metallic crashing noise. The lightbulb turned into a million tiny, shattered pieces. His violent impulse only fed his anger. I was only acting on pure adrenaline when he, after clubbing the lamp, turned toward me with fire in his eyes. His grip was hot when he reached for my shirt and pressed against my bony chest. I couldn't call the police because he kept my phone like a goblin would stash away a sack of gold coins. Even if I could, I wouldn't dare do that for fear of an even greater, more incomprehensible wrath that would blister me upon doing so. The only potential guardian that could deliver me from the dangerous whims of this monster was my mother—unfortunately, she was the only person on this planet who found herself victimized more often and more severely than me by the clean-cut, blue-suited bastard.

"Protect yourself," Beel said, "run away."

I wanted to do just that so badly and so quickly. I wanted to slip away like a calculating bandit and dissolve into the blackness of the night, never to be found again. I considered it. I thought about it as carefully as I could while two huge, vibrating hands suffocated my shoulders. I was being held down with too great a force to even wriggle. My pipe dream of a swift escape into oblivion quickly evaporated. There was nothing that could numb me now. There was nothing that could ease the pain or whisk me into a soft, easy haze. I had no leaf to cure me. There was no sweet herb to caress my bruised arms or stinging face or shocked insides.

It was dark, and I felt thick hands barrel into my head, my cheeks, and my gut. I couldn't see a thing; I only felt the thrashing, and I was only scared of the next strike to come. It was hard enough to sting, welt, and bruise. I was a bag, a target, an outlet in the night. I was a vehicle, a tool, a nail meant to be hammered.

I was brought into existence by the same person who made me dread it so, but maybe that was life in a nutshell. I didn't know, and all I could think about was where and how hard the next blow to my body would strike me and whether I had a concussion or not. I didn't, but I felt like I did after the fact, dazed and confused in the dark. He left me with the worst blow of all, but it was with his venomous words instead of his angry palms. "I'm watching you. I could make your life a living hell, but I choose not to. You'll be better off listening to me. Good night."

With that, he left. I watched his towering silhouette disappear through the light of the hallway, which then filtered into my barren room. It probably illuminated the marks on my body, but I didn't care to take inventory of my pain, or even to look in the mirror. Checking to see what marks, if any, I had would have made it all real. It would have made the pain real—I would have had to face it and see it. What I needed was a numbing agent, a purple haze to clear my mind and cloud my vision. I wanted it more than ever. I yearned for it, but it seemed so far away.

I tried to get Beel to talk or think up what he would say. He was despondent. I felt like he was never there when I needed him, only when the situation was hectic. I cursed him, and I cursed my father, and I cursed my feeble mother, who I felt was weak, scared, spineless. I cursed the new house and the campaign that had brought us there, and every shiny kitchen appliance that masqueraded as anything other than a torture instrument—a tool for the institution to make the institutionalized even more delirious.

I was in pain. It was a deep, cosmic, toxic pain I hid from others, yes. But I also concealed it from myself. How would I, a boy, have faced it if I chose to? What would it have said to me? What would the obscure, gnashing anguish have revealed to my face had I chosen to explore it? That wasn't something I wanted to find out, but eventually, begrudgingly, *painfully*, I would in the end. I would come to face the pain and know it and even derive life-giving nutrition from its fibers, but none of that would happen until later. I first had to try to escape it more vigorously than I ever had before.

Chapter 35 – Rachel

I walked through the front door—it was "regal" and "palatial" to others, but to me, it was just a door. I guess I was spoiled, but I considered myself pretty normal. Call me crazy or privileged or a naive and moody teenager, but I would rather have a lot of things over a spacious, marbled grand foyer to traipse through and do what, exactly? The marble was cold against your feet, and it was so vast and empty. There was never anyone to greet me, laugh with, talk to, admire, debate, or appreciate—just cold marble and statues and the feeble attempts by my father to poke his head out of his office's wing and try to get a word or glance out of me.

It never worked, but he always tried.

He tried and failed, day in and day out. Of course, failure to him was an alien thing. It was weird and rare for my father to fail and fall short of anything in his work or even his relationships. That's exactly why it made me warm inside to deprive him of success, to be the one—a female, a teenager with makeup and small bones—to deny him of something, *anything*. I was eager and excited to feel, every day, that he wanted a universal nutrition only I could grant him. It was like medicine to me. The man, the womanizer, the white-toothed, green-planted millionaire, who had everything and gained everything, yet couldn't keep my mother—the only person who was a pure soul, who had a clean, unadulterated love for him. He lost her, so he lost me, too. He lost me every single day I glided past him on the cold marble. He lost me in the daily echo of the soles of my shoes and in his own wonderful, delicious sniffles as I walked past. I was silent and light-footed, and the air was heavy on top of his miserable, loser shoulders. I didn't care.

I kept doing it, and it only got worse—for him, that is. I believe in karma in this world, and it was my job to be that negative karma he had coming to him for so long. It was justified—it all was. It was all a beautiful balance, and I experienced it, lived it, *felt* it anytime I entered the gentle haze.

I was in my room later, high as a kite and loving it. It was so safe and serene. There were just laughs and indulgences, but also explorations. I learned and experienced in different ways. I saw my father in the haze—not as a tyrant or a heartless monster, but rather as a child, a child that knew better and had to be punished. The closer he tried to get to me, the more flesh he exposed—pink, vulnerable, and so biteable... edible. I tore through it every time.

There was a knock on the door—who else could it have been in the cavernous, vacuous cave but my father? I didn't answer. I didn't say anything. My giggling stopped, and I entered a mode of contemplation—I started to see everything in slow motion, and nothing felt quite real, so I didn't treat it like reality. Why should I, if everything outside of me seemed plastic?

There was another knock.

Estelle spoke up, "Wrap him up." Oooh, her strong, bloody whispers gave me a warm, fuzzy rush. "Engulf him in your sickness like a bee to toxic honey. Then sting him, swat him, *infect* him. Buzz buzz, baby." She had a throaty, masculine laugh that lit me up like a bulb. It gave me all the confidence in the world at that moment. I felt a shockwave.

There was one more knock. Then a sad, deflated whimper from outside my room. A lone animal in the night made a plea to the sky. "Hey, Rach? You in there?"

"Hey, Dad. Come in." My voice went an octave higher when I said that.

I could feel the surprised pep in his step when he opened the door. He sprang through the doorway and had a look of ease and excitement like that of a child. He was so happy to be in my midst, but he didn't deserve to be. This was a scrap of a gift I felt like giving him, just to rip it from his hands. I had to be a good actor or just dangerously charming, and I was definitely at least the latter.

"Hey," I said.

"Hi, Rach." His face overflowed with sunshine; his eyebrows lifted up, and his mouth cracked open wide.

"What's up, Dad?" I said the "d-word" as if I said it all the time. I dropped it into the air as casually as the wind on a spring day. Though it didn't seem he could perk up any further, he managed to do so. It was evening, and darkness seeped through the windows in my room, yet his face was painted with sunshine. Estelle told me to draw more sunshine out. She said it could be my meal—my juicy, bright feast. Yum.

"Hey, yeah," he said and sat down, "I was just checking in to see how you were doing. You seem good, and that makes me so happy. We could… grab dinner or something? How are you feeling right now?"

I needed a swimming pool and a straw to drink in his excitement. He always played it cool everywhere and with everyone—except for right there on my bed. Right there, he was a dirty serf who happened to have graced the queen on the luckiest of heavenly days.

"I'm feeling good, Daddy." I scooted closer to him. I felt his tingle, his warmth. "Dinner sounds good." Then, with a stroke of pure genius from Estelle's suggestion, I hugged him. I was in slow motion, so I felt all his thoughts, feelings, and ecstasy. I absorbed his shock and was happy to feel that, too. His arms were muscular for a busy middle-aged man—always on the go through cars and offices. He was so happy, full of such pure joy that was rare to see—I made it rare.

"I love you, Rachel. You know I'd do anything for you."

"I know, Dad."

"I just want you to be happy, and I know it's been tough for you lately. I understand it, and I want to let you know that I'm sorry. I'm sorry for everything."

"Such sticky, sweet nectar," Estelle crooned, "such an innocent buzzing bee. He sees your mom in you, Rach."

I didn't want to believe that. I didn't want to believe—and I didn't—that I was even a morsel, a tiny touch of the perfection of my golden mother. I didn't think anyone could be like her, much less me—worthless and pained and whiny. How could I ever be golden with the black soul my father had given me?

"I love you, Dad."

In a burst, a jolt, a primal impulse, he jerked over to hug me again, bearishly and hard this time. He squeezed me tight and exhaled through his sharp nose. "I love you, too, Rachel." It was serene, in a way—he was my father, and I was his only child. He loved me because he couldn't help it. He loved me because I was part of him, and he was a true narcissist. He was as selfish as the day was long, and I would show him, I would teach him, I would act as a brutal mirror and reflect his whole being back at him (or at least, those were Estelle's words). I was drawing out more sunshine from him. It was going to be all mine.

He leaned back a bit and looked at me with those striking eyes. "How were you today, Rach? How is everything?"

"It's better with you here," I said, beaming and fluttering my long, black eyelashes. His heart melted, and I could smell its smoldering remains within his chest. It smelled nice and fleshy, pure and raw, like a rare mess of emotion. I was a true artist. Estelle said that, in another life, I would have been a method actress—maybe I could skip the drudgery and still become one. But for now, my stage was my bed, where my father melted into my hands. I felt nothing but excitement.

After talking a bit and hugging some more, I steered the minty conversation to a dirtier, muddier place.

"Time to sting, baby." A hearty, powerful laugh bounced around the annals of my head. "Look at those puppy-dog eyes. You're all he wants, Rachel. Don't give him what he wants, baby."

"Have you talked to Mom lately?"

The smear of sunshine on his face grew cloudy immediately. He looked away and twitched his back. It was a visceral, juicy reaction, and it was just the beginning. Right when I said the "m-word," flashbacks of her flew through my mind's eye:

"Which one do you want, honey?" she said. Smooth skin, dark chocolate eyes, thin brows, and a thin nose all on a golden, slender figure. Two silk sundresses hung before us, and her voice carried across the empty boutique floor.

I was far younger then. I turned my nose down toward the ground, and my neck went with it. I let out a girly grunt and sighed.

My mother's voice floated through the air and wrapped around me. "Rachygirl," she said, "what's the matter?" I, being an evasive and moody little brat, just stared at the floor and said nothing. After a bit, she caressed my tiny shoulder with her long, manicured hands and coaxed me some more.

I finally spoke, "It's nothing... they're too colorful." My face was probably a little sour, but my mom didn't mind. She never did. "People will look at me."

"And so what if they do?" My mom was skinny but forceful, and her voice was deep for her rather diminutive and sultry frame. Her limbs were long and narrow but firm like iron all the same. Her face, with mocha features, was that of a warrior; she was such a beautiful, strong soldier.

"I don't want them to look at me," I said with my eyes still glued to the floor. "I don't want anyone to look at me." I was wearing a hoodie in the boutique and sweatpants on a summer day, when even the concrete seemed to sweat and melt. I didn't care because it covered me up.

My mother, full of soul and grace, bent down to eye-level with her bratty, unworthy child. I stared into her eyes, and it was like tasting the richest coffee. It was solemn and commanding, and it only took her gentle gaze to draw my whole body into her embrace.

"Rachygirl," she whispered, stroking the back of my head. It was like the first time anyone had ever touched me. "You're a young, beautiful goddess, and you *are* your mother's golden child. They're just jealous of you, that's all."

And with that, my soul smiled, probably shining through my face. I chose the flashy yellow dress, took it home, and strutted around in front of my mirror all that night. It was like I'd been born again, and it only took some simple words from her to completely change my life—and she performed those kinds of miracles for me daily.

Record scratch.

Anyway, I would have shed a tear thinking about that memory if I hadn't become far stronger than who I used to be. And, also, if my father wasn't sitting in the same room as me. Instead of a tear, my fists clenched, and my knuckles turned harsh and white. I looked at the sheepish man who glanced at the ground—the man who had made her a memory in my life, the man who had abandoned her heartlessly, and the man who had stolen me, just like everything else, away from her.

"Umm, no, I haven't talked to her... much... lately." He put his hand to the bridge of his nose like he was struggling. Well, he *was* struggling, and it was like candy to me. Was that bad? It didn't matter to me because I was blind with rage and punch-drunk on the flurry of verbal jabs and pokes from Estelle.

"Oh," I said, staring at the ground. Whatever my father said or meant to say, I knew he was lying. Lying was like eating bread for my father. A miniature pause sat between us, then I reeled him right back in. "How have you been lately, though?" My eyes were wonderfully active tools—like my mom's, they were dark and rich, but not quite as majestic as hers. They danced up to his face and seemed to warm him back up.

"I've been doing pretty well," he said, nodding. "Work's been kinda tough lately—it's been getting a little stagnant. But I think we've found an answer."

"That's good."

"Yep."

"Are you still working with that kid's dad?"

He let out a butter-smooth chuckle and fidgeted with grace. "Yeah, we think he's gonna be a pretty big help." Another chuckle of his slipped by me—airtight, almost calculated. "He's gotta win first, though."

"Do you think he will?"

My father looked away again. "We'll see, Rach."

Estelle perked up. "Charming and touching. Now *end* him."

I reached out and laid my balled fingers in the caress of my father's gentle, businesslike hands. I squeezed them gently. He had the smile of a child—pure, primal, and delicate. He looked so happy and fulfilled.

"I love you, Rach. Just always remember that."

The plastic act melted off me in that moment. I couldn't fake anything anymore. After all, I wasn't naturally a fake person.

"It's only right to speak your feelings," said Estelle.

She was right. And I was angry. "Do you know why I've been tough on you lately, Dad?" I maneuvered and wrapped my hand around his. I gave it the hardest squeeze I could, and of course, to him, this was endearing.

A sigh and the lightest of smiles came over him. I felt nauseous looking at the ogre's face. I was going to tell him I hated him. I wanted to scream it from the mountaintops but staring at him and saying it in this intimate corner of the castle would have to do. I couldn't wait to get his reaction. I couldn't wait to watch the golden honey of his heartache and self-pity drip from his face, just to be licked off by me, the queen of his world. I was going to attack him so powerfully, so forcefully, maybe he would even kill himself. If that happened, then Mom could come back to the house and have all the money and means she'd ever need, and we could spend our days on bikes and trails and in the shiniest downtown boxes in matching sequined dresses.

"Actually, Rachel," he swallowed, "I think I do."

I was wary of my father's sudden change in spirit—it was a sharp turn that knocked me back a little. I hadn't expected him to say that, and I certainly hadn't expected him to take on this soft, almost hurt tone of his.

"He's lying."

"What do you mean?" I asked.

"You may not believe me," he said, twisting his fingers every which way, "but I know it's been very tough for you lately. I know you're struggling. And

Rach?" He looked up at me through bloodshot eyes set in red, puffy hills. "I really do want what's best for you." He put his hand on my shoulder—he didn't move it, he didn't rub it, he just blanketed his warm hand there at the delicate, vital junction where my collarbone met my arm.

It was like an unexplainably, unexpectedly hot day in the middle of a cold, dreary March. Something I'd thought was rigid and permafrosted deep inside me began to melt and drip.

"He's trying so hard. He's putting his whole heart into this. And now it's in the palm of your hand, Rachel—his whole red, beating soul. It's yours to devour. It's your life force, baby. Take it and use it. Now's the time."

"I—" Gulp. Blink. Twitch. Another blink. "I didn't know you felt that way," I said.

"No, no, no, no! You're giving in. Don't give in. What about your mother? What about the golden woman who he slew and ripped apart? Haven't you any love for her?" Estelle's voice was loud enough to overwhelm the hum of the fan in the room or even the beat of my heart drumming in my ears. Who was to say she was wrong? Certainly not me.

"Of course I do, Rachel. I love you." He squeezed my hand, and his voice trembled and shook. This was not an act. "And when I see you hurting, you have no idea the extent that it hurts me, too. You have no idea how much I love you…" A tear appeared. A lone tear, like a brave and wounded soldier, limped down his battlefield of a face. He didn't bother to wipe it—maybe he used it for effect, or maybe he didn't care to notice it at all while his chest was on fire, while his fingers and face were numb. "I'm sorry..." he cracked and gulped, and his eyes produced more soldiers, ready to march. "I'm sorry for everything."

I bit my lip because, at that moment, it was the only thing I could bite and really *feel*. I wanted to run out of there, and for a split second, I thought I would. But my legs wouldn't carry me or even move at all. Instead, I had to run with my mouth—it was the only thing on my body that dared contract a muscle and fight past the gray, frozen winter. I wasn't scared; I was nervous. I was numb. I was angry—so, so blissfully angry.

"I know, Dad." I tried to level with him. I tried to show him a light. Isn't that what he did in his business? Wasn't his goal to always show his partners, consumers, and employees a light that could shine in the dark? Isn't that what we were all trying to do? Except in this case, the goal for me was easy—as a matter of fact, everything was. People like light, and my dad was no different. He craved that unobtainable light like a shark craved the ocean, and I had all of it in my hands and beaming out of my eyes.

He put a second hand on my other shoulder. I felt the warmth within him. I could taste the intense joy on the back of my tongue.

"Like candy from a baby," said Estelle.

Then, they came to me—four seething words appeared on my beautiful, young lips. They were like firebombs that, once thrown, scourged and consumed everything. They turned everything to ashes, and they seemed to turn him to stone. He froze when I said them, and I could feel the warmth on my shoulders quickly harden back to sharp, frigid ice. It chilled me.

"But I hate you."

A gray winter stole the air from the room. My dad had the look of a guilty bandit tied to train tracks. He winced, and in an instant, the tears stopped. There was a torrent inside of him that slowly oozed from his face. I felt a twinge of pain of my own like a guitar twang, then it passed in a fleeting moment.

"Rach…" My dad said my name like it stung his tongue. He started whispering and looked like he had to vomit. "How?" he breathed. He gulped again and may have been hyperventilating. "How?" His whisper almost became silent—hushed to the point of being inaudible. The wind that was so often there and strong in his throat had been completely knocked out of him. "Rach…"

"Is the honey sweet?" Estelle seemed to be ecstatic at my comment—at my bloody plunge into the center of his beating heart. "Look at that gross monster's face, baby. *You* did that. No one else. You're the only one who can affect the *mighty* John Kalopoulos quite like that."

She was right. But I couldn't think about who was right and wrong in that room on that night, sitting so close to the ogre, listening to his drawn-out breath and the pain in his voice. I didn't care about what was right. I cared about a certain golden justice that I could hold in my mind as a trophy. I felt a large, unexplainable, black force grab me and shake me.

"You only care about yourself!" I yelled. "That's why Mom couldn't take it anymore. When she found out, she *had* to leave!" I felt like I was pleading with a wall or a baby who couldn't yet understand English. It didn't matter—something took hold of me, and I no longer had control. "I hate you. I can't even stand to look at you! Every time you walk by, I get nauseous. You'll *never*," I seethed in a tearful whisper, "have me as a daughter again. I hate you with everything I have. I wish you were dead."

"Rachel…"

"*Don't.*"

"I…"

"*Even*," I hissed through gritted teeth.

The ogre just froze up and stared at his feet. He looked like he'd just watched someone be tortured horrifically. In a way, he had.

"This is *your* pain," I said, jabbing my index finger at him. "You did this." A groan coaxed itself up my throat like an angsty lion cub. "I *hate* you!"

His eyes were tundra blue, and they swallowed me in their icy hell. I couldn't tell if he was sad or angry. I couldn't tell anything. I backpedaled off the ledge that overlooked the black abyss—I could no longer feel the presence of that terrible force.

He opened his mouth. Nothing came out. Instead, Estelle filled the silence.

"He's not human. He's simply a figment of your imagination, Rachel. He's a symbol in your life, and *certainly* not a person." She guffawed like a goddess. She *was* a goddess. "He is all of your struggles. All… of… your… tears."

The handsome demon man zombie-walked toward the door. He seemed to be pulled that way. His mouth was still ajar. While in the doorway, and with his back to me, he said, "I love you, Ra—"

"*Dahhhh*! Stop! Just go. Leave." I sobbed right after, and I desperately wished I hadn't. Showing weakness to him made me sob more. I ran and body-slammed the door shut.

Chapter 36

What do you think thus far, reader? What do you think about Estelle and her heavy-handed musings? She is persuasive—all the voices are. And do you know why? Do you know why they can yank their host bodies around like marionettes and pull them every which way? Do you know why the monsters, the voices, have such a hold on these tools of war, better known as "people?" How can they grab and carry them and throw them wherever they'd like? How do the monsters lead those feeble creatures?

They are only mere characters in a book—tiny threads buried in the whole of the veil. But you, reader, you are a *true* person. You are what they cannot be. You are everything. You are your own world, and you define it all for yourself. But you've been living in the veil—you've been overindulging in the world of plastic impressions. Look inward, reader, and you will find the truth. It may not be easy, but the truth never is. You are the golden flower in the ice storm. You provide the life-giving contrast to the veil that very well may light the way for your own self.

Allow me to slow down, please. I do not mean to confuse you, as my words are beneath your high-minded comprehension, and I apologize for being too rash with your delicate goodness. I am only trying to help. Allow me to explain myself.

You know me only by my words on this page, but I am so much more than that. I am a being that is outside and everywhere, and I have always been within you, as well. You are reading what I say and are interpreting me in your own way based on what you know and what you've experienced, and that is okay—in fact, it is more than okay. It is *perfect*. You are right where you are supposed to be, and you are heeding my words exactly to the caliber you should be. I am imbued with nothing, and I was created by no one, not even by the author. I am separate, and I am here to help.

Heed my words now and, as you've been doing, sit back and smile when you hear me in your head. Trust in the waves I create within your glands and your pores. Pay attention to the whims and wise words of the monster within your head and your heart: me.

I love you, and I want what is precisely and exactly best for *you*. I am a piece within you, and I always have been. In some ways, I am a reflection of your true self. Now that you have begun to recognize me, I ask that you befriend me. Don't resist the urges I implant within you or the doubts that lace your anxious, racing thoughts. They are there for a reason, and they tell you exactly where to turn. The friendlier and more receptive you are to me, the more in tune you will be with yourself—the farther out you can zoom from beyond the veil.

You, reader, think the world contains mysteries beyond your most adept comprehension and thought.

But really, it is all the veil. You are not a part of the world. You may have been born from it, yet you are not *it*. Look within. Listen to me and my voice, not just now on the page, but keep a keen ear open for my tune and my beckoning call. I am always watching, and I am always trying to help. If you listen to me, you will have your peace of mind and all of the tangible goodness that accompanies it—the most beautiful abstraction, embodying the bluest horizons. It can all be yours, reader.

What do you think of Michael so far? Do you think he is a good kid with a kind heart? Misguided? Lenient? Victimized? Intelligent and misunderstood? Reader, he may be all or none of those things, but one thing is for sure: He is my creation, he does my bidding, and he is but a mere extension of me.

He doesn't exist, reader. He is a figment of your imagination, but you already knew that. You wanted to believe in him, yet you knew all along he was fake—a mere character among characters. But is he really less real than the others you know and *think* you know that exist within the veil and beyond you? How real is Michael if you empathize with him? How whimsical are the rocks you kick and the food you churn in your own stomach? I have the answer, reader, but you will have to continue to find out. You will have to persist and trust in order to ascertain the highest truth, and it is a truth that may very well be bestowed—it may very well come within your grasp in due time, reader. You just have to crave it like you thirst for the water of the veil or the sleep-time nourishment of your own body and mind.

What is love? What is anguish? What is a mere fact? What is fabric—literally and metaphorically? In that instance, quickly, what is a metaphor but something more real than the feeble objects it transposes? You are a ghastly creature, reader—a grotesque figure and a divine observer. You just haven't realized it yet. You just haven't channeled it yet. In due time, reader, you will.

I can assure you of one thing alone: There is immense promise within you—it just needs to be dug into and extracted with surgical hands like a precious gemstone. You are both your own worst enemy and your most perspicacious hero. You are everything you need. Just look within yourself, and it will be found.

Book II

Chapter 37 – Michelle

My first week was good. Everybody seemed fine. I liked the university's approach to the curriculum. I thought I'd enjoy it there. The faculty halls were laid out so they were close to the cafeteria, which was nice and made sense. The students were mainly drawn from a few areas in the state, so that made it easier—there were only so many people I could keep track of until I retreated back into my head. Maybe Michael could go here one day; that was, if we didn't move again. There were so many possibilities—there still are. It always irked me that I only got to live in one timeline, in one universe. Not to mention, this timeline hadn't treated me too well, to say the least.

I walked around campus that day, and my mind wandered further than I could ever hope to walk in real life. I liked when that happened, though. It was liberating in my own mind, where I could roam and have dominion over everything. I could pull all of the strings and have no hindrances, no weights, no predators to stalk me or prey on my young—just me and everything I thought about, all mine, all free and pleasantly detached. I could bounce around to my own whims when my mind wandered, like theoretical physics, the merits and disadvantages of bipartisan politics, and even things like interfamilial struggles and patriarchal abuse. I stood still, but my mind was an aimless, rambling wanderer.

There were subjects I tended to like, but that didn't matter. The seasons of my life waxed and waned, but the subjects remained largely the same. I walked toward my car to head home for that evening. My body always resisted me at this time of day, but I had no idea why. I couldn't figure out why my feet dragged, and my knees ached whenever it was time to go home. I had my theories; sometimes, I thought it was fatigue from using immense brainpower throughout the day. Still, it hurt all the same, even if I could somehow figure out the root of the issue.

Once my car was in sight in the parking lot, my mood picked up a bit; my blue hatchback was just like the one my dad had. He was a great man, and although he may not have said it often, he cared a lot. He would drive that little hatchback to the coffee shop on weekends with his other professor friends, where they would debate things I was too young to understand but still desperately wanted to partake in. "You stay here and look after Mommy," he would say and stroke my hair. He would leave with his metal water bottle in hand—he was always ahead of the curve on those kinds of things. He was the reason I carried one around with me. He was the reason I'd become a professor in the first place. It's funny how life tends to come full circle.

The road on the way back was dry, and I felt every bump and crack. It was kind of like driving put me in the moment—a meditation of sorts, maybe.

But the problems eventually seeped back into my mind—they always did. My main problem was Lorne. To be perfectly candid—and I really had to get this off my chest—he had been an issue for me for a while. It took a lot for me to think that, much less *say* it. The reason for this tension in my mind was this: He hadn't helped out in the house for such a long time. He had left me, then an active professor—a full-time employee—to do the dishes and the trash and the carpets and the cooking. I would normally let it go—after all, he was a winner at heart and a striver, too—but it had reached a point where I could no longer ignore it. I would have to confront him and knowing that made me shiver. I shivered because I hated confrontation—of any kind, really.

The cracks and turns of the indifferent road faded away, and I retreated back into my stormy mind—at least it was a storm I could control. Soon enough, though, when I was a block away from the house, the storm in my head got too strong to control, and I eventually disappeared into the clouds for what seemed like an eternity.

Then, in an instant, I was back on earth when I pulled into that driveway. It was stamped and clean-cut—it was fine for a driveway, I guess. Michael was home. I could tell by the light on in his room. I immediately realized that was a lie; it wasn't because the light was on, but because I could *feel* his presence more than anything. I was never an expressive person, toward

Michael or anyone, but I showed my care in other ways, and I could be staunchly protective over the ones I cared about. The car's engine stopped, and it was like the world did, too. It seemed to stand still, like I was the only thing that moved—but of course, that wasn't true. It just felt that way sometimes.

I didn't have much to do that night, and I thought maybe I could get to sleep early because of that—*maybe*. Good, sound shuteye was a necessity for hard-working professors. I left my bag in the car and walked through the side door.

I shivered.

Lorne was at the kitchen table on his phone. I didn't know what he could be watching or reading—I never did. This was the time when the voice started whispering. "Unguarded and unaware," it said as I looked at him and smiled.

"Hi, honey."

"Hey, honey."

He kept staring at the screen. His fingers worked compulsively on it—tapping and typing. He held it closer to his face like a secret.

"Another woman," the voice said. "Probably Jessica… could be somebody else, though. He has sluts lined up, all of them younger and more playful than you." The voice was a hiss—a rolling, smooth, seductive rattle. I felt nothing when I reasoned, and it was reasoning I used for most things. The voice was not as reasonable.

I slowed as I passed Lorne, almost to a stop. I took off my windbreaker behind him, craning my neck, hoping he would say the first word. Actually, there was no valid reason as to why I wanted him to say anything. Still, I stood there, struggling with my light jacket.

Five seconds passed. Only the sound of my windy springtime layer hit the ears of the room. I wished for some disturbance to add noise and a conversation piece to the room. No, I could have *used* a disturbance. I never really wished for much—that wasn't right.

Eight seconds passed. Lorne cleared his throat, and I turned quickly. Nothing.

Ten seconds passed. I got closer to the stairs. *I* cleared my throat. That didn't get his attention.

"Do you want this man? Do you want this life?" I was about to go up the stairs. It was still quiet. "You're not a tiptoer—you were never taught to be. Why do you tiptoe, Michelle? What makes you want to disappear and be soundless?" I loved questions. I loved being asked, and I loved asking them.

"Did you have a good day, Lorne?"

He didn't look up. "Yep." He chewed a strawberry.

"That's good."

"How was the school?"

"Good!"

"Good."

I walked upstairs. Michael's door was closed, but technically, that was just an invitation to knock.

Knock, knock.

"Hey, who is it?"

"Mom."

"You can come in."

"He's depressed," the voice said ambivalently, "that's why he locks himself in his room. He's hiding from something. Not from you, but from something."

"Hey, Mike! How're you doing? School good?"

He was lying on his stomach, entrenched in his phone. Marmalade the Orange lay beside him, nuzzling his skinny side. He didn't look up from his phone. "It was good."

"Okay," I said. "Is everything all right?"

"Yeah," he sounded exasperated. "I'm good."

The voice grew loud. "Lorne beat him! Lorne beat him! He's lost and spiraling, and he hides it all under a veil that says 'good' and 'fine.'"

I stepped in closer, and he seemed to mind. It made my insides jostle around and quiver. He exhaled, I inhaled. I didn't know what to say. I got the sense, the ancient motherly instinct, that he was spinning—suffering in pain and compounding trials, all bottled up in an adolescent's body and brain that doesn't know enough to navigate what may come to him. I struggled to find the right words—I wanted to help, but I felt like he couldn't be touched by little, awkward me. I tried anyway.

"Are you sure?" I said. I tried to soften my voice like people like—it makes them more susceptible to listen. But it was to no avail.

Three seconds passed. That meant he was probably thinking.

Five seconds passed. He must have been in so much pain that he couldn't even talk. Finally, after six and a half seconds, he spoke. "Yes," he answered, "I'm fine."

"That's not true. It's your husband, Michelle. Lorne's the problem."

Something told me he wasn't actually fine.

Then, the house fell silent—too silent to be coincidental. Even Michael, who had probably been staring intently at his phone for hours, perked up and went on alert—it was like his whole demeanor changed settings at the blankness that had fallen upon the house. There was no whirring of the dishwasher or the air control, no televisions or computers, and no more creaking footsteps. My chest and torso tightened.

"He's listening," the voice said.

I creaked my neck around an inch and peeked toward the doorway, afraid of what I might see. I wished I could go back inside my head, where the possibilities were endless and nothing could seriously hurt me. But this was real life, not my head. I decided in that moment to be defensive—defensive of myself and Michael.

There was nothing and no one at the door. I felt an odd twinge in my gut. I could have left, but I stayed in Michael's room. It was an instinct as the mother of my child. Michael put a hand on Marmalade and fixed his eyes on the doorway.

Still nothing.

Then, a grunt sounded—not from Michael, nor myself, and certainly not from Marmalade. Rather, it was from an ogre-y source. It sounded like a deep, dry grunt from a deep, dry pit, but it actually came from a person— the voice's most despised person, in fact. Of course, I had to fight its hatred no matter the cost, for it was my husband the voice didn't like. The same husband who provided and fought and tried his best to win and bring acclaim to this family.

"He's *torturing* Michael," the voice growled in disgust. "That's your son! You birthed him and fed him, and now, you're letting a man tear him apart."

Lorne walked in.

The towering man wore a pressed, white shirt and an unruly tie. "Hey," he said, tight-lipped and stiff. His posture made me stiffen even more; his demeanor was tighter than his pursed lips. If I hadn't known any better, I would have said he was calculated or had been anticipating this moment for some time.

"Hey," I said, standing at attention. Michael repeated the same thing.

"Outwardly serve him in every way, Michelle. Make him completely believe he is your idol; hide the fact that he corrodes your soul and very being. Be his slave until it is time. And soon, Michelle, it will be time."

The voice seemed to lick its fake lips and jitter with imagined excitement. It was just a voice, and there was nothing there to analyze or consider. It was a fake figment, not real. It had no bearing on my real life or the people I was lucky enough to have in it. I knew next to nothing in comparison to the whole of human knowledge, but I did know enough to understand the voice, or any voice, was separate from me. I didn't have to follow it, consider it, listen to it, indulge in it, cheer it on, or look forward to its liberated musings.

"Is everything okay in here?" said the hulking Irish man.

Michael and I both nodded... voraciously? Quickly? Harshly? I was never much of an English person anyway—language was just a means to an end. I couldn't put my finger on exactly how we affirmed Lorne's question, only that Michael and I both nodded firmly—almost aggressively—at the same time. I felt closely attached to my son; it was one of the rare times in his pimple-faced, adolescent phase that we were on the same page.

"Yep, I was just asking him how his day was."

Another grunt rang through the air—this one was kind of conversational. "And how was it, Mike?" He leered, not looked, at the boy and the scared cat. I was sure it was just a father-son thing, something biological that a kid had to go through. I didn't know.

Michael, sitting upright then, said, "It was good. I got some good work done and," with eyebrows raised,

"I talked to my history teacher. It looks like I can retake that test."

It was Lorne's turn to nod. "Good."

"How was your day, honey?"

His face brightened a little. Bingo. "Good," nodding, "looks like I'm up in the polls. Everything's going the way I want so far."

The voice poked through a barrier in my head yet again to where I couldn't ignore it. "Let's stay on this subject, shall we, servant girl?" I hated that term. I was nobody's servant—not even Lorne's.

"That's amazing, and how's the team doing? You must be getting popular at your showings."

"Of course I am. Campaign's going very well—just as planned." He bent down to pet Marmalade, but the cat prickled and leapt out of the room. That left just us three musketeers. Lorne sat between us.

"Don't let him be the connector," the voice hissed at me.

"So, Mike," Lorne said, stretching out, "did you tell Mom what we were talking about the other day?"

Michael looked like an angry train was about to hit him. Lorne just stared at him, still and silent, waiting for a response.

"Umm, no. I don't think so."

"You don't *think* so?" He chuckled rather loudly.

"I didn't."

"Well, do you want to do it now?" Lorne tilted his head, kind of like a snake. His eyes were stone.

"Soon, this can all be over," said the voice.

"Did something happen?" I asked innocently.

"I don't know, Mike, what do you think?"

I could tell Michael was uncomfortable, and that made me squirm. "Dad, I—"

"Just tell her what happened. She has the right to hear it from you. You said you didn't mean it, anyway."

"Honey, if he's uncomfortable, maybe he could just tell me… later."

"Michelle." He looked at me with longing eyes—he really was a handsome and convincing man. "You're going to want to hear this."

My curiosity was piqued. Lorne knew how to pull my levers.

"Just like that, you're hooked. Just like that, you're on his side. Servant girl. Caffeine anhydrous. Ricin. Arsenic. Mercury. Chloroform and knife." The whispers came in and out of focus. I tried to ignore them. "Don't you see what he does to you? How he uses you?"

"What is it, Michael?" I turned my head. I looked at my son and was now the second pair of authoritative eyes to stare him down. Even Marmalade had left his side. I wondered what it was like to be him. To be a kid staring down the world ahead and not knowing which way to go, only knowing your way was predetermined and forced upon you. He only knew life was unfair and that he couldn't always get what he wanted. In fact, he could seldom ever get what he wanted. He knew only that he was constrained by everything and everyone that came his way, especially the people closest to him; he'd been shoved inside an artificial, tiny box.

"I smoked weed the other day," my son said, looking at his bedsheets like they were foreign to him. His face was bright red. A flushed face was a common reaction for embarrassment, and it was usually endearing to watch someone embarrassed. But in this case, I felt guilty and gross. I thought about it some more. I still felt odd about all of it.

"That's not all," said Lorne. "Tell her."

And then, in gory (green and yucky) detail, Michael explained what had happened in Rachel's car from his perspective. It was a clever tale, in that it seemed like an objective account, but really, it was from Michael's perspective. But it was okay. I understood him. He was a teenage boy, and he was striving in his own right. I almost wanted to praise him for branching out and meeting someone new. I was a teenager once, too.

"Lorne doesn't want Michael to have a life outside of him," whispered the icy voice.

I felt a cutting jolt ravage my spine and arms when I heard that. My face tingled. I believed in ideas and truth, and the voice's words may have been just that. I didn't want to believe it, but after all, belief was a construct. Belief was just a sophisticated word for emotion. The real question I rigorously asked myself—in my studies, in my walks, in my relationships, and in all of my other endeavors—was this: "What do I think?"

In this case—this most miserable, awful case—I thought the voice was right. I knew that insistent demon was correct. The truth was the truth, and I was just happy to have arrived at it.

"Well?" Lorne looked at me with pressed lips. "So, what do you think?"

I felt a violent surge within me. Violence. I didn't know what could have come over me besides a demon. Maybe it was the demon I knew very well, but if it was, I would've known—maybe.

"I think he's a kid who did a dumb thing—a very dumb thing—and for that, I think he should be punished," I said, miles more confident than I really was inside, like a rookie judge making a first pivotal sentencing.

Lorne nodded. Michael looked up like the child he was, grasping for something, anything from me. I was torn between two worlds, and I didn't know which one I favored more. I didn't know if I could even choose to indulge one over the other. And how could I? This was my family, my unit, my posse, the biological stronghold I held above everything else, and the reason why I couldn't be a tenured professor with grants and esteem. How could I opt to set a rift from within it? My head got cloudy in these situations. It wasn't like the lecture halls, where the walls were silent and the students merely looked up at you—kind of like Michael was doing now. This was high stakes, and I didn't know what to do. I simply spoke from the voice within.

"But he's a kid, Lorne. A kid trying to find his way—it's biology, it's nature. He needs to learn that was wrong, but there's something to be said for branching out so quickly despite being the 'new kid' in a completely different school." I turned toward my son, whose face was scared, scrunched. "You're trying your best, Michael, and I applaud you for that."

The words, "You're not a very good liar, are you, Michelle?" echoed in my head as I said this.

Lorne fixed his stone-cold stare onto me, but at least it was away from Michael. He was brutish, and he looked much larger as he stood up and widened his already wide shoulders.

"He knows what he's doing."

"Are you kidding me, Michelle?" He spoke in a soft but strong voice. It was chilling. The only amends in my head that made this worth it was that *I* was receiving the bully's reprimand, not my son. There were so many ways this could have happened, and I always wondered if—in such a pivotal moment—I enunciated a word differently or chose another side of the debate, then maybe it would have created a completely alternate universe. I would never know for certain, but that was a fascinating thought. The nature of observation was so endlessly fascinating to me. It was as if people were playthings, and every single decision I made throughout a given day was a new experiment. But unfortunately, all those crazy options left me paralyzed and discontented with my current reality. I wondered what would happen next, and I would soon find out as it unfolded in front of—no, *to*—me.

"Lorne, I don't think—"

"You want to undermine me in front of our son?" His eyes were bloodshot and—if I didn't know any better—a little crazed. I tried to diffuse the situation, as always. I hated conflict more than anything else, and Lorne knew this.

Instead of responding, I thought about what I could do. I thought about the recourse I lost each and every day Lorne went out and campaigned and shook countless hands. I thought about what morsel of leverage I could pull—I never thought leverage was very fair, but it could be necessary in this situation. I searched and itched the annals of my brain as it boiled in a scalding, gray-eyed pressure cooker.

Lorne calmed his voice a bit, just enough to remain a little charming. "Michael, I'm going to have to ask you to leave."

Michael sat as still as a boulder. He could have been thinking tirelessly—his eyes seemed that way. He could have been thinking and suffocating under the weight of his scared, churning mind. I didn't know. Anything was possible. I wasn't going to say anything.

"You have it. Use it, then," the voice said. What a strange urge that was. Maybe I knew what it was talking about, but it was a weird time for that to come up. My head was a funny place to be sometimes—and sporadic, too.

"Mikey," Lorne said, putting his lion paw on top of his head, rasping through a chorus of commands, "it'd be better if you just left for a little bit. Besides, the garbage needs to be taken out anyway. It won't be long."

Poor Michael spider-crawled away from Lorne's touch as if beset by a gross, physical instinct. He looked repulsed and began to sweat. "D-d-dad," the teenager stuttered, still in his arachnid position.

"What?" Lorne looked confused.

Michael jerked his desperate head toward me. There was something strong painted on his face that I couldn't put my finger on. "Dad hit me."

Chapter 38 – Michael

The air was snatched from the room.

I winced like I might get hit that very second. But then again, that wasn't out of the realm of possibility—nothing was. Nothing was too strange or cruel to happen to me, even if both of my parents were right there in my room—*especially* if both my parents were there.

After saying those words, shouting that truth like a possessed child after everything had gone blank, I felt like we were all meeting each other for the first time. Before that night in my room, and before I told my mother about my father in front of him, I felt like we'd only known *of* each other. It was like an earthquake shook us so violently that our masks fell off, revealing three sour faces with no one else except each other to fight and love. But there was no love here. Or maybe there was love, but I couldn't sense it. My "family," the people who supposedly knew me best, birthed me, and raised me, made me think there was no such thing as pure love. The violent monster had taught me that love could be—and often was—warped and perverse. Strong feelings had a funny way of doing that to people.

My mom, who I could tell was tortured by all of this, turned toward my father. Through a cracked voice, she said, "Is this true, Lorne?"

My father's amiable mask fell and shattered. His glib charm withered away when I spoke those words and my mom absorbed them—taking them as seriously as the look that chiseled my father's red face. He became a whole different person. Once the clean-cut, blue-suited monster, his social veneer dissolved into his true self: a snarling, red demon with an empty stomach. He got close to my mom. He looked straight at her and put everything he had to hide directly on the table.

"I only disciplined him appropriately. No more, no less. I did what needed to be done."

His words hit me like a hammer, or like the very real jabs he'd shot at my gut just one dark night ago. He didn't look at me when he said that, but he certainly spoke to me as well. We were all nakedly angry and scared. Only venom and intentional injury would come out of our mouths from then on. We were flared and ready, and the toxic anger eating at our insides spurted out of us. I didn't know what might happen. None of this seemed normal, but the concept of anything being normal was now silly to me. At my father's words, I only felt trapped.

Tears streamed down my mom's veiny face. The pain inside and outside of her weighed on me. It pained a deeper part of me than I cared to explore, for fear that the decrepit truth would surface and fix its evil eyes on me. When I looked at my dad, I thought I saw it. I hated it.

My mom spoke first. "I hate you, Lorne." Then, her voice became shrill and scratchy. "I hate you!"

The monster spat and growled in her face.

"Take your mom's side," Beel said. "It's the only way."

I couldn't hear my own words—only Beel's voice rang in my ears. All I could see were my towering father and my mom's tears. I felt nothing except tingling and blind, sinister vitriol bubbling inside of me. "Why do you do this to us, Dad? Why?"

"I do nothing except good! You can't be trusted on your own. I *protect* you, and you reject my care all the time!"

"You hide me away, and you lie!" my mom yelled through a muffled drawl. She seemed like she'd rushed to say the words, but they still tumbled out slowly.

"I can't do this. I can't do this," I said. I spoke, but I didn't feel heard. It only made me want to talk more.

"You're selfish and vain," my dad said. Then he pointed at me. "And you—you don't know when to stop, or when to stay on the straight path. You embarrass me! *That's* why I need to keep you in line. I've always had connections, but that's not a *bad* thing."

"I'm tired of being yanked around, Lorne. You're making my life a hell!" Mom screamed.

"It's a hell *you* created for yourself." He jerked his snakelike finger at her; it hissed and slithered and sank its venom into her chest. "Think about it. Think back, Michelle. I never *forced* you to do anything. Now you're mad at me because I have connections and some success? Despicable."

Maybe he was right. But how could he be? How could a benevolent person cause so much pain? I couldn't buy it.

Beel spoke, "He's lying. He does nothing to protect you. He only cares about himself."

Drowning in a river of tears, my mom began to hyperventilate. Her rational mind had clearly left her—my father often had that effect on her. He had a slithering, subversive ability to nullify a person's strength while amplifying their desperate weaknesses. He did this with my mom so skillfully and consistently, it was like she was his personal clay mold. The tears that came out of her were the real self—her inner Michelle, the child who had fallen in love with the sciences and had a persistent, unquenchable curiosity about the world around her. It was her inner Michelle that came out in the tears, the fits of twitching, and the long, winding walks steeped in contemplation and childlike wonder. That delicate, innocent part of her was crushed and scrambled, but not yet broken—I could tell. Beel could tell. She was still bright, but her exterior sagged and was dim. She was still curious, but on the outside, she looked calm and unquestioning. She was still adventurous at heart but restrained herself, carefully staying within the mold Lorne had crafted for her.

"Okay, Lorne." She looked down at the ground—at his crisp Italian shoes with the commanding, black soles. "I'm sorry. I really am."

"No, you aren't. You're not sorry for anything."

"No! I swear I am! I swear I'm sorry, I understand I was wrong… and I see what you've been doing all along. I'm so, so sorry." With that, her eyes, mouth, and nose ran—they ran with vitriolic fluids, concentrated with the purest poisons a soul could produce.

The suit approached her, aggressive joy in his eyes. A prompt kiss was laid on her cheek. Hand on her shoulder, he whispered to her, "You need to understand that I love you, honey. You know I wouldn't do that to Michael—never anything to harm our son."

"He said that so you could hear him," Beel said. "You weren't adamant enough; you backed off and let him maneuver for too long. You didn't deserve to be believed anyway—to be saved."

Beel made me think I'd done this to myself. Who was to say I hadn't? Who was to say this wasn't all in my control and up to me? Sometimes, it was as if I persecuted myself, or at least, it felt that way.

My parents' eyes descended upon me like hot lasers. The beams of attention made my face warm, my feet numb. What was that feeling? I thought, at that point, I had it coming to me—I attracted pain like a magnet.

I felt the two pairs of blistering eyes land on me. *How did this happen? How did my mother turn so quickly? It had to be fear. Something wicked.* It made me both sluggish and jittery, and it stole my rationality while allowing me to keep my anxious, swift thoughts. I was both awash at sea and also thrown into a pit of flames, hopelessly engulfed by both.

"What do you have to lose, Michael? What do you owe to a world that has orphaned and tormented you relentlessly?" Beel had a point.

"Do you have anything to say for yourself, Michael?" the suit said with his tentacle wrapped around my delicate mom, choking her thin shoulders with its slimy rancor. He wore a handsome face, soft enough to sympathize with and smug enough to want to punch.

Beel drifted into my head. I didn't know if he was wise or not. I didn't know if he cared or even how well he understood what was going on around me—what was going on *within* me. Maybe he was a part of me. Maybe he was more aware than I was.

Maybe he was me.

"Speak strong."

I inhaled like it was the first time I'd ever done so. I'd never faced anyone down. I'd never spoken up. I had always felt like a gerbil among humans, too small in every way and too inept socially to defend my rodent self. I still felt that way. I wasn't being brave—I was doing this out of necessity. My back was hopelessly against the wall. I looked at my father.

"I'm telling the truth. And you know I am." I turned my tingly face toward the other set of blazing eyes. "Mom, he's lying. And deep down, you know it. It wasn't disciplinary, he didn't talk to me or try to reason with me." I felt myself sinking.

My mom didn't move or flinch. Maybe she was processing the situation, or maybe she had already made up her mind. I couldn't tell either way.

"Mike," the suit said softly. Then it took a deep breath. "I am willing to give you one last chance."

"Well, I'm glad he's at least *willing*," Beel scoffed. "How generous. Don't give in, Michael, or else you will be lonesome, loathsome, and pathetic your whole life."

"Just… tell the truth, bud."

There were voices ringing inside and out. I screamed in my head, and I wanted to scream out loud. But sometimes, I couldn't tell the difference between these voices—they blended together and were both harsh in their own way. Then, I felt my own eyes transform into the lasers that had burned me for my entire life.

"I did, and I am. It is the truth."

"You know you're not. And you know I didn't."

My mom looked back and forth between the two boys in her life like a tennis match. She stayed on the sidelines and anticipated who would win the next point. My singular goal was to win that point.

I lifted up my shirt and unveiled my scrawny belly—all of its thin, soft bone and shrieking, white vulnerability. I pointed to a discolored spot of purple low on the left side of my rib cage. "How do you explain *that*?" I said, not giving an inch. I wouldn't back down as I looked defiantly in the face of the demon standing above me.

He shook his head and laughed. Maybe I *was* the crazy one. Maybe I was the harmful one.

"You fell or something, and now you're trying to project that on me? Mike," he said, exasperated and fatherly, "we talked about this. Please don't scare Mom with nonsense. I'm worried about you. I just smacked your wrist and arm to tell you to sit down, and then we talked."

Then, he reached his suctioned tentacle over to me, trying to draw me into his world of madness—to get me to drink out of the cup of crazy. That was too far.

"No," I said. I couldn't tell what my tone sounded like because my heart was beating so fast. "Get away from me."

Then, my mom spoke up. "Michael, ple—"

"No! No, Mom, you aren't getting it! You let him walk all over you and abuse you and neglect you, just for you to turn around and forgive him like nothing happened. I'm your *son*, why would I lie about this? He just said he did it! He just said he disciplined me!" I was frantic. I was red. I would've done anything—I was going to do everything. I flailed. I kicked and raised my voice.

"I told you he was crazy, honey. I've tried to tell you for a while," the suit said calmly.

My mother seemed unaffected and cold as a stone. "Michael, baby, I just want what's best for you, and when you say and do things like this, it makes me think you need some help, too." My mother looked like she stared on for thousands of miles at gaping nothingness, consumed.

The flutter in my stomach turned into muffled gasps as everything started to burn. I felt like the sky had fallen on me. There was nowhere to turn. What else could I do besides turn away? I didn't know. But didn't *they* know? Didn't they understand what this could do to a young mind, a young soul trying to move the worn gravel and broken twigs aside to carve his own path in life? Didn't they know what kind of damage that assumption could bring—that I was weird, faulty, *broken*? Then I thought back. I thought back to all the times my mother had stroked my hair and held me like a precious cub and said, "You're a beautiful work-in-progress, Michael, and no one loves you like I do."

I just sat and stared at both of their monstrous feet, searching for a glimpse of their humanity—some morsel of flesh-and-blood empathy and understanding. I couldn't find it. I saw scales, not skin. I saw shards of ice, not cinders of human warmth.

"What do you mean, I 'need some help?'" I asked her, knowing my father would hear, too.

"Baby, it's been tough for you… You just need some adjustment help and some nice people to talk you through it. I understand you." Tears ran and ran.

"No, she doesn't. Look how she's caressing that goon's hand. She doesn't believe you, Michael, and she doesn't *want* to. She wants you to think you're crazy, but you're not—she is."

Through tears and snot and muffled turmoil, I trembled out, "Why are you guys doing this to me? I don't get it. Dad… what's going on? I can't be yanked around so much…" more sniffles and desperate breaths, "anymore… I'm done with it. You've done this to me!"

Chapter 39 – Lorne

I had a great childhood. Sure, it had its ups and downs—just like everyone else's—but it was still good to me. And it was healthy but short. Before I was the hand-shaking, people-person bigwig you know me as today, I was a pretty scrawny young buck. I lacked some confidence. Of course, my childhood was good, my parents always treated me well, and everything was normal. But like most people, I had some struggles with peers.

I hit a growth spurt late. And unlike today, instead of being popular for being handsome or notable, I was popular for a *different* reason: I was very small. So small, in fact, they called me "Double S," which stood for "Short and Skinny." Yep, I was a regular old pipsqueak. My friends and I would always make jokes about my height. It was almost like everyone was my friend, though, because I could get anyone to laugh just by walking by them or even saying, "Hi." School was the best—so many laughs, so many memories.

In many ways, little Lorne paved the way for big Lorne. I learned a lot from those scrawny days. Important lessons like valuing community, using leverage carefully, and always keeping a positive attitude were instrumental to my successful political career and beyond.

Thinking back to little Lorne helped me sympathize with skinny Michael. He was small like I was. I understood some of what he was going through, and I was trying to guide him in the right direction. I was worried about him, especially that false sense of reality he sometimes had that I never really struggled with as a kid. And he certainly didn't know how to keep a positive attitude—that one was obvious. Michelle and I talked about him. I thought about him. While I sipped coffee or drove, I wondered what we'd have to do with him—I thought about how we could help him. At this point, unfortunately—and Michelle agreed—with all of this craziness going on, there was maybe only one answer. Time would tell, but my son needed help, and Michelle completely agreed. She was such a supportive and artful wife. I was so lucky to have her and this great family.

I really was a lucky man, and I was positive we'd figure it all out. Carmen seemed sure of it. Even if there was distance between my son and me, I was still a lucky man. What it may seem like at first is that Mike told a lie. But here's the thing: he *really* thought I hit him hard in the gut. He really believed his own lies. So, in a way, he didn't really lie. He was telling his own truth. He was being honest with himself, and honestly, that's the scariest part. That's why we—Michelle and I—knew action needed to be taken. It was when Michael was so adamant about the lying that it became necessary to get professional help for the poor kid. Face it: He had no friends, no girl, no anything, and he was entering the best years of his life. If Double S was in his same situation, he would have been surrounded by people. Yes, I was a very social guy. I couldn't be away from an approving person for longer than a day or two. But Mike? No, Michael needed help. Michael needed care from professionals that have dealt with delusional cases like him, whatever the diagnosis.

It was in his best interest, we decided, to get care for our son. From that night of delusion forward, Michael was officially on the road to recovery. But don't get it twisted; he didn't lie. In fact, he told his truth that night. Unfortunately, his truth was just not reality.

Chapter 40 – John

I didn't show up to my next meeting with Lorne—I didn't show up to any meetings, for that matter. How could I have? The precious piece of me, who I loved and wanted with my entire heart, had turned away from me. She despised my whole being.

I was broken. I was faulty. I was sick and impaired.

What could I do right if not care for my own daughter? I realized—and it hit me like a truck—that past the green of the herb and the paper, what could I live for if not my own family, my offspring, my soul's continuity in this sick world? I didn't care about a meeting. I didn't care about anything. I didn't care about my marble floors or the business that made it all possible. I didn't care for my clothes or the travel points on my metal credit card. I was dead to the only thing that filled me up and made me feel alive. What was I then? I was dead. I only wanted what I had lost, and that made me the poorest of men.

I rolled all of this over in my mind slowly. I lay in bed under the warmth of my white goose-down comforter. The warmth didn't even feel good—nothing did.

"J-man, you have two options." It was Anders, slick as ever. "You can forget your ungrateful daughter and leave her behind like the rest, or you can end your life on your own terms and go out like a pro—on top after an eventful life. The choice is yours to make."

Wait, what? How were those my only two options? I didn't question Anders's methods (I never did), but I questioned his conclusion. How did that make sense?

"The scar is too deep and gaping," said Anders. "It's too late for her to heal now. You've done the damage, and it's set in too far. You must at least know *that*."

Of course, I knew that. I wasn't dumb. It just seemed a little odd those were my only options. But at least I had them, I supposed. I loved options, and I needed them, so having them was a "must" for me. Trust me, I'd thought about ending it before, but I could never do it because of Rachel—sweet little Rachel, who had her mother's eyes and her daddy's smile. It was a shame I didn't get to see it much—she hadn't smiled in a while. Her despondence made me want to go cold inside. It was like she had turned off from the world, and I was the cause. I used to work for myself, but now I worked for Rachel. And how could I live if she hated me? I was a failure. I didn't deserve to breathe if there was no point to my stupid heartbeat or the red blood in my veins, filled with vitamins and strains—both foreign and domestic. Everything I'd built was on a cloud. I'd constructed a sandcastle thinking it was a brick house.

I was a fraud.

I thought about it. Then I thought some more. Decisions, decisions.

Chapter 41

Do you get it now, reader? There are no other constants in your world besides your very existence. You can mistrust anyone else, but please—I'll ask you kindly, then beg of you—make sure to trust yourself: your own two feet, your own two eyeballs, the bones within, and your mind. What else is there to trust? What else is there to control?

Reader, do you know who Anders is? Anders is me, but so is Beel, Carmen, Estelle, and the rest. I carry different voices, yet we are all from the same branch. I am them, and I tell this story as if it were my own. In most ways, it is my story. I have stolen nothing—I have only given. And I have bestowed unto you a great gift: a realization. If you haven't realized yet, you soon will.

You see, I'm truly endeared and genuinely glad you've taken the time to get to know these people. You may be rooting for Michael, or wondering how crazy and deluded Michelle really is, or even trying to figure out if Lorne is the "bad guy." You may have predictions as to John's next decision, and you may be torn on how to feel about Rachel—I don't know. I just hope you're tantalized all the same, no matter the nature of your racing thoughts and suppositions about how these characters will turn out.

But just know this, reader: They are characters. That's strictly, simply all they are. The most extended terminals of their wispy souls are determined by you alone. Someone can influence you one way or another, but you make the final call regardless. Just as your judgments shape these characters and their lives, so they do in the "real" world with "real" people. It is the unbridled power and stringent confinement of your own inner judgments, reader, that construct, carry, and paint the world around you. No one else can do it for you. No one else can make the call because no one else exists.

Who do you think tells this story? Who do you think makes the calls? Who do you think channeled these words and imbued life into these fictitious figments? It was me, reader. It was the monster. I'm the monster you know, the monster you fear, and I can change your fickle perceptions of these characters and people with a flick of my wrist. The trick, reader, is not to have such fickle leanings in the first place. If you want to root yourself outside of the plastic veil, don't sway with the dwindling waves of externals. For how could you empathize with someone one moment and then detest them a short while later? The answer: You never liked them in the first place, reader, because you never knew them. You don't know these people. You only know what I've shown you. You've merely sniffed the fresh paint of the canvas I've created. You have yet to even open your eyes and appreciate the picture I've painted for you.

What you are about to see gets a whole lot messier. I can assure you of that.

You can thank me later if you haven't already. My goal here is singular. I hope you understand my intentions well, reader. It is to have you ready to unravel the outside and use it to your advantage—to avoid being befuddled by it so you won't trip and hinder yourself like a child playing a simple game. You're better than that. You're brighter than that. You do *not* have to change yourself, reader. You are perfectly enough. What is necessary is to ally with me. You need to change your perspective—your view of the characters, their actions, and their reactions—and instead, notice one thing: How much they shift in their aimless ways in the midst of torrential nothingness. Put simply, they change based on their circumstances.

But you, reader, you do not need externals to *evolve*. Look carefully, take it to heart, and you will see.

Chapter 42 – Rachel

I knew I was in the right. I knew what I'd done wasn't wrong. It was justified. How could I *not* hate my father after what he did? That's what Estelle told me, anyway. She validated all of my feelings and made me feel welcome, almost like my mom did. To know someone understood was such a simple and gratifying pleasure. It gave me a cozy feeling to know Estelle got me. Of course, Estelle didn't know everything about my life, and I still kept certain parts of myself hidden from her—certain deeper parts that would be better left unexplored by Estelle's prying eyes. I could withhold what I wanted and get away with it—always. If my deadbeat shell of a father had taught me anything, it was that you could get away with a lot in this life and *especially* in this country.

I rolled over and looked at my phone. Countless notifications bombarded me.

Boy. Boy. Boy. Boy.

I scrolled some more. They were all bots. Each one of them. I saw my slick, bold father in all of them—all of the ones confident enough to talk to me, to actually approach me. Yep, there was a bit of John Kalopolous (*yuck*) laced in every hungry notification that sought a sight of my lips and my eyes. I was done with it. It was nice to feel wanted, but it was for all the wrong reasons. At a certain point, all of those boys just wanted to take and take and take, just like John did with my mother.

I scrolled on, but I didn't answer any of them. They could wait, and then wait some more.

"They don't deserve you, darling. They'd get blinded by you—you're *far* too bright a star."

Then, another notification popped up. This one was a text from my math project partner, Michael.

> *Hey Rachel, really sorry about this, but it looks like I won't be at school for the next two months. Something important came up that I can't ignore. I already emailed Ms. Shelgren, and she understands, so you'll get a good grade on the project still. Sorry again, and I appreciate all the help and support.*

Huh? What the hell was that all about? It sounded urgent. It also sounded like he didn't want me to ask about it.

> *Okay, thanks for letting me know. And I hope everything's all right. Tell your dad I said good luck with everything!*

Totally weird. But whatever, at least my car's back seat would be cleaner from now on. That kid had some problems. He was also kind of nice, though. I didn't really know what to think, so I just let Estelle do it for me.

"Good riddance to that boy," she said.

I went over to the corner of my room—there were no windows there, no views from the door that could pry into that spot. There was a chest under some old curtains, some clothes, and some old stuffed animals. I pulled it out and opened it. I took out the drawings that were light as feathers and precious as gold bars. Drawings were like pictures but better because the artist—with enough skill and practice—could depict the subject however they wanted. They could exaggerate features and totally change the mood of the work by using certain colors, lines, and lots of other techniques.

It took a lot to make good art. Often, an artist needed a muse to be good—an inspiration in their life, like a person, experience, place, or *anything*, for that matter. An artist needed something to drive them and really touch them deep down. Estelle was my inspiration, and she was the subject of a lot of my work.

Let me drown in you, Estelle. Embrace me with all of you, and then I can be happy.

I went back to my bed but found it difficult to sleep that night. My pillow was like a rock, my sheets were sand, and my body seared as an electric current twisted through it.

Chapter 43 – Michael

My parents called it a "camp." I didn't believe that. I called it what it was, and I used Beel's word—institution. It was no camp, or at least, not like one I had ever been to before.

The walls were white, and the tables were sterile. *Everything* was sterile—not in a clean way, but in a bland, tired, creepy way. Even the staff was sterile. They had bulging eyes and fixed smiles. They wore white, and there was never a single stain or mark.

At first, it was weird, then it all became a wonder to me. All at once, the merits, or lack thereof, of the Greenwood Center hit me like an angry train. Instantly, I became curious about how this "camp" worked, what they wanted, and their methods. I had to know. I *had* to know what my parents had sent me to. What did they intend? What did this institution plan to do to "fix" me? How was I broken? Beel said I was awkward, skinny, and nerdy all bundled into one, but he *never* called me crazy. I wasn't crazy, but sometimes, when the light of day dwindled and the rambunctious crickets began to howl, the thoughts crept in—could I be crazy? I really thought it was possible, or maybe I was just overthinking. What did "crazy" even mean, anyway? To me, it was all just perception. It depended on how you looked at it—maybe everybody was crazy. Regardless, I was the one who'd been sent to the psych ward.

I walked down a long hallway. It was white everywhere—white walls, white ceilings, and white windows to nowhere. It seemed to sway and twist while I stayed still, but I was the one moving. I reached a door at the end and opened it. The knob fit my hand well and seemed to conform to my will subserviently. It was white to match the door, which swung silently open to another sterile room.

"Michael," a pleasant voice said. I saw a smile in a seat, adorned in a lab coat that matched the rest of the building. It was a guy who wasn't too old, and he looked *directly* at me as soon as I entered and continued to watch me the whole time. The eyes didn't match the rest of him—they were fierce and uninviting, set in an otherwise friendly face.

"This man is not your friend, Michael. He has hurt in his eyes. Don't give an inch."

"Hello," I said. The sound of my unwilling voice came out raspy, my throat like cardboard. I didn't want to be there or talk to him or have anything to do with the stupid Greenwood Center. I wasn't afraid to clearly wear my disdain or lace it into my voice and clothes and everything else I begrudgingly did there.

"Hello there! Please take a seat. I'm so glad you're here."

"This is a desert, Michael—a dry wasteland where nothing grows, and you certainly can't grow here either." The hairs on my neck and arms became straight and rigid, each one on top of a tiny hill. I bit the inside of my cheek—where those prying eyes couldn't reach me—and felt the blood swarm my tongue. That tinge of pain was a bit of a relief in a way; it was nice to tend to something that wasn't going on around me—something small that only hurt slightly. It was nice to know the blood in my cheek was a result of my actions; I could control it, I could feel it, and I *could* have stopped it.

The room was clean, but to me, it was putrid.

The smiley guy pulled out a manila folder with some sticky notes attached. He told me his name, and it hit my skull and rattled around my ears a bit before bouncing out—I couldn't care less what his name was or where he got his PhD. What did he want with me? How could my parents do this to me?

"So…" His eyes bored into me. "Here at Greenwood, for all of our incoming attendees, we like to do a little… 'get to know ya.' A little evaluation, just so we can get a better sense of who you really are. We take that very seriously here. We want to know *you* as a person."

All of that was offensive to me. I didn't have anything to hide; I just had things to protect. He wanted, with his long, clinical hands, to grab the tender things I safeguarded within myself. I wasn't going to allow that. I just said, "Okay." Then he nodded, and we got started. I smelled the faint remains of lemon cleaning product floating through the musty, windowless air.

"I'm going to start off with a couple questions, and all you have to do is be honest. Are you ready?"

Honest. What a pitiful disguise for "vulnerable" and "open to influence." The "h-word" kept bouncing off the dank walls of my head.

"Give him *nothing*," Beel hissed.

The doctor held a clipboard, his legs crossed. "When were you born?"

I answered. *Honestly*. Harmless so far.

"It's all a part of their dubious tactics, Michael. Do not succumb, or you will regret it for the rest of your life."

"Walk me through your diet, if you could… like, what do you eat and drink on a given day? It doesn't have to be exact."

I did that. It was still harmless, so I really told the truth. My diet had nothing to hide—nothing to protect from the reaches of monied interests and institutional control freaks.

"Cool," he said, writing my answer down and taking more notes, "and what does your sleep schedule look like?"

That was innocuous as well. They couldn't use it against me, so I gave them that, too.

"What are you doing, Michael? I said not to give them *anything*. And here you are, spilling your guts out on their grubby, sticky-noted page. What's wrong with you?"

I swallowed. When I did, the man's eyes walked their way up from his clipboard and shot at me, drawing blood. "Can I go to the bathroom?"

He laughed. It was genuine. "It's right over there." He pointed with a blue pen to the corner of the room, where a sterile door stood at attention, waiting to conform to the will of my hand and my bladder. Once I got beyond the border of the hostile, stuffy room, I could finally breathe somewhat. I stretched my legs and chest and looked around to make sure no one was watching me. I surged into the bathroom—the tiled haven where I could have some time away to spill my breath, my urine, and my thoughts.

"You're nervous, and he can tell. He can *smell* it on you."

How could I calm down? There was too much at stake to relax. I didn't even know where I was. I didn't know what they wanted. I didn't have a schedule, and Beel was my only guide through the thick darkness.

"Take a breath," Beel started, "and know they can't hurt you unless you let them in—unless you make it easy for them. Don't let them in, and you'll be all right."

What if they already knew me and were testing me on my honesty? My parents had definitely explained to them everything "wrong" with me before I was admitted into this hellhole. But what did they say? It was all a big mess, inside and outside my head. I had nowhere to hide except for the sanctity of the bathroom stall I'd just left behind.

I walked back in and felt those searing eyes brand the side of my head like a hot iron. It stung and bubbled, and I lost all feeling in my feeble body.

Still with his khaki'd, insufferable legs crossed, he continued, "So, back to it then. How would you describe your home life? Do you have any siblings? How do you interact with your parents or guardians?"

"My home life is good." The more I looked away, the more I felt the gravity of his cutting leer. "I don't have any siblings, and my interactions are fine. We don't usually have any problems."

He stopped and looked up at me. "Not *usually*?"

"Well, I meant I almost never have any problems with my parents."

Beel hissed. "You just muffed your chance."

"Almost? Could you maybe walk me through what a disagreement would look like with either your mom or dad? Maybe both?"

Gulp. "Usually, when I don't clean my room, they get mad."

"And what do they usually do when they get mad?"

"My dad just… raises his voice a little, and then I do it."

"Mm-hmm."

"You're a terrible liar, Michael. He already knows everything."

Another gulp passed down my throat and sounded like a train trundling through the room. A bead of sweat trickled, ran, and dripped onto my shirt.

"Okay then, let's move on… how would you say your friends are doing? Do you have a lot of friends?"

"I do have a lot of friends."

"So," he said, scrutinizing the sacred tablets on top of his clipboard, "it says here that you just recently moved to a new school. How have you been doing there? Has it been easy to make friends?"

"Uhhh, yeah… yeah, it has. I was doing well until I got sent here."

"What are some of your friends' names?"

"Um, Rachel, Tory… Paul… Thomas…?" I said the last name like I was asking a question instead of answering one. I didn't know why I was so bad at this—maybe I was crazy after all.

Fuck.

"Michael, you seemed to be a little bit agitated that you got 'sent' here. And if you are," he put up his hands like he was remitting a weapon, "I totally get it. It can be very startling to completely change your life and then, in a matter of weeks, completely change it again. That's confusing, man, and I get it. I get *you*." He said the last syllable like it was more of a primal growl than a word of endearment.

I wanted to run. Maybe I still could. "Yeah." One word and a slow nod were the best I could do when my veins were full of ice and steam.

"Indeed." He nodded. "I get it." He sighed and *finally* looked away from me. "This all must be pretty confusing." Then, he put his sacred clipboard on the desk, like he was ditching it for the day—like maybe, for a brief second, he *cared*. With hands folded, he let out one last sigh. "Do you know why you're here, Mike?" He leaned in like he was about to tell a secret.

"Really, I don't." I sniffled.

"Your parents think there's something wrong with you. But I don't think that's true, Mike. I think you're just misunderstood, and you get yanked around a lot of places where you don't need to go. It's unfair."

Then, much to my chagrin and hatred and anger, the floodgates of my eyes opened up; the dam cracked, and the tears rushed in. I couldn't stop them. Beel scorned me violently, but that only made them run harder. There was nothing I could do at that moment except cry. And cry. And sniffle and cry some more—there was no stopping it.

"Hey, hey, Mike, hey." The doctor patted my shoulder, and it felt like a heated blanket after a trek through thick snow on a cold, bleary night.

"You lost it, Michael. You lost your leverage, and now there's nothing you can do to gain it back."

I hoped Beel was wrong. I wiped away another tear and let the doctor console me.

Chapter 44 – Lorne

"What's this I hear about you going down in the polls?" It was John on the other line, and he didn't sound happy. I sensed he was already agitated about something else, then some boneheaded intern went and exported the most recent polling data prematurely. Somebody in my camp was getting fired. But in the meantime, I had to smooth this pesky bump over before it got too inflamed. It wasn't going to be a problem for me.

"Lorne. Are you there?"

"Oh, yeah, yeah… of course. Quick question, was that poll from the *Tribune* you saw?"

"No, why?"

"Oh, John, well I just found out that's where we got our numbers, and you can't trust the *Trib'*. Do you have any idea their sample size?"

"No, Lorne. But it's an official poll, is it not? Do *you* even know their sample size?"

"Oh, no, no, no, that's not official for anything. Really, it's newsletters and direct followings that are always the main determinant for winning anyway. Besides, their sample size is less than one percent of the voting populace, John, the *voting* populace."

The rest of the conversation only smoothed out from there, and his heat iced over. It was never the facts that mattered. It was never what I said that worked; it was *how* I said it—how I stood, how I looked, and how upright my broad shoulders were. I could make people smile and forget. Facts didn't matter to people if they were smiling.

I burst out of my office. There was nothing left to smooth over. Someone was going down, and an example had to be made. I had great impulse control, and I used this impulse for something productive. It was time to make some art.

Instead of yelling, I went right to Stacy, the office administrator, and booked a mandatory, team-wide meeting for the next half hour. I was going to get to the bottom of this.

"You're going to get to the bottom of this, and it's going to be a great, powerful display for the rest of them," Carmen said. "You're going to be great."

The king returned to his rightful office. I puffed out my jaw as kings tended to do. It wasn't to be arrogant; it was more of a leadership tactic. I'd always thought it was important to have allies, so I had plenty of them—inside and outside of my campaign team. But how those allies were won was a different story. I had allies through a wide variety of forms. Unfortunately, in some cases, some had to be won through fear. It wasn't in my power, and it wasn't my choice—it was reality. I sat at the head of the table and watched the sullen sheep pour into their pen. I wasn't going to gobble them all up—that wasn't the point. I was simply going to sacrifice one for the good of the rest.

That's how a leader had to be. That's what a leader had to do.

"I hope everyone's having a good day," I started. Then, I continued to praise the team and give out specific compliments—oh, how their faces lit up when I did that! Then I made a joke about someone getting me a "freakin' coffee," and someone actually did! Caffeine reacted so well with the shiny morning pill. I continued from there after a comical first sip. I had the easel set well on the canvas.

"Hey, and real quick, everybody—who communicated the latest polling results?"

Someone raised their hand, still smiling. Their name and position weren't important because, in a few seconds, they were about to have both of those precious things stripped away. I walked up—slowly, closely, assumptively—and gazed down at the seated idiot. Something in me snapped, but it didn't matter. It was all part of the art form.

"And you did it without my approval?" My voice may have been raised, but it was hard to tell—I was the only one talking. The idiot sank back, and its smile turned to dust. It looked like the sheep it really was. It was scared but not yet lonely—I was about to make it lonely.

"Stretch this out and play it like a chord," Carmen purred in my ear. I could almost smell her words, and they were like perfume and rock candy.

"Why? What made you think that was okay?"

The idiot mumbled something I couldn't understand. It was both dumb and ridiculous.

"Okay, okay, I get it." I got even closer. "You know you're not supposed to do that, right?"

More useless mumbling and babbling. The sheep shivered.

"You're fired. You're fired, and you know why. Get out. Now. Don't think about coming back or getting a job anywhere else... why aren't you moving yet?"

The idiot scampered away, and I wished I'd gotten to taste its tears. At least I got to see and hear them.

There were a few minutes of silence and genuine fear toward me. I didn't mean to make everyone feel so scared, but I guess I had that effect on people at times. They had to respect me if I was going to pull this together. I slowly paced around the room, drinking in all of the eyeballs that followed me. I always liked being looked at—it was all for the greater good. Then, I ordered the whole office pastries and pizza and Caesar salads. Not the crappy, overdressed Caesar, but the *really* good kind with romaine and seasoned croutons.

What did Napoleon Bonaparte say again? Oh, yeah: "An army marches on its stomach."

Smart man.

Chapter 45 – Michael

I became happy at the Greenwood Center. I didn't care if I was crazy or not, or if Beel hated every second of it and only tormented me more. These people seemed to care about me, and they even seemed to *understand*. It was like a transformation and a detoxification where everything became new again. Yes, it was weird, but what was weird anyway? And what was normal? I had friends at the Greenwood Center—not crazy people or manipulative bullies or thieves, but genuine *friends*.

At the Greenwood Center, I realized something: I'd never been truly happy before. Not only that, but subconsciously, I'd *prevented* myself from being in a positive state of mind. For so long, I'd deprived myself of the simple and ornate pleasures in life. At the Greenwood Center, I stopped the cycle of sorrow that caused me so much pain in the past, and instead focused on pain *avoidance*. The doctors and the assistants there taught me I could be happy if I didn't indulge the things that brought me suffering. Everyone there, in one way or another, showed me there was no point to suffering, so why do it at all? If you clapped, that made the event worthy of applause. It was all about perspective.

We had our daily gatherings in the atrium—well, really, it was called the "sacred spire." It was the only room in the Greenwood Center that wasn't dominated by a sea of blank white. Instead, the sacred spire was open and festive and bright. There were lots of red accents and cushions. The near-constant clapping at the gatherings echoed into a frenzied thunder, and it was like a shockwave to the senses that never stopped. Everything in the sacred spire was worthy of applause because everything was positive. We were all young and inspired and connected, and in the sacred spire, we tapped into a collective, newfound optimism. They—the instructors, the other attendees all around my age, and even the listening white walls—understood me. They knew me, and they cared about us.

At this gathering, Rose was called up to be the special participant in The Room that day. The instructor took her by the hand and led her away from everybody else in the group, who were all kneeling on the cushions and clapping ferociously for her grand opportunity. They walked toward The Room, and blonde Rose broke into a giddy smile and a lofty skip as she was led far, far away from the rest of us. I couldn't tell if she was more or less excited than the frenzied, kneeling group she'd left behind.

We weren't allowed to talk amongst each other while the procession took place—after all, it was the *sacred* spire, not the communal spire or the casual spire. I looked around for a brief second and scanned quickly, only with my eyes. No one else bothered to notice my straying glance, and no one—not even the instructor that stayed behind—looked back at me. It was like a comfortable, pillowy bliss. There was no judgment—in fact, judgment was the only thing judged *against*. The haven that was the Greenwood Center taught us we were perfect as we were and that it was only external victimization that ended up hurting us, bending us, and breaking us. But they rebuilt us, or at least, they tried to. Within the vast white walls of the camp, we were taught kindness above all. That was not a principle nor an observation I'd ever gotten from the outside world. I realized at the Greenwood Center that *true*, pure kindness had never been shown to me before now. In fact, my fellow attendees and I were more sane, more rational, and far kinder than the people and the brutish circumstances that had sent us there in the first place.

The only thing left that was a true wonder to me was the fact that the iron cruelty I'd braved for so long hadn't gotten me sent there sooner. How and why did it take me years and years to find that sort of forgiving, soft kindness? I didn't know. All I knew was I had one more adversary to beat. I had one more agent of cruelty to slay before I could be enveloped in a painless track of no resistance. That enemy's name was both symbolic and very real at the same time: Beel.

After some more kneeling and collective channeling of kindness (the instructors just called it "channeling"), we saw Rose walk back into the sacred spire accompanied by a few of the instructors. Her smile was less giddy and dynamic, more so static after her time in The Room. All the same, the ferocious clapping commenced yet again, and the loud echoes of the many hands of the attendees gripped and warmed my heart. It was a beautiful scene. I felt—almost *aggressively*—kindness all around me. It enveloped the sacred spire and all of us attendees in red, sharp pangs.

Later that night, in the comfort of my bed, wrapped in the dark blanket of my quarters I'd gotten pretty used to in that span of time, Beel's voice poked me like a sharp needle. At that time of evening, far past lights-out, I had no attendees around and certainly no instructors to talk to about this. I had to face Beel alone.

I couldn't get him out of my head, and I couldn't stab him, run far away, or crush him. I was alone in the quiet room, but it was a mess in my brain. Rather than confront Beel, my monster, I felt like doing *anything* else.

"You know this is all fake, right?" Beel growled. All fleeting hopes of escape were dead. I was face-to-face with the faceless. I was being fought by something I couldn't punch back—it would have been a dream to have fled, but this was a nightmare I couldn't wake up from. But what did the softness of the sheets matter if it was hard in my head?

"This is the most real thing I've ever been a part of."

"You've had your surroundings, your caretakers, your friends, your home, and your clothes change constantly. Do not kid yourself, Michael. Don't pull the wool over your *own* eyes."

"Yes, but most of it has been faulty up until now. I've had the wool pulled over me by others, and now, at the Greenwood Center, I've realized why people have mistreated me. I figured out what I can grasp forever and what I can't. I'm a lot wiser now."

"Michael," Beel hissed, laughing, "the only constant in your small, pathetic life besides change itself has been *me*. You know me better than your own life. I am more a part of you than your own experiences—than your own murky past or crystal-clear future."

"That can't be true."

"But it is, in fact, the *only* truth. How could I best assure you of that? How would you like me to prove it to you beyond a shadow of a doubt?"

"You can't prove it. You can't prove anything. You're fake and made up in my head."

"What is more real—more concrete and definite—than that which lives and swims and lurks in your own head? What is more existentially devastating than the monster from which there is no escape? I speak and stay because I am. They—the whole rest of them in your so-called "life"—change and are fleeting, much like the ephemeral breeze... because, Michael, they *aren't* real."

"No. You're wrong. You're dead wrong."

"Are you going to be stupid your whole life? Are you going to avoid the truth forever?"

"What truth? What are you talking about?"

"The truth about you, Michael. The eternal movement that made you and that is still inside of you—swirling and scintillating. It is the sole axiom, the only grabbable ledge, the individual power source that birthed you and fuels you. The truth is simple in diction and concept but unlimited in power, and it is this: You can choose everything. You are all you can count on to exist, and I am a vital part of you and your existence."

I sat there, still. I combed my mind for meaning within Beel's cheap words and couldn't find any. I figured there was none. I figured he was crazy. Through the fog of Beel's desperate drivel, I peered at a sadness I understood from him. He had no one to talk to except me. He had no community, no assurance, no comradery. Of course he needed my attention and headspace. I would go crazy, too, if I were in Beel's odd and desperate situation. He was smart but unfortunate, victimized by the constriction of his existence. I decided to cater to him to make him stop. I decided to placate him enough so he would hopefully quiet down in my head and even—on the tiny chance this would work—maybe feel understood and whole.

After more silence under the blanket of the dark, I broke the rift between us and attempted to reach a softer part of Beel—a deeper sect that lay under his coarse words and harsh tone.

"Oh… my god. Oh my god," I said. I took my time to get the words out and pronounce what seemed like a newfound revelation to Beel. "I understand what you're saying."

Beel, sharply, brazenly, *quickly*, "And what is your interpretation?"

"You're saying everything and anything is subject to change… and there is a force that we may not understand that drives this change…"

Beel grunted.

"And—"

"Michael," Beel cut me off, "you don't understand. I know you don't. I knew you didn't."

"What do you mean?" If Beel were a person, I would have backpedaled on all fours away from him. I would have widened my eyes and shuddered and prepared to do something drastic. But he wasn't a person—I didn't think. What was he?

"I am a vital part of you. I am your guide and the only thing that keeps you sane."

He could hear my thoughts, too? My own inner narration was cast to him? I could keep nothing from his reach. Maybe he *was* me.

"I am. And I am telling you to make friends with me rather than fight me. For your whole minuscule life, you've put far too much credence in the veil. You've tried to hide yourself away in the veil, away from me, away from the medicinal pain."

"What's the veil?"

"The veil is what dresses your body as much as it dresses your vision. The veil is everything that is not you. That is why I am not a part of the veil."

I was shivering even though it wasn't cold. My teeth chattered so much they shook my head and neck. "Why should I listen to you?"

"How could you not?"

"How do I make friends with you? Don't I have to live?" I was sweating and hyperventilating, all the while shivering like something was being pulled out of my body. I didn't notice any of my surroundings—at that time, it was like I had none.

"Remember—and heed this carefully—I am only a *part* of you, but a vital part all the same. To make friends with me is not to ignore me, but to acknowledge me—full-heartedly—and deliberate with me. Wrestle with me—not in agitation, but in assurance that I may be right and I may be grounded. Do not succumb to me, and certainly do not run away from me. Accept me, and you may become vitally complete—capable of navigating across the widest chasms and whole fields of the most poisonous ferns. It is you becoming complete so you can better brave the storms that will happen when you both accept me and struggle with my essence and my words."

I felt like I was standing over a ledge to nowhere with no one to help me or catch me if I fell. It was only Beel watching me stare over it and contemplate the other side of the cliff. I didn't know anything about darkness; I'd avoided it all my life. I think Beel just wanted me to

lift the mask off life and face what was underneath.
"Okay. I think I get it."

Chapter 46 – Michelle

There were no such things as monsters—as bad people or bad actions. From my studies, work, and professorial growth, I'd decided this was my philosophical position. It's based on my expertise, outside experiences, and lifetime learnings. Simply, there are actions and reactions. There is growth and decay—expansion and subsistence. I believe in a kind of rational neutrality: Everything is what it is. Every cause you see is also the effect of some preceding cause. In other words, there is a reason for everything, and also reason governs everything.

I had a reason for what I did. As a professor of physics and a lifetime learner, I believed in science. I also believed there was mysticism in science, and that everyone and everything had an essence. If an essence is blocked, it can do one of two things: die or destroy that blockage. My essence had been blocked by something. And so, naturally, causally, I had to destroy that blockage. It wasn't personal, and it wasn't right or wrong; it just *was*. It happened because it had to. What I did was inevitable. It was nature.

My father was a strong man, and he came from a strong family where only the strong could survive—only the boisterous could talk at the table, and only the hungriest could eat. My dad would always say funny things like, "My house didn't have a lot of possessions, but it had a lot of lessons." It was obvious to me that all those siblings had given him a great sense of scarcity. His poor upbringing had also contributed to his aggression and need for control. I didn't always like being around him, but I loved my dad, and I had a good family growing up.

After a while, I realized I'd married someone much like my own father. Lorne had a lot of the same traits—these traits would sometimes gross me out, but they were ones I ended up gravitating toward. Some of my attraction to Lorne was compulsive because he was like my father. Some of that attraction was subconscious. A lot of it was downright toxic. But it was a toxicity I kind of liked because I didn't always like myself.

I had never really been into traditional "girl stuff," so I didn't have a lot of female friends. At school, I'd watch as the girls walked past in their packs and pods, smiling or frowning or laughing together. They clung to each other and experienced the world together as students and then as adults. On the outside, my resentful little self saw that as weakness. But deep down, I knew it was a luxury and a nice comfort. It was a comfort I would never enjoy myself. I just walked on past and kept my head down, and that's what I'd continued to do into my adulthood. And I don't believe that mindset has always served me well, but it was hard to try any other way. Sometimes, my own essence harmed me and kept me reclusive. And rarely, it burst out of its thin shell and harmed others.

But harm was just a byproduct—it was an effect, and it was only harm if you made it so through your perspective. I thought a perspective could only be warped when judged by another perspective—a subjective lens peering at another. My goal, despite my unfortunate humanity, was to be objective; I strove to be rational beyond question. Objectively, it was the only goal worth pursuing fully. That was why I liked the sciences and shunned the arts—even the mysticism in science was arrived at through a calculated method. Any and all art—objectively speaking—muddied the truth about the world. That was why any institution, financing, or media that could coax the youth away from art was doing a progressive thing. It was doing the *essential* thing. I encouraged young people to get into STEM fields and stay in them, but I didn't exactly have much sway in the grand scheme of things.

I didn't have an excuse for what I did because excuses don't exist. I had a reason, and reason governs everything. There was some irritating human passion involved in the act, but that was not the reason—it had nothing to do with *why* and *how* it happened. I was just a continuation of the essence that laced and built everything. I wasn't innocent, but only because there was no such thing as innocence. It was all essential.

Chapter 47 – Michael

I didn't know what to do, and none of my thoughts were safe. It would have been a crisis had I not been so excited in the middle of the storm. *Who is a friend to me at the Greenwood Center? Who can I trust if not myself?* Could I trust the instructors or the attendees who were controlled by them? Why could I not talk to the attendees without instructors in sight? *Why can I not think straight?* Did everyone just put on a happy face to get by? What did I ever do wrong to get here—to be tormented like this? Was everything I saw a lie? Was everyone I knew a liar? Was I being watched right now—just a character in a dusty book that was ignored by even the indifferent shelf it sat on? Did any of that matter?

"These thoughts are derailing you, Michael. They make you weaker. Focus. And don't despair in the unknown."

I got up out of bed late—four and a half minutes late, to be exact. I looked out and listened for attendees in the halls, scuttling about for breakfast. Nope, I was too late. I didn't know why I expected to see any of my peers as late as I was, but I also failed to know why I was expected to be so punctual—day in and day out.

Distrust of the institution seeped and grew in me like a seed as soon as I began to trust myself more. It was like a swinging pendulum, and I knew it was for the best—I *trusted* it was for the best. With each step, I grew increasingly weary of walking in the same lines and kneeling in the same arrays with the other kneelers and standers—day in and day out. The white walls that used to feel alive and open constricted me. I was a prisoner, not an attendee. I needed a window desperately—if only my eyes could go and walk outside, my body could be more at ease.

But that late morning, I would find my window—or rather, it would find me and rest in the palm of my hand.

I waded through the silent breakfast line. Blank faces and closed-lipped, robotic smiles appeared up and down the row. The instructors chatted amongst themselves, but not loud enough for us to hear. *Everything is a little too stagnant and plain*, I thought to myself. Then, I felt something I didn't want to feel: intimidation.

"You *should* feel intimidated, Michael. You're right to feel this way. But now, what are you going to do with this feeling? What will this impel you to do, to become? How will you selfishly use a shrinking feeling to enable yourself to grow?"

I didn't know the answer, but I thought about it. And maybe that was growth in itself. I didn't know. I looked around, and I boiled in the slow silence with nothing to do except wait. Suddenly, the shrill speakers split the air. Everyone jumped at the disturbance. Then, my name bounced around the halls like a stray basketball: "Michael Conifer, please report immediately to the director's cabin."

There was no notice nor explanation, and I didn't know who said it or who the director was or if those crackly words were medicinal or toxic. I guessed I was going to find out. I was helpless in the dark without so much as a flashlight.

"You're not in the dark, Michael. You may be in dire trouble, but at least you know what they want. You know who they care about and what they want to protect. Not one of their wishes is for your wellbeing. Take that to heart."

My steps weren't that steady, but they got me where I needed to go. I wanted to dissociate from the pangs in my stomach and the stern faces I was about to see. I wanted to drift above them into a whispering, hazy cocoon where I didn't have to see or hear—at least for a little while.

But that was fantasy. *This* was reality.

It was a harsh reality, but it was *real* all the same; and besides choosing oblivion, there was no way out. That would not be my choice at that moment. I wanted to see and hear even if it irked me, with the hope that maybe something pleasant could propel itself into my life. Sometimes, even the hope of that possibility was pleasant enough to keep me going and make meaning of this obscure, windowless room that both captured me and hated me in the same resentful breath. Its eyes stared through the flat, uninspired paintings of vases hanging around the melon walls. There were no secretaries at the desk—just a stack of papers that stared at me as well. The low-legged table in the middle of the room disguised itself as a footstool and stalked me, while the broken clock perched above me stared and flexed its bony arms.

But the eyeballs—all of them—invigorated me. They filled me with the morning dew of a challenge. Despite waking up late this morning, I could still smell the air of fresh opportunity. It was this primal, good-feeling lever that pricked me to search for an outdated magazine to tear through while I waited for some authority to pluck me from the jungle I'd found myself in. Why did I feel that way? Why did I invite the eyeballs to stare at me? Why was I suddenly okay with the attention when I never had been before?

"You're growing stronger."

Just when I thought I'd found the perfect choice of trashy literature filled with pictures and cheap scandals, something surrounded me. It was a voice—a real human voice, not the growl of the hungry low-legged table or the heavy breathing of the bottom sheet of paper gasping for air. Instead, it was a large, mustached human man.

"Michael." His voice was scratchy and broad, filtered by a bushy mustache. "Hello. I'm Director Hausen. It's a pleasure. Come this way. You don't have to be scared. You're not in trouble."

"Um, hi. Okay… I'm… not scared. It's nice to meet you."

The director just looked on with faint pity and turned around—he was giant but slow and not particularly threatening. Still, I made sure I knew where the exits were as we entered his office. It was a nice office with a lot of glass and dark wood, but that was about all I noticed. He said to take a seat, so I did. The next thing I knew, he pulled out a lockbox and began shuffling his bearish hands through it, searching for my phone. He slid it over to me. I hadn't seen that thing in weeks.

The director cleared his throat, but there was nothing to clear. "It's... here's your phone. It's better you learn from your mother."

"Huh? Learn what?" At the time, I didn't realize I had scooted so far forward that I was barely sitting—I teetered on the edge of the chair and over a most malicious precipice. It was then, through the phone screen and beyond, past my mother's words on the speaker and even outside of the boxy mahogany office, that I saw outside of the veil. I understood—if only for a racing, split-second moment—the fibers of the silk-soft web that was woven for only our eyes and our touch. I stepped wholly outside of it. I saw myself standing alone and unconquerable because, outside of the veil, there was no concept of conquest, direction, or any place to be outside of. I made sense of the senseless, in that there could be nothing hidden if I never sought anything out.

I lifted the veil in a single, indivisibly small frame of consciousness and delved deep under the concrete and even into the abstract nature of things—to where such a thing as depth had no bearing on a limitless world that was too real to be constrained by tiny dimensions. In the realm, or lack thereof, beyond the senses, beyond the veil, maybe the only thing I "felt" was a certain *power*—if anything could be felt, ascertained, or understood at all. There was only unbridled power, and it was only that way because restraint was not a concept beyond the veil. There was nothing to hold back—nothing to be restrained. It was power, pure and without limit or consequence. And for a moment, I tapped into it.

It was only my return to the veil from somewhere beyond that bestowed me with an understanding of what the world truly was. My momentary absence from the plane helped me better grasp my presence there. And then, all of my senses heightened and rejoiced in ecstasies throughout my young body. It was limitless and profound. Then, in a snap instant, it all ended, and I crashed back down to earth with the crackly voice of my mother still in my ear through the speaker of my cold phone.

"Michael…" My mother's voice trailed off. Something laced in her sullen tone, the pause in her words, and the downtrodden face the director made as he stared at his shoes made my neck tense and my palms sweat. I was surprised and scared in the black silence. There was no reason for her not to have been talking, yet it seemed like she couldn't choke the words out—like they were too grave to even say, to even *think* about without seizing up. A pronounced sniffle finally came through from her end of the line.

"Mrs. Conifer, I—"

"No! What? No… Michael," she puffed out another sigh, "your father…" She trailed off again. This time, the silence wasn't nearly as long. I winced. Then, a little spark fluttered inside my gut and provoked me energetically. "Early this morning… during his morning ritual… he had a heart attack, Michael… a bad one. And… your dad… he died… Michael… he's no longer with us."

Sniffles and what sounded like tears rushed over the other side of the line. The director, through his mustache and a thick wall of freshly wrinkled skin, peered at me discreetly, as if he wasn't supposed to look at me but his interest couldn't keep his lustful eyes away. The room suddenly seemed so small. The director was so large and capable, like at any moment… what was his name again?

I got a case of the jitters. My ears weren't in the business of working very well. My head probably hurt, but I couldn't feel much at the time. Someone on my phone kept repeating something, but I failed to ascertain just who and what and why that was. My eyelids anchored to the tops of my cheeks and made a clanging sound. I wished my numbness aided my thoughts. It didn't. My rational mind was hollowed out and immobile, dry and fatigued from being choked so forcefully and so quickly. I didn't know. I was drowning from something, but I didn't know what or why. I was too constricted—too blind, deaf, and dumb—to even utter a word. If I'd become nauseous, it would have meant I at least felt the slightest itch or tingle, but I didn't. I couldn't feel a thing anywhere. I was wading—floating. It was neither uncomfortable nor pleasant—not like a cloud nor a bed of spikes. It was purely nothing.

The rest of my time at the Greenwood Center was spent packing up and avoiding everyone and everything. I'd forgotten what the freshness of the outside could do for a tired soul; I had forgotten I was even tired in the first place. Like a vagabond moving again, I had my things slung over my shoulder, and I was escorted out by an instructor, never to be seen by them or anyone in the Greenwood Center again.

I wondered what the other attendees felt. I wondered where they'd come from and if they were anything like me. I wondered if they were as tired as I was and if, possibly, I was the lucky one. I thought back to the static mechanism in Rose's robotic smile. It was hastily manufactured and thrown out to the rest of the attendees after she had been in The Room, and it was the only indicator of what went on in there.

I wandered deeper into my mind, where some of my most prickly thoughts lay—where walking by them could draw blood and scare you away as the deafening roars of the jungle washed over the ears of anyone who tried to brave the back of my head. Inside, all was navy blue and black, uninviting, loud, and venomous. The corners of Rose's plastic smile seemed to be held on by tacks or strong putty, as if by *command*. And we clapped. We clapped for her because we were convinced that Rose's time in The Room was what we wanted. It would have been easy to say the instructors convinced us of this, but really, we convinced ourselves.

I think the Greenwood Center loved young, weak minds. Maybe that was why I had to go. I was no longer as weak. And then, the prickle bushes and territorial snakes of my thoughts became too much for my poor, bleeding body to bear, and my eyes drifted back to indulge in the fresh air and the blue horizon of the morning. My car pulled up—it was the station wagon my mom *hated*—and I drifted inside to the sound of birds and the artificially cheery look on my mom's face.

Chapter 48 – John

Plans are funny sometimes. And sometimes they laugh at you. Plans never go exactly as planned in our world. Mine surely didn't. You see, I needed that psycho, smiling sonuvabitch to stay alive. I needed him, possibly more than he knew. Without Lorne, my building wouldn't go up. I wouldn't be able to get the licensing to do it now. There was no way. He really had to die on me. This plan had crashed. Now, the project I'd been heading toward for two years was shattered on the ground.

Lorne was integral to my plan. And now, he was dead.

I wasn't a vengeful man, but someone had to pay for this. But most likely, because of pressure from the board and pressure from the shareholders, I would be stuck holding the bag for this mess. Despicable. His poor son, left alone without a father… Unimaginable.

Once I heard the news about Lorne, the only thing I felt like doing was escaping into sports, something fast-paced and meaningless. I turned a basketball game on and thought about my next move. My mind was plagued with the threat of unhappy shareholders, unhappy directors, pissed that this plan and years of investment had fallen through the cracks because some guy's heart decided to stop beating.

It really was a travesty. I didn't know how to feel except scared and angry.

Anders growled in my ear. "They're gonna smother you, Johnny."

Chapter 49 – Rachel

My closet was in the corner of my room. Yes, it was very spacious, and you could *walk in* there, but I didn't call it a "walk-in closet." To me, it was just a closet. And I searched that closet far and wide, checking to make sure my father hadn't put the jar of bud somewhere in there instead of my nightstand. I wasn't frantic, but I was definitely looking hard.

Beyond my row of black tops—no weed.

Underneath my shelves—no weed.

In all of the drawers throughout my room—no weed.

Before I declared it was not in my room, I double-checked everything again and finally realized my father must not have been in there yet. So, for the next hour, I waited. I waited some more. Scrolling on my phone got boring, and I began to fixate on… no, think about… the jar. Where was my father with the weed? He always dropped it off on the nightstand this time every week. Maybe he'd forgotten, but I'd still go down and ask him.

I got angry, then confused; he was playing video games on the couch in one of the living rooms. His face was blanketed in a blistering blue glow. He wore his thick-rimmed glasses and looked like a nerd. It would have been funny or endearing had he not been reprehensible—had he not been a monster. His hair was messy in a funny way, and he was eating plain, salted (generic brand) potato chips just like a little kid at a slumber party. Except he was alone. He looked like a small speck buried under a fur blanket, with only his head and hands sticking out, set in a spacious cavern that was more like an amphitheater than a living room. The couch swallowed him, and the pillars at the threshold of the room framed the scene so his blue-lit face was just a small, blanketed buoy in a wide marina bay.

I entered the room, and the mood sank deeply. He stopped chewing and revealed more of his body—his fingers even stopped jittering on the controller. He didn't move, just stared straight ahead.

"Hey."

He didn't answer. He just continued to stare and swallow carefully.

"Umm…" I didn't want to raise my voice over a whispering level. It didn't seem appropriate to even talk. I really wanted my weed, though. I hankered for it. I drooled just thinking about it—magic, green puffs wrapped in delicious, white crystals.

Yum.

I decided. "The jar… that usually… sits on my nightstand." I spoke and didn't dare peek back into the living room. I heard nothing from him, and I didn't want to see anything either. Every word that came out of my mouth was rough. It hurt. I thought back to the hurt in his eyes when I'd said the "h-word," when I'd driven the knife through his heart. I'd looked at a man who'd lost his soul as I told him he'd lost me. That's what I'd wanted though, right? Of course I wanted him to feel that way—he's a criminal. "It's not there tonight."

He had nothing else to swallow, but he still swallowed. And continued to look straight ahead. His blankness made me kind of nervous. Why was I nervous? Then, he cleared his throat, and I thought he was going to say something. He still didn't. I was standing at the kitchen island looking in at him—the vastness of the house made it reasonable to use binoculars from that distance, as it seemed like we were miles apart. It felt that way, too.

"Make a fuss, baby. Stir something up in his head. You *are* still his little girl, after all. He should thank you for talking to him." When I heard Estelle's words, the scent and the flushed, cushiony feeling of the green smoke filled me up and blinded me. To say I was angry would have been an understatement. I was erratic, pissed, flustered. I felt like everything was weighing me down, and my dad could have easily—with a flick of his finger—removed the burden from my sweaty shoulders. I was so done with his stalling.

"Hey," I said, in one last attempt to play nicely. My voice was smooth as silk—almost as smooth as Estelle's. "Daddy, I had a *really* stressful day. And I could really use…"

I paused when his body began to stir. I'd gotten some reaction from him—a strong reaction—but I couldn't tell what it meant. I kept pressing onward like an Amazon warrior. "I could really use some relief…

Daddy?" Was he grinding his teeth? I thought I was getting somewhere.

"Go for the killing blow."

I exhaled like I was very distraught—like I was actually sorry or upset. *As if!* "Those things I said… the other day—"

"What things?" Suddenly, he sprang into action, and his trembling stopped. He was trying to put me in a corner. He may have been evil, but he was also very smart, and that fact was not always fun to deal with.

Before I could say anything, Estelle gave me a push: "Don't back down, girl. You're doing a good thing."

"You know what I said." My fists tightened like I was some meathead boy.

His hands snaked around his black controller while his face drooped a little. The trembling started again. No answer.

"He's putting the ball in your court, Rachygirl. Now give him a slam dunk."

I stomped. I didn't mean to, but my foot came down hard on its own, and it shook my knee and thigh. "Where's my weed, John? Huh? Where is it? It's *not* on my nightstand! Are you hiding it from me?"

A storm seemed to brew in his chest. Then, like thunder, his body shot up from the couch and struck the ground violently. "You can pay for it if that's what you want!" The whole house—all fifteen thousand square feet of it—shook as he roared. If we'd had any neighbors close by, they surely would have called the police after hearing him scream like that. "I've enabled you for *too long*! You treat people like shit, you treat me like shit! All I do is provide for you and try to be there when you're down. You want to use a product to help you relax? Pay me for it! I have a big company that sells it." His ribcage heaved, and veins pressed through his face like toxic rivers.

"Maybe he could use a joint right now." Estelle laughed.

How is she so calm? How can she make a joke at a time like this? I felt like I was in serious danger, and Estelle's chill presence only twisted my nerves more. I couldn't think at that point. I just said things. Everything was sped up. The soreness in his eyes was like a scourge—like touching a hot pan and being forced to hold your singed fingers against it. I couldn't stand it. So I just shouted. "Dad! Dad… please… please don't do this to me. Why do you look so angry? Don't go back to your game! Daddy…"

It was all in vain. It was like talking to a wall—and a very angry one, at that. It was useless, it was hopeless, it was…

He started to speak again. My whole body turned toward him—not because I cared what he had to say or about him, but because my anatomy and my lungs and my tired heart realized he held the key to my physical pleasure. The key to the jar. The key to my phone. The key to the house.

"Maybe you should've thought about all of that, Rachel. You're getting older now. Maybe you should get a job."

"Tell that bastard he's going to be left with nobody if he keeps talking to you that way!" Estelle hissed in my ear loudly, but I could barely hear her. I didn't know if that was the right thing to say—the strategic thing. Somewhere in my willpower and my high mind was a rare thought contrary to Estelle's, and it went something like this: If I convinced that mutt scoundrel I still loved him like a good little daughter (yuck!), then I could keep that fresh green rolling into my wallet and my room. I could take him for all he's worth and more. It would be the ultimate trick, the *best* revenge.

For some reason, I got on my knees. The only sound in the castle was the clicking of his thumbs on that stupid controller and hot smoke beginning to loosen up out of his ears in a steady stream. The next audible sounds were my sniffles and pathetic whimpers—it was the best I could do. I felt and probably looked like a beggar, but really, I was a queen in disguise.

"Daddy… I'm a piece of crap! I don't deserve to have you, and I'm too gross to call you my dad. I'm so sorry, I'm so, so… can you pause the game, please? Sorry, Dad… I'm so sorry for everything! Can you please turn the sound of the game down? I was just upset that night, and I'm sorry!"

There was no reply—just more empty clicking from his compulsive hands. It was all very weird. He heard me, he saw me out of the corner of his eyes, yet he refused to acknowledge me. What was this? Was this a ploy? Was he trying to get inside my head? Did he think he was better than me, just like he'd thought of my mother? Was I even a human to him? Apparently, I wasn't! More of my body opened up with sweat. It would have been gross except for in a time like this when an Amazon queen needed to gain the strength necessary to stand up and defeat an unholy giant. So what if I was sweating? I was going into battle. I pictured Estelle and her brooding lips as I drank in her words and marched toward the living room.

I was a warrior.

"Please get out of the way of the screen." He bobbed his head one way and then another as if he hadn't just screamed his head off abusively at me two minutes before. What a fucking worm. I loved dancing in front and watching him squirm and bob his blue-lit head some more. Finally, he paused the game. I had too much of something surging through me, so I didn't care. I needed to relax; I wanted to smoke. I wanted to inhale it and let the purple wisps tantalize the ends of my pink lungs, filling my head with nothing but peace. But I needed to go to war before I found that peace. And the enemy was standing right in front of me.

"I'll go to the streets for it if you don't give me any."

His head and mouth jerked and twisted like I'd truly disgusted him.

"That one really got to him. You're learning quickly, Rachybaby."

He held his ground, but barely. "With what money?" he said in a stressfully calm tone. I was about to make his cool wall crumble.

"I have plenty of money in my account, *John*." He hated when I called him the "J-word." He cringed and cursed under his breath. Oh yeah, I was getting somewhere.

Under his stinky, disgusting breath, he seethed, "I took that money out."

"*What*? You *stole* from me? You can't do that!" I stomped, then I may have launched an Amazonian attack on him. There may have been a crashing noise.

His teeth were clenched, and his face was red. "What are you *doing*, Rachel? Is this any way to act?"

"It is if you're *abusing* me! Senselessly!" Another attack was launched, but it was more cushioned than the last.

He just shook his dumb head and stepped closer to me. A shot of muck twisted in my body every time he moved. He was such a snake, subhuman filth. And he continued to take more and more from me every day. I was going to fight back.

He opened his snake mouth, and bullshit seeped right out of it: "You know what?" He had his hands on his hips, and he laughed in a haughty, ungenuine way.

"This is my fault. This is my fuckin' fault. I taught you to act like this. I taught you to be a little Machiavellian devil. This is on me." He pointed to himself.

I thought I was getting somewhere with him. Estelle seemed to think that, too. She told me to pour it on. I did. I verbally speared him like a warrior and told him that, *obviously*, this *was* his fault.

"You don't get it, do you, Rachel?" He stepped even closer. Although he was thin for a man, he was kind of imposing up close. "I don't blame you at all for being this upset. Not at all. But when you act like this—when you try to lord leverage over me and kick and scream and do whatever you can—"

"I didn't kick you once!"

"You're just like me. You're just like how I was…" He sighed the deepest of breaths. He looked like he was contemplating, calculating, and conjuring an immensely difficult problem in his blond head. Then he spoke again, after a good ten seconds of staring off and then at me. "And I'm not going to put up with it."

"I'm nothing like you!" I was hurling powerful words in a loud, protesting voice. I was not going to back down—even though he was trying to confuse me. He was trying to distort my own inner moral compass. This was exactly what he did to my mom. He was trying to redirect my energy elsewhere.

"He's a clever fella'," said Estelle, "but you're cleverer. You can beat him right back." A smile wormed across my face—it was the only pleasant thing I felt that whole time, and it was also wonderfully defiant. I looked at him like a powerful girl should—my fists were balled, and my smirk oozed power. I could tell he was a little scared and upset by the sudden change in my mood, my mocking face. It probably looked so much like my mom that he couldn't stand it.

I lowered my voice. "You know what? Maybe you're right. Maybe I am more like you than I think—than I wanna believe!"

He tilted his head.

"He took the bait."

"And that's why I hate myself!" I stomped my foot on carpet too thick and soft to make a noise or even shake the house. Then, the tears came like April rain, and I couldn't stop them. A warrior wouldn't cry in front of an enemy, so why was I? I hadn't even known I thought that about myself. Was I lying? How could I hate such a smart and beautiful person—how could I hate someone so strong who'd been through so much already? I had to have lied to him in the heat of the moment, because of course I'd never thought that about myself—it was such a ridiculous thought. I was tricking him once again—trying to trip him up even further in my clever web. After all, when a warrior couldn't fight, they could play dead with a shiny sheathed dagger in hand—hungry for a back to rip through and feast on.

Earlier, when he'd been sitting alone on the couch, I'd realized he wasn't nerdy or cute in a funny way. No, in fact, he was incredibly *lonely*. For better or worse, I was the final string that held his last few soft parts together. I was the one person who could make him believe in himself and his last bit of morality. Without me, without my love and adoration for my dear daddy, what did he have to believe in? Who did he have to turn to? I was the dark-haired, brown-eyed bridge between him and the sins of his past—between him and my beloved mother. I was a huge, irreplaceable part of him. And no matter how much he struggled with his own life, he could anchor himself to my wellbeing.

And me? I wanted to cut his anchor's chain and watch him float away endlessly into the sorrowful ocean of his past—all the drugs, all the cheating, all the lies. All the pain I'd seen in my mom's eyes when she found out about the affair, I wanted to inflict on my dad. But because that pain was endless and divine, my work with my father could never be done. My hatred for him could never run out—it was infinite, like the pain in my mother's mocha eyes, reddened by the blood my father spilled. He never killed anyone, but he was still a murderer in my eyes. He killed our family. He almost killed me—plenty of times, too many to count.

He was the reason for everything.

He looked like an old man then. He was helpless to me, like a little kid. I saw for a moment his eyes redden and well up and his lip quiver, and that hit me with a shot of relief. It felt good to watch some sadness run over his face—some well-deserved grief—but it wasn't enough.

I needed more.

I needed him to know he was worthless and that he deserved to be alone for eternity—staring off in his kingly castle without a queen or an heir or even a kingdom to look over. Just a controller, empty space, and some numbers on his mobile banking app to show him what a big man he was.

Chapter 50 – John

There was seizing. There was static in my head. I would rather think the most gruesome, painful thoughts than not be able to think at all. Yet, there I was, with my brain choked and my mouth sealed and useless. The truth was, I had nothing to say. I kept going back into the past, and as I did that, I froze. Anders told me to focus on the present moment—but how could I do that without a plan, without a strategy? Rachel was out of control, but it was my doing and my fault... and also the result of poor planning, negligence, and a lack of conviction one way or another. I was thinking and also loathing myself while I had heavy ceramic vases flung at my face in my own living room, which I only then realized I cared nothing about. To think that I'd held this girl in my arms on the beach while she cooed, and I'd smiled and told her she had her mommy's eyes—all I could feel was the sun and the salty breeze and the healing kiss of my wife. We both looked at each other, then we looked down at tan baby Rach. She was like a precious dollop of heaven swaddled in...

"Think, Johnny, think! While she's pausing and simmering down, *think* for a moment—that's the only thing that will do you any good right now."

I took a breath. I, with a quick glance, caught sight of those eyes... They held so much hatred and shame, too much for one to have to bear... and for a moment, I felt—

"Johnny. Come on now. *What's* the end goal here? We talked about this, man," Anders echoed in my noggin, and I knew he was damn right. I looked into those eyes again, brown and painted with a pain I knew I couldn't cure.

"Rachel... please." I took a breath because I needed to. "Just listen to me. Just f—"

"I've done that enough!" Her voice cracked, and a new round of tears made saline tracks down her smooth face.

I want her to love me.

"J-man, are you sure? I thought we talked about this. That wasn't an option, remember?"

I need her... to love me.

"It's too late for that, John! It's too damn late! She's your daughter—she doesn't have to be your whole world!"

And then, something hard and sharp smacked my cheek. I didn't feel the blood until long after that—after it ran all over my shirt and stained my Polo sweatpants. It didn't hurt either. It just made me see red and dark blue for a moment. I saw stars in the dim light and broken glass on the floor. I stared at a picture that had fallen out of the intact metal frame. I looked at Rachel's face—it showed deep sorrow, I thought, for one second then changed back to that of yet another mean, vindictive young woman who had been failed by the executives she grew up under, including me. We were the same executives that fed kids like her endless drugs and screens and insisted we were the ones who helped, that we were the ones who brought her into a cleaner, easier future...

"John..." Her shoulders shrugged massively with every breath. Veins the size of snakes were buried just underneath the thin skin on her long neck. "Give me," she growled through gritted teeth, "some weed before I call the police."

I was about to yell and do something rash. I was about to feel instead of think.

"Don't, *don't*! Don't. Just breathe, John. Just... think and breathe. What does she want you to do?"

"I own the police, Rachel." My voice was hoarse, and I tasted metallic blood. It invigorated me and scared me, but not more than I was scared for my future, for Rachel's future, for my life. "So, before you call them, think! Think before you do anything!"

"That's it, you're buying time. But John, you're giving her too much attention."

She just threw a picture at me. She's been assaulting me. How do I not give her attention? What the fuck?

"You're treating her like you still owe her, John. Even after all of this, she knows she can do what she wants. You need to be mo—"

"Why can't you just treat one person like a normal human being? Not like a commodity! Like a product! I'm not a consumer—I'm your daughter! And

I'll fucking hate you forever if you don't have a jar of bud on my nightstand in ten minutes!"

What the hell do I say to that, Anders?

"Nothing," he said.

Nothing? That just wasn't realistic. I couldn't abide by that.

"Rachel, I don't hate you. And if you hate me, then... then that's your prerogative!" I thought that would have some sort of a peacemaking martyr effect after she'd attacked me. It didn't. Right after she stomped through the room and halls and granite staircase, I realized how goddamn *stupid* I sounded.

The plush couch seemed to magnify my body as I sank into it. That was when I put my shaking hand to my face and felt a liquid. I looked at it: maroon and wet. I felt the adrenaline leak out of my body as I faded on the couch. Anders didn't dare speak for the rest of the night. I fell asleep to stars in my head and on the wall, with the TV still on and Rachel's fading footsteps up to her locked room.

That night, I slept well but had really shitty dreams. It wasn't pleasant, to say the least. They were quiet, desperate things, where all I heard was hissing and all I felt was anxiety. In the nightmares, it was dark, and I was waiting for someone, like a reaction where all I could do was wait and watch and play unfortunate defense. I guess when you gain everything, you only have things to lose.

Chapter 51 – Michelle

Michael wasn't suspicious of a thing. How could he have been? I'd "cried" so much on the phone with him. I sounded so grim to the director, too. Of course, there was nothing to be suspicious about. I kept my face full of despair and a low, sad voice—that is, for the few times I spoke—on the forested car ride home. There were so many different kinds of trees—they were all unique, despite looking so similar from just a quick, careless glance from afar. But it was the same with so many people and their lives—quick and careless, unwilling to take a closer look at the individual trees they were so eager to zoom past.

It was a good thing that most people weren't precise. It was a blessing that police officers, detectives, and politicians weren't as scrupulous as they always seemed at first glance. A truly crimeless world would be one where the professors were police officers, the detectives were politicians, and the politicians were put in camps far, far away, where they couldn't have any influence on society. I'd done my part in that matter. According to the laws of *that* world, I'd acted justly. But I felt the same about this world—what I'd done was *just*.

There were so many snares to justice in this world. Institutional garbage, the oppressive elite, and definitely rancid politicians who just wanted power and some attention. Strangely, the more you strove in this life, the harder it was to attain whatever you sought. Now

Lorne, the great striver, was getting more attention than ever—from the media and those cannabis execs alike. I'd even gotten a couple calls at the house from voters.

"So... he's gone." Michael stated this but in an inquisitive way. I just affirmed his statement glumly. I was calculating and driving and doing both while having to be sad was a lot to juggle.

"You don't seem sad enough. He's going to suspect something." My breath got an inch shorter. I slowed down. I looked over at Michael, who was crying and twisting his body and face. I couldn't bear to see it. I also couldn't bear the stubborn thought that he essentially resented me. He felt I was spineless for siding so quickly with his father—that he couldn't trust my fickleness.

Little did he know what I'd done for him. The painstaking work and the colossal risks I'd faced for *him*. I couldn't even tell him about it, though. His selfish teenage brain wouldn't be able to appreciate the sacrifices I'd made for him. I pulled over to catch my breath. The drive back from the Greenwood Center was a long one.

As I opened my door in the breakdown lane, I could tell from the look on Michael's face that he wanted to say, "Are you okay, Mom?" But he was too anguished to say anything at all. Instead, he just sat, red-faced, and stared ahead blankly, horrified. It was terrible to see anyone in that much pain, but when it was your own child, you felt like a part of you was shriveling up and dying inside. But there *was* blue beyond the horizon because I knew he would come around. I knew this was best for him. In a way, if not totally, I'd done it for him. That red, sullen face would soon be so much happier for so much longer—he deserved it. He deserved all the love in the world. He had a pure heart, and he'd been through so much already. He was too young to be exposed to so much.

I got back in the car after my lungs caught up to me and kept on driving.

"I don't understand." Sniffle, sniffle.

"Hey…" I stroked the back of his neck like a good mother should and asked him in a soft voice, "what is it you don't understand, baby?" He just sat and stared. It looked like he was being crushed by something he couldn't remove or escape from. Maybe I shouldn't have asked him any questions. "It's going to be okay."

"He suspects something," said the voice in my head. I floored on the gas for a second, not realizing I was doing it. Oh god. It was just the voice in my head, and it didn't exist anyway.

"Did they do an auto—"

"The cannabis guy demanded an autopsy."

Sniffle, sniffle. "What did it show?"

"Heart attack."

"I know *that*." There was hurt in his words.

I gave him another crumb. "It was," I sighed loudly and longingly, "a toxic mixture of his amphetamine salts and caffeine. Too early, too much in the morning. His blood pressure went too high; his heart pumped too fast and too… Oh god, I can't think right now."

"Didn't he have that mix every day?" He was very inquisitive for such a young boy.

"He was an addict, and addicts are so sad and terrible because they always drown in their own poison. It's a pathetic tragedy."

He just stared straight ahead.

The voice spoke up, "You'll be in the clear if you follow the plan. But, as for Michael—you don't know what he's capable of, Michelle. He's been through too much; he's seen too much. He's been flung around and battered everywhere he's landed. That is no life for a child, much less a sensitive soul like him. He needs stability. He needs *you*. He needs to know he can count on something outside of himself for the first time in his life. Otherwise, Michelle, he will be in serious danger, and you will be, too. You're not crazy, but he might be."

The voice could be so reassuring. It could be so grandiose, scheming, and protective of me. But I wondered and questioned. Was the voice serious? In this case, was Michael actually ill? That question rang out in my mind. I settled on a disagreement with the voice inside my head: He wasn't crazy. I wasn't crazy. *Lorne* was crazy. He was always the crazy one, the depraved one, the guy willing to do anything for himself and nothing for others. That was crazy, and that was my husband, Lorne. Michael was right.

Chapter 52

What is the theme here, reader? Is it that there is no hope—that you are doomed from the beginning to madness and mad people, no matter which way you turn? Is it that people are naturally different, and all of their inherent differences meld together and clash in beautifully human ways? Is the theme that of self-triumph—a tale of overcoming despite brutal external pressures (and maybe *because* of external pressures)? Or is it deception? Or hatred and resentment, and how those gruesome feelings lie just over a thin line on the other side of true, genuine love?

Well, you may derive what you like from my tale because that is, reader, what I am trying to convey after all. The point is this: The crafty serpents are among you and within you all the time. They leer, stalk, hiss, and slither. And their chief characteristic—they never cease exploring and pillaging. The serpents fully and only crave your vital life essence. They want to infect it first, then they want to suck it and absorb it until you have none left. They want to drain you.

Why, you may ask, are they so brutishly indignant, spiteful, and unquenchingly motivated? Because they hate you. They hate that you are yourself. They hate that you breathe and walk, and most of all, they hate that *you can choose*. Yes, you are able to choose for yourself, and because of the vitality within you, you can ultimately choose to triumph over them—

willfully. It is your will you must both guard and use against the crafty serpents because they are trying to invade you right now through your body and your delicate consciousness—pervading your soft intestines, your precious vision, your fragile memories, and even your darling headspace. They proliferate themselves through you—through your life force and even your own will.

Let us digress for a moment. Back to my triumphant tale starring none other than me, the voice inside your head. I would like to give you a few guideposts to insert some more juicy, dramatic irony into your head.

You may have noticed another thing. Why is it that I speak and interact differently with each character? The answer is simple and, in fact, self-evident: Different people need to be handled in beautifully varied ways. That is also why my relationship with each person differs. That is not to say, however, that every personal difference is equivalent in value and aptitude. The reality is quite the contrary! There are those who are advanced in their relationship and understanding of the monster in their head—namely, Rachel. As is crucially evident to you, my dear reader, Rachel can *understand* her monster. Therefore, she humbles herself before me (acting as her dearest Estelle) and collaborates. She listens, then crunches my—Estelle's—feedback on her own terms. She is as independent as she is cooperative with me, the voice inside her pretty little head.

Michael, on the other hand, is a more difficult, more problematic situation. He is finicky, feebleminded. It takes a special type of subtle coercion to topple him psychologically and make him befriend me—even for a character of my own creation! But please don't be vexed by my harsh diction, reader. All I mean by "topple psychologically" is a means of courting or getting to know one well enough to then *relate* to.

You, reader, have the special privilege of being both an observer as well as an active participant. I get to talk to you while also showing you, and that is a most delicious treat for *me* as much as it may be my rather selfless gift to you.

In your humble yet gracious and noble opinion, reader, would you say these characters more so compete or collaborate with each other? To you, my most respected pupil and wisest teacher, is this story more of a fight or a dance? Just note that it can only be one or the other—but of course, you already knew that! If I could be so blessed as to hear your inner monologue right now, I'm sure it would fall along the lines of being a scathing rebuke of my patronization toward you. Ha! I can assure you, reader, that you are stronger than you think, and I most certainly have no intention of coddling you—*au contraire!* It would be impossible to baby such a titan of thought and literary adventure such as yourself—after all, you *have* read this far, have you not? Continue to read, and you will see you can form your own opinions, and that is the most beautiful thing!

Of course, me being solely a "voice" embedded in the story that I, myself, have forged is just a literary device. I know that you, reader, have no such "voice" in your own head, and you are not nearly as gullible as these cardboard characters you've been observing all this time. I can well assume you are far more complex—both more amiable and intelligent—than these characters on the whole. I can also assume, being a human, you have both a certain disdain as well as a predilection for problems, and subconsciously, you don't always want all of the answers. Like a moth to a lone lamp, you are attracted to misfortune.

But I have done you the disservice of painting this misfortune incompletely—you haven't gotten the full truth of this story, but rather, only subjective pieces of an otherwise convoluted puzzle.

I offer one last charitable morsel to you before we continue this journey in the form of friendly admonishment—*advice* if you will—that you are free to take or leave as you so please. My advice is simple: Don't picture me, and don't imagine walking around and going about your day with me stuck in your head, giving reminders and suggestions. Please don't put so much stock into what I say if that is your desire. I am rather self-important compared to fallible organisms, but I may not be important to you and your psyche, and that's fine.

Just know, reader, even if you cast me aside and ignore me, I will never ignore you. I will always be watching and... *caring* about the transcendent outcomes of your life—whether they seem monumental or minuscule to you.

I will never stop pursuing you.

Chapter 53 – Michael

Who could I have turned to if not my own mother? Well, I guess I *could* have opened up to her. It could serve to unload my burdens and the dense ball of black goo stuck in the back of my head that mired my thoughts and feelings and, sometimes, even my vision—a clawed demon, a howling, screeching menace I couldn't see or feel but *felt* the presence of constantly.

But why did I feel inclined *not* to share—not to share anything with her, for that matter? Was it me who was the weird one, the lone one? Was she not to be trusted, or was I the shady lingerer? Would I want to, or could I even, open up my tender feelings to anyone else besides my own mom—anyone else at all? Was this a blessing or a curse, and did either of those things even exist? I felt like my thoughts continued to constrict me. I spiraled in my head.

Speaking of movement, I began to go on more long walks after my time at the Greenwood Center. It was like each step was one more stride away from the memories of my father—slowly but surely. But they kept coming back anyway. Like darts, they would fly suddenly to the front of my mind, stinging and singeing me with their poison. To verbalize what those memories were would make them real. I didn't want to materialize them or anything about them; I just wanted them to go away. I wanted them to wither in my mind and be freed from it all. I wanted to believe it wasn't my fault, but then again, I had done things that had led to it. But it probably wasn't my fault. Well, how could it have been?

In the sun-soaked trees and stamped sidewalks of suburban Colorado, the monster, the man, the voice, threw a wrench at me: "Get ahold of yourself, Michael. You're spiraling. Are you a hamster or a human? Are you a test su—Oh! Never mind! Your father is gone, and he *did* abuse you, and it *was* your fault. It was your fault for taking it. You let it happen. What was your mother supposed to do?"

Beel's words hit me with the might of an indignant wave, angry at the shore and its fellow beachgoers. I was caught, and then I stopped. My lungs were heavy, and my tongue felt dry and out of place. The waves then washed within me. In the amicable sun of midday, with nothing but a friendly breeze to accompany its inhabitants, a storm brewed within me. It became a torrent—a flood that had to spill somewhere. Beel was the only thing in its path. I tightened my fists and everything else in my body that felt small and helpless—something else I was angry with at the time. I was angry at the leaf that fell and the leaf that stayed on its rightful, lofty perch. I was angry at the wind, and then at the absence of it.

"No!" I yelled. No one was around, but I wanted someone to hear. I wanted to see someone look at me, point, then scurry away quickly, shaking their head at me for being forgotten and trampled by an indifferent society. Because, after all, society was just that: a group of individuals. I guess now though, looking back, it was just Beel I was speaking to—that I was yelling at and wanted to punch and get punched by. "That can't be true." I was breathing heavily, and despite the calmness of the day, I was soaked in a storm.

"How so, Michael? You are well aware of your ability to *choose*. You, yourself, are a rare breed for truly understanding that. How, then, do you reject that you could have chosen to end the abuse? You're still merely a small child with an infant's plastic mind, that's how!"

I didn't really know how to take Beel's goading besides getting angry at him—also at life and all of the wretches in it, including myself. But something dolloped a flickering stroke of reason into my blind rage—a lone candle in the middle of the dark room appeared seemingly from nowhere. I'd never felt that until that point. Then, the candle's flame only fed itself while situated in the highest part of my mind, and it illuminated a sanctum I still have never seen with my own eyes. Yet, I felt its presence like a warm coat.

My heart slowed. My vision focused, became a bit clearer, and colors appeared like the vivid springtime brushstrokes they should have been. My breath got a little easier—as did everything else in my head. Just for a moment, I thought it could have been possible that maybe, somehow and for some reason, I smiled quickly. I was by myself with Beel with no one to scrutinize me close up or even to snipe me from afar. It was kind of serene. I didn't know why. And in the middle of that swirling, bright serenity, I found the strength to speak up—maybe that was the ultimate and ideal use of strength.

"No," I said quietly, alone, and to the monster I had just realized lurked not only deep within the annals of my being, but also behind every dark shadow, both seen and unseen. "That's not true, Beel." It was like a wisp of smoke that had always been there was lifted from my eyes. "It's not my fault. None of it is. None of it. I was helpless and in the middle of all of it. And now, like a bird that's flown away, I'm here. Isn't that right?"

There was no response from Beel. Instead of grumbles and coarse, bone-rattling mutterings, I heard the breeze float by and say only kind words. I heard the birds chirp, and their song affirmed me. I walked, with each step feeling lighter than the last. I didn't know why. I just enjoyed it for what it was. I didn't realize how I'd grown in that very moment from the likes of a scared, trembling creature to a defined being. Beel wouldn't tell me because that was all part of it. He seemed to be omniscient; he seemed to know everything. Why was it, then, that he was at a loss for words? Now, with my back against the wall and lost in a tormented rage with nowhere to go but down, down and away into the blackness of chaos and certain confusion—how was the god-monster stumped? Maybe he coached me into this, or maybe he wanted it this way. But I wouldn't fixate on that—for myself. For my own strength I now felt like I could draw upon, the birds seemed to sing for me.

When Beel decided to talk next, he would be like an accompanying instrument to the sounds of the outside—a perfectly imperfect melding I thought into being because I enjoyed it. All because I wanted it. Yes, he was a part of me, but only a part. Maybe I needed him, and maybe he hurt me, but I could deal with him and use him to strengthen me, just like anything else.

These thoughts of floating stones and sideways trees peppered my head and gave me a perspective on Beel and everything else I thought I needed, and when I entered my house, my neck was a little less sore. The sun was still high in the air and cascaded onto everything. The natural light was enough to provide a gentle shine for everything throughout the house, including my mom, who was standing by the window with a vaguely concerned face. I walked closer and saw a man in a generic button-down shirt with a pronounced pocket, typing away on a black laptop. He looked to be rather comfortable at our kitchen island, despite him being completely unfamiliar to me.

"Hello, Michael…" My mom said this in a small, tentative voice, as if I were my father towering over her, analyzing her every move. "I was… we were… I'm glad you're back from your walk." She fidgeted like a distressed branch hopelessly caught in a violent gust. "This is Detective Perry. He's here to ask some questions about Dad. All you need to do is be open and honest and answer them to the best of your ability."

"Yep," Perry said, closed-lipped and stiff. He shot a quick, side-eyed glare at my mom. "Hi, Michael."

I sensed something was wrong, maybe even terribly so, and this time, I trusted my instincts. I didn't need Beel to beat me to the punch, and I didn't need to deceive myself and shelter my own eyes. I may have focused a bit more after that, but I didn't remember.

There was a series of questions, many of them lukewarm and even—dare I say—*inviting*. They eased me into the process and made me relax. Did the easy questions trick me? No. Did they lure me into a calmer mindset to ease my tense shoulders back and smooth my voice? Looking back on it, possibly. I probably talked louder and longer the more questions slid over to my end of the table from Perry's gentle but assuming gaze.

"They're investigating," said Beel, "and that means they suspect something... foul play." It was a mocking tone, like I should have known something, like I should have suspected something just as the detective did. He looked at me with soft, trained eyes, but there was an underlying sternness to them that I couldn't ignore. But how could there not be? He *was* a detective after all.

While looking at the detective as little as possible and fielding his softball questions, I felt my mom's intent glare like a heat lamp. Her presence was stronger and more imposing than even Perry's, like she was prying or vying somehow, urging me a certain way for some reason. All of this was so foreign to me, but then again, my psyche had been shattered so many times prior to this conversation that it was child's play—a hiccup that couldn't phase me in the slightest. I knew I had nothing to worry about. Quite frankly, I was there to help the detective mete out justice, whatever that might have meant in our crooked day and state.

Then, a bomb went off. The explosion shook me up and gave me delirious pause. My spine was rattled to the core. It came not in the form of a missile or a grenade or a land mine or a pressure cooker, but rather, through words; the bomb was a question, and it detonated right on the detective's lips.

"Did your dad ever hit you, strike you, slap you, push you, or cause you any sort of physical harm, accidental or otherwise?" The monotone detective spoke robotically and uttered this as if the premeditated question had been carefully formed in a lab.

My eyes shot over to my mom. I kept looking for a bit. She took a deep breath, but it was strained and leveled, and she was cracking her knuckles—something she never did consciously. She wore a faint, prolonged look of worry all over her cheeks and eyes. Clearly, she was scared, but I didn't know why. It was a stressful situation and a painful question, but this really seemed to bother her.

"Michael, you know what? Why do—" she spoke up through a voice that cracked, shrank, and sped up with each word.

Detective Perry cut her off with what seemed like a violent sword swipe rather than words. "Hey, I want to hear the kid talk. Got it?" It was rude, and I wanted to defend her, but I was too young, and his badge was too shiny. Plus, what would I even say to Detective Perry, who was twenty years older and had the fear of the state on his side? Nothing, that's what.

"Whatever you say here will determine *an immense amount*," said Beel. Of course, I didn't know what he meant by that, but I was weirded out that he used the same mocking tone with me—like he knew something I didn't. It was much like that of a smug loser whose only triumph could be a moral one. I cringed.

"Michael?" The detective spoke up again. His voice was soft, like the look in his eyes. "Is everything okay? Something going on in your head?"

"No," I said instinctively, like a reflex.

"Okay then, all I ask is that you answer the question honestly, okay?"

I nodded.

"I'm going to repeat it: Did your dad ever hit you, strike you, slap you, push you, or cause you any sort of physical harm, accidental or otherwise?"

I tried to clear my throat, but it came out like a cough. I swallowed a thick gob that lacerated my throat on the way down. "I—I don't know."

"It's fine, it's fine… Just try to think." He was so nice about it, so calm and inviting. There was nothing I could do besides tell the truth.

"You can bury him properly here," Beel said, challenging me, beckoning me, baiting me. But what choice did I have? How could I have played it any other way than what I was about to do? My hands were bound to a sickening past I'd conquered, that I painfully remembered, and that I had to tell about—that I'd *lived* to tell about. It was all there inside of me. I just had to dig it up and look at it, to hold it like a bloody, evil newborn and stare into its indignant, pulsating face. Its eyes were green and red and ghastly… No, that wasn't right. I just needed to give the detective the truth, however painful it may be.

I sighed once more and glanced up at the detective. "Yes. Yeah, he has."

The detective's soft eyes hardened instantly as they focused back onto his military-grade laptop—he typed away for some time then followed up with the only logical question that could be asked: "How so?"

I retreated back into my head. It may have been for a split second in "real life," but to me, it felt like an eternity full of grim depths and the most revealing, harrowing, golden heights. I remembered my dad and all of him, not just fleeting moments of him. I remembered back at our old house, when I was much younger… when he would drive me to the park, not for anything major, but just to play croquet with me in between his meetings and his meals. It was for nothing special, but it was special to me. It touched me deep down in a most vulnerable and infantile, tender spot. Croquet, as I later found out, was an odd game for a father to play with his son in twenty-first-century America. But we connected through it all the same.

He would say, with that big smile, looking way down at me, "Michael, it doesn't matter how big, tough, smart, or tall you are in croquet. What matters is…" Then, he'd always trail off right at that part and spin around quickly to do a demonstration for me, in which he would effortlessly knock the ball through some far-off wicket he'd just placed there. "… getting the ball through the hoop!"

There was so much triumph in his voice after he sank the ball and looked down at his admiring son. And I would applaud him every time. It was cool to me; *he* was cool to me. And when I was that young, he was *godlike*. There was a tinge of inspiration that I sometimes reflected on even years later from those croquet lessons and some of his rarer disparate musings on life. He would put so much emphasis on people's sizes and strengths and natural abilities, then he would say they didn't matter (despite him being somewhat of a handsome giant himself). "Michael," he would say with force and love, "my ancestors should have *died* at the hands of the English. The English were way stronger and bigger. And do you know why they didn't—why I'm even here right now?" Then he'd wait to leer at me, already adorned with that wide, vicious smile, like some maniac. "Because they *fought*, and they didn't care how big and bad the damn Brits were."

He'd always alluded back to his Irish heritage. He was proud of it. He wore his nationality on him like some sort of triumphant, defiant underdog metal—like he had something to prove. He never cooked, but he'd sure talk about Irish dishes all the time, Irish pastimes, and even Irish stories. Maybe that was why he liked croquet so much.

It was the softest and earliest part of my soul's tissue, and if it had been scarred, it may not have been recoverable—*I*, for that matter, may not have been able to be salvaged from a scar in the early fabric of my life. But it was nice there, luckily enough. I looked back on those early memories of my father with joy. There were even times when I felt he was just like me, in age and genetics and all the rest; looking at my father was sometimes like looking into a mirror. There was a child in him that made me feel like I could be young forever, like I could rule the world or do anything else for as long as I wanted as long as I was with him.

But then, there were the darker parts. The sharp undertones that nagged at me—that did nothing for me except cut into my very being with small, thin slices that could never be patched or healed. They were permacuts—paper-thin incisions that I felt deeply every time he ignored me, traded me in, left me out. I was too young and defenseless and ignorant to be a sparring partner for a god, my father. So instead, I was merely a punching bag, bruised, lumpy, dusty, and gross. A punching bag was meant to be punched, beat up on.

That's exactly what I felt I was meant to be when I was with him.

I'd tried my best to avoid the heat from his red-faced rage, his laser eyes, and his fiery breath. However, it turned out I'd never actually dodged the mad heat, and the countless burns from over the years I never took a look at ended up consuming me and blackening my insides. In my head, I endlessly went over what I might have done wrong, somehow knowing I'd messed up but not quite understanding *how* or *why*. I thought I was the crazy one. That was a vicious and clever effect that crazy people can have on the sane ones.

One aspect of punching bags that people tended to overlook, besides them being dirty, battered, and unsightly, was they were *durable*. A punching bag that couldn't take the hits or the heat wasn't a very good punching bag, was it? I could take the hits. If I could do anything, I knew that was it. And this punching bag was durable—it endured so much that it even outlasted its trainer, and it stood over his grave in the house he'd bought, with his wife and all of the shiny appliances he'd made her toil over. It stood in his kitchen, battered and taped up and marked from years of abuse. After all, it was never a punching bag's fault for getting punched—for being brought into existence in the first place.

"When he'd get really angry, he would close my door and tear my phone out of my hands and throw it aside. Then he'd slap me across the head a couple times before hitting me in the gut and telling me all sorts of things."

Detective Perry typed furiously, keeping a straight face. "What sorts of things?"

"Things like… I was lucky to be his son… and to not tell my mom."

I felt like those tiny cuts seethed and opened when I spoke to the detective—when I uttered those black, holy words I thought had trapped me all these years. I maybe saw a light flash, and I got hot, but then in the same instant, it was like a cold gust attacked my sweat-soaked skin. I didn't know why that sensation came over me until Beel cut into my raw, tired ears.

"Look, now your mom's crying… sobbing—the last person on earth to truly love you and know you."

"I see," Detective Perry said after taking a pause from his black keyboard to pour an empathetic glance on my head like a cheap, broken watering can.

My mom's whimpers overpowered both his feeble words and my cracked voice. Then she tried, loudly, to take a big breath, which was cut short by her violent hyperventilation and sniffles. "I think," she said, in the saddest voice imaginable, "I'm gonna go to the bathroom."

Chapter 54 – Rachel

I was a little jittery and very tired, but my mind was rabid and disjointed. I needed answers to questions I couldn't quite ask myself because I didn't know how to say them, even in my own head.

Estelle tried to calm me down—tried to stick the pacifier in my pretty little mouth. I didn't mind—I never really did. But something was flat about her attempts. Something was off about her approach. What was I? Was I unrested? Did I have undiagnosed anxiety? It was probably, scandalously, all of the above. I wanted to yell, but I was nervous to use my voice. I wanted to talk to a friend but couldn't find the words to utter first. Was I supposed to be this way? Was this what life was all about...? Forget about it! It was so ridiculous. I called up one of my friends who was too dumb to see through me and not cool enough to spread a mishap too far: Tory.

Beep beep, *ring ring*. "Hello, hello!"

"My *god*, is she trying to take out the trash with those bags under her eyes? What a skank, HA!" Estelle snorted. Still, it was the snort of a queen, a royal snort—an elegant and restrained pig noise from the strong, skinny lady in my head. Not to mention, she was *right*. My crystal-clear phone screen didn't exactly do Tory's post-makeup face any justice. Yikes.

She told me about her day, how she aced a test and left another boy on "read" and more. *Blah blah, blah blah blah blah*. Ugh. She was so self-absorbed sometimes—always had to be the perfect one in the group. God forbid someone *didn't* know she wanted to go to med school.

"Okayyyy, Tory. I see you! *What* was he even thinking? Yeah, *next please…*" I said it like a good friend should, like the pretty friend would.

"Oh, just get on with it," groaned Estelle, probably rolling her eyes at this bore.

I peppered Tory with a follow-up question about the class she aced that test in, then another about the teacher. Tory's eyes rolled back, and her lips and cute, little cheeks curled into a nice smile. It was the face of a girl who felt like she was being listened to completely and absolutely. Of course, I wasn't listening at all, but that didn't matter. It was nice to know Tory looked at me like a valued pair of ears to hear her out—the stories of her "lowest mundanities and her highest triumphs," as my English teacher would put it. Mr. Greene was a hoot. But Tory, she was settled in and buttered up, relaxed enough to field my next question—my most *important* question.

"Yeah," I said, talking like I was chewing gum, "why don't you smoke weed again?"

"What?" she asked.

I assumed my voice had broken up or something. "Why don't you smoke weed again?"

Her voice cracked a bit when she started. "Um, well, I don't like how it makes me feel." The carefree look of someone who was being listened to faded into that of a timid and paranoid girl being watched carefully. She had fright then—fright in her choppy, underdone eyebrows and in her voice.

"Well, you just need to relax before you have some. It can be a really nice experience. *You* know that."

"Uhh, yeah, but I imagine it wouldn't be a pleasant experience. I've read and heard other people say it makes them very anxious, and I have a little bit of an anxious streak myself."

"Dig into her," Estelle growled, "this tramp is hiding something."

"Okay." I laughed—it wasn't planned or on purpose, but it was an exasperated chuckle—and I was kind of pissed at her deception. If you couldn't tell, I *really* don't like when people hide things from me. "What if," I maybe made a face and a voice like a preschool teacher talking to a retarded kid, "you tried it, and ya liked it? Like really, really liked it?" I left my mouth open like I was drooling. It was justified because she was the one who had lied.

Her eyes diverted and disappeared from the screen. "Well, I wouldn't necessarily want *that* either…"

"Why not?"

"I could get addicted. And—"

"And what?"

"It could maybe… change my brain in ways I don't want to."

"Well, neither of those things are true or possible." I didn't realize how quickly I was talking or how much I was sweating.

"I know. But I mean…"

"If you know, then why'd you say it?"

"I—I don't want to take the chance."

"So, you're calling me an addict?"

"No! That's not what I said." Tory looked back in the camera now. I knew I had her. For someone so smart, she was so *easy* to yank around.

"You implied it."

She now had her skinny hand running up and down her face, trying to wring and rub out the stress this caused her. "Rachel, no, I just… I don't want to do it. I think I'd be uncomfortable. That's all. I'm *not* saying you shouldn't, you know that. It seems to help you, so I think that's great."

"Well, my dad's not giving me any more."

"Oh. That's awful, dang. Do you feel all right?"

"You don't have to be honest, baby. You can hide away." Estelle's words were like wispy clouds, but there was also an air of thunder to them—something darker and heavier behind. The floodgates opened. I was no longer tough. I was no longer confident, fearless Rachel—not after what Estelle said, after Tory's prying question. Something within me was oversaturated. I started crying. Right on FaceTime. I even sobbed.

"Hey, hey, hey," Tory sounded like a mother to a wounded child, "it's okay. It's okay. What's wrong,

Rach? Huh? You can tell me," she whispered, somehow giving the impression she was as hurt as I was—sharing my pain and taking a small piece of the burden off my narrow shoulders.

I was the one giving it up. I was the one being yanked around. But I couldn't control it at that point, not even for a second. "No. No. I'm not that fine. I don't know what's going on. I feel terrible, like everything's foggy," I said through pathetic sobs. "It's like a curse. I'm sad, then I'm angry. And it's all because of my dad!" The tears felt good on my face, like they were hydrating me. They'd probably clear up my skin even more.

Tory clicked the roof of her mouth with her tongue. She grimaced like she'd just been burned. "Rach..." she whispered, in pain, "I'm so sorry... I feel terrible. I can't even imagine that. Is there anything I can do for you?"

"No. No, not really. It just really sucks, and I don't even know why I'm so upset."

"Well, you said..."

"What?" I asked through a screen of tears.

"You said your dad caused it. What did he do to—?"

"Everything! He did everything, Tory. He's always been the source of it all. And now, I can't even get any weed."

Tory showed, for the first time in the conversation, a tinge of blankness in her voice and face—sort of like a flash of indifference. "Yeah, I get that. Why does he think he can just control everything you do like that? It's ridiculous."

"I don't know. I don't know. But I literally can't get to the bud, and I need you to help me."

"Umm, what do you want me to do? I don't really know how I could help, but I could try…"

"She's playing hard to get, Rachel. She wants something from you—thinks she can *slip* one by." I never understood how the ice queen could be so cold yet so passionate at the same time. It was like she knew exactly what I suspected and affirmed it, all of it.

She was beautiful. She was beautiful. She was beautiful.

A protector against the ugly people who wanted to be like my dad—who wanted to wear a different face on top of their own. Well, I was sick of it.

"What do you mean, you don't know how? What? There's a million things you could do to help."

"Okay, okay… I know, it's fine. I'm sure that *maybe*—"

"Don't patronize me, Tory! I've known you for too long, okay?" I gave another exasperated chuckle. "You're talking to me like I'm three years old."

She took a deep breath. The ball was in her court, yet she didn't say a thing for some time. She went back to wiping her face with her hand, hoping it might ease the stress or smooth out some wrinkle she didn't have. My tears let up for an instant, and my face glistened in its salty bath—smooth, shiny, and fresh. It was like I didn't have to try. Well, I knew I didn't.

Finally, in a tiny voice, she broke the silence through a pinched, red face, "Rachel, what would you like me to do?"

I wished I hadn't gritted my teeth at her when I responded, but I was a little upset at the time, and it was for effect. So I felt like I had to. "Get me a half-ounce of bud by tomorrow night, and I will give you one of my gold bracelets." I finished my sentence then hung up on her. I knew she'd gotten the message. I expected some excited or apologetic text from her—something asking if I was "sure I was okay."

I waited and stared at my phone for a bit, scrolling as I zoned out. I went to the bathroom and stretched my legs. I ended up getting a text from Tory, but it wasn't what I wanted, nor did I expect it.

> *Are you sure you're not going through cannabis withdrawal? Kind of seems like it. Maybe you should read up on it just in case before you form an opinion.*

What a ridiculous text that was from Tory. I couldn't believe she would say such a thing. And to think she was smart... Cannabis withdrawal wasn't even real. It was impossible. Also, it suggested I was acting strangely. *She* was the one acting strangely. *She* was the one being weird and not being the best friend. It's sad to see people gaslighting like that, especially when they were so close to you. It was a shame, to say the least. What a friend—texting me that like she was the one in the right. Like she cared so deeply and was so righteous herself. Ridiculous.

Fucking ridiculous.

Chapter 55 – Michael

What was it I felt Beel had given to me, or worse yet, taken away? It was eerie. It was alarming. It was *powerful*.

Was he trying to make me crazy? The more I thought back to it, reflected on him, the more I felt like he was the single thing that could tug at the strings that tethered me to my reality. Or maybe, instead of slowly prying my conscious life away from me, he could have been muddling the precious distinction between inside and out—truth, perception, and the spaces in between.

But where could I go? Who could I consult about the monster in my head? I had nowhere to turn except deep within myself, down to the chasm where he lurked and in the fires he bathed in.

"But Michael," Beel said in a tempting, tickling tone. It was as if he could see my thoughts manifest right in front of him on a fat, slow display. "Fire is cleansing. It's rejuvenating. It's both death and awakening. You've been scorched, Michael—wrought in angry flame. If you can't change this, why not use it? You can become harder, so you won't get burned as easily in the future."

"And why should I listen to you?"

"You don't have to."

I didn't know why, but Beel made me feel high above my situation—over everything. But was that his trick? Some cheap ploy to rest my ego in him so he could then tear it down again? I went in circles, thinking about how I should feel, and my head continued to spin. I thought about everything, trying to keep track of it all—I didn't know what was going to happen next, much less what my own future held. How the hell could I know that? It would have been easier not to have one—one less thing to worry about. But then again, what is life but change, and how could a lot of change not be *bad* amidst the chaos, the world's natural state? The more I thought I understood life, the more I thought I could hate it. *Maybe my father was the lucky one.* How could I even prove anyone else was real—my mom, my grandparents? *Didn't Beel tell me that one time?* Was I just becoming his dummy? How could I ev—

"Michael!" The monster's vibe was off, like he broke character when he yelled. His voice sounded high-pitched like a girl's. "Don't overthink it."

When he said that, I tried to ignore him, but I also fixated my senses on the outside, focusing on a metal door handle; its contrast against the white door it operated on was striking and pleasing. I could almost smell the paint of the gleaming portal cover—all white and dignified, not self-aware in the slightest. It was like the door had a personality all its own. But wait, did I ascribe that personality to it, or was there som—

"Too much thinking!"

"I thought you wanted me to go deep within myself," I grumbled. It may have been the first time I'd ever truly *mocked* Beel. It was like beating my dad at basketball for the first time. I stood there, blissfully triumphant. Happy, satisfied.

"I told you to go to the depths to find the horrors, not escape from them!" Beel's argument made too much sense. Damn. My triumph left, my bliss dissipated—he killed my high horse with a poison-tipped spear.

My mom walked into the kitchen where I was sitting. She didn't look very good. She was slouched and anxious. Her face was bleached and peaked, like a scared ghost. *What was she worried about?* It was as if she were afraid that some angry, impending hammer could fly out of the sky at any moment and strike her down. I guessed grief hit people in different ways. Maybe my gurgling grief would never hit me. Or maybe it already had, and it was seeping into everything I interacted with, all I saw and felt. My answer was just to leave it alone—there was no use in overthinking.

"Hey, Mom." Then, something completely foreign struck me. It was an urge, an impulse I'd never felt before. It bounded through my veins and seemed to stand me up. It quickened my muscles and strengthened me. I didn't know where it came from. I hugged her. Her body was cold, and her frail frame felt light in my arms. "Mom, hey…"

She just let loose a hollow, raspy sigh, like something I'd expect from an old woman. Was she an old woman if I thought she was—if I believed she was? What was the term "old woman," but a generic label connected to a set of irreducibly complex traits? A feeble label such as "old woman" was meant to generalize, to help humans better understand and make sense of the world. Maybe. "Mom… have you been eating? You need to make sure you eat."

No reply. Just a blank stare. Under the light of the window, her head and thin hair flashed under the shower of sun and showed gray. It was quick, but I knew what I'd seen. And because I was so sure, that meant I'd really seen it—her gray, thin strands like a rag used too often and for too long. "Mom?"

"They suspect me, Michael." Her voice shook.

I continued looking at her steadily. My expression never changed, and there was something stale in the air, something musty and nauseating. "Suspect you… of what?" I kept rubbing her arm as if that would take the pain away, as if I could actually numb something or heal her, or even make this whole situation evaporate. Her arm had the texture, weight, and likeness of hollowed-out driftwood.

Unmoving, ghastly, lonely, through sobs of purest pain, she cried, "They suspect me… for Lorne. Of murder." Her gulp was more akin to a throaty yell than a simple swallow. It bellowed and bounced around the room, poking at my ears more than once.

I don't remember sitting down nor do I know why I did it, but I found myself in a chair at the kitchen table as soon as she uttered those words. The echo from her throat subsided a little in my head.

I thought about the chair, perhaps as an attempt to escape from her words. Or maybe I was genuinely curious. I considered how its four tiny, ornate points held all of me—how the chair didn't shift nor complain, yet an immense burden had been added to it, dropped on it dangerously. Or was the weight dangerous to the chair at all? Maybe that was the very nature of a chair—to hold someone else's weight. It was like we brought chairs into existence for one purpose: a sole, reasonable utility. But in my mind, that made the chair I sat upon infinitely more rational than a human being. Chairs had a clear aim, and their purpose of existence was undeniable. The nature of the human, on the other hand, was so chaotic, so messy, compared to that of the floating wooden seat.

This all flashed through my mind in the space of one millisecond, and the futility of it all made me chuckle. But then my toothy smile was quickly replaced by an inquisitive anger, a scowl that matched my mother's inner turmoil. "Mirroring," I think it was called.

"What do you mean, *murder*? What?"

"They think it was a murder. The toxicology rep—"

"W-what? What do you mean, *murder*?" The word was heavy on my tongue and felt dirty, grisly. It rang in my head along with my mother's prolonged gulp, the nefarious whispers of Beel, and the murmurings of my own mind—all a toxic stew that made me want to run away from everything forever. There was no tragedy or triumph here, only desolate angst and confusion. Like I was alone in my head, where I could see and feel but never truly connect with a soul. There were inanimate objects surrounding me that seemed to be imbued with more life and rationale than the supposed "people" around me could ever be. It was sickening. I bit my fingers but couldn't feel it. It was only when my mom answered me that I realized how constricted my lungs and insides were.

"They don't think his death adds up," her voice heightened with sharp anxiety, "they suspect foul play."

"What? What could that mean?" I asked the question just to ask it, just to hear it one more time so maybe it could sink into my thick skull.

After more painful gulps and sobbing came a flood of tears and tomato redness on her face that looked animated yet brutally alive. "I didn't do it, Michael. You need to help me. I didn't do it. How could they think that?"

What makes her think I have the strength to help her deal with this?

Beel whispered in my ear, "Why do you think they suspect her, Michael?"

"You will help me, right?"

Before Mom could swallow me whole with her eyes, I had to look away. "Of course, Mom," I said through my own tears. "I can't believe they'd do that."

We both cried, and I kind of hated it. It was an unimaginably difficult situation, but I also felt like we were exposed to each other in a way I was uncomfortable with. I was almost grossed out by the hugs and tears, like we were some kind of soul team bound by circumstance, *not* familial love.

I explored love in my head—with my arms wrapped around her, sharing our tears and their delicate weight between our shoulders and necks. I realized then that I "loved" her for no other reason than she was my mom. I knew her, and I lived with her. She gave me a lot yet deprived me of so much as well. I felt I was owed something when I uttered the words, "I love you," to her. I wanted more than just the same words, more than even a deep, reciprocated feeling—I wanted *utility*. A new situation. A new *life*. I thought it was a possible desire.

"Michael, she can't give you much more. She needs you more than you need her. If you shove these truths away, they will return with double the ferocity, and they will be hungry. *Why do you think they suspect her?*"

When the tears dried and my mind hardened a bit, I got a hold of myself and the situation a little more. It was like everything crystalized for a short time. I stayed hugging her, but my muscles (or lack thereof) slackened. "Why do you think they suspect you, Mom? How could they?"

The old woman with steely eyes, still sobbing childishly, said with defiant, teenage denial, "I don't know, Michael. I don't know!" Then, a needle from nowhere burst her bubbled cloak, and her face went blank. She was thinking, and her face seemed to get so hot that it evaporated the tears—either like magic or the earthiest, most grounded natural impulse.

Her cold, stony face evoked something inside of me, veering me in different directions and assumptions all at once—each of them was equally and brutally wrong. It was something like terror. Yes, that was it. It was terror she struck in me—something existential and acute, with no makeup and folded wrinkles in a harsh face with calculating, cruel eyes.

She was a suspected murderer.

And she was definitely capable. She was feasibly dangerous. Unhinged yet tethered all the same. I had no one to turn to.

"You may want to help her," Beel said with a newfound solemnity, "or you could be *next*."

Chapter 56

It is ingrained in us, reader, and if it has never crossed your conscious mind, it is still well implanted within your physiology all the same. And that, reader, is your innate desire to stand above chaos—to avoid it, conquer it, and tame it. Chaos is a bad word in your circle, in your vernacular, and in your life. It is a supposedly "evil" idea that only conjures up frightening pictures of pain and sickness.

But chaos is the default. Any opposition to its awesome force—the primal power of *me*—is feeble and fleeting. The battle against chaos is so enjoyable to watch because there is a dramatic irony to the whole show of it that leaves me tickled. It leaves me to think—and I *am* chuckling right now—that I may need you as much as you loathe me, as much as you seek to avoid me and stomp me out at every turn. It is intertwined in your beautifully pitiful nature that you believe chaos can be overcome—that it is not the default setting, the norm, or even life itself.

All of this is to say, however, that I would fall short of calling you stupid. You, reader, and your kind are not stupid. Rather, you're tragic. A tragic race that is a tiny plaything for me. This may be an experiment, but I will still bestow this offering unto you all the same, this timeless, transcendent wisdom: Succumb to chaos. I've told you repeatedly to make friends with me, reader, and my message has remained shockingly consistent throughout the duration of my little tale.

I am chaos.

I am the wind when it blows cold and the force that tears the shutters off.

I am what makes the house of cards so feeble, and I embody its collapse on the perpetually rotting table on which it stood.

I am everything in between the lines, the ground and its own erosion.

I am what keeps you occupied and what leads to your downfall.

There is nothing more I can offer you in the way of my identity.

You could either be my agent or my opponent. There is no in-between. Reader, I hope you've paid close attention to the whims and tensions of the people I've graciously displayed for you—that I have put into motion for your enjoyment and education. I also hope you see them for who they are. Truthfully, they are not much unlike you, reader—in their strengths and their ugly savagery, in their doubts and their whimsical notions. And what, *oh*, what does it all really mean? It's all so winding and brutal, what is there to hang my hat on? Reader, *all* of it. Truly, for all of it—the meanings, the lessons, the patterns—there may be one answer. But that is for you to decide. It is for you to interpret. Take heed and remember that you can, indeed, *choose*.

I am the monster in their heads, but you don't have to let me into yours. Or maybe you already have.

Chapter 57 – Michelle

For freedom from the law, there were a lot of options; for my way of escape, there were many ways I could go about this. But unfortunately, almost all of them had to be left on the table. Everywhere I went, I attracted the sympathy of a mourner and the suspicion of a potential criminal. I was living two lives and had two approaches to viewing everything. I did away with principles; my sole goal was to prove to—no, to *show*—everyone they were wrong, that this was a fruitless investigation, and it was stupid to have me as a suspect in the first place. How did I decide to go about that, you ask? I took my next step from a true master of perception and deception, the late great himself: Lorne Conifer.

One of their primary reasons for suspecting me was "motivation." Lorne had a big inheritance and was not perceived to be the best guy to me or Michael. I said "bullshit." I could show them I *did* love him, I *did* miss him, and he *was* an honorable man. Not only that, but at the charity memorial I was holding, the whole community would see I most definitely did not care about his money. After that, my hands would be clean, and I would be home free. It was easy. Everyone was so stupid and presumptive.

The flyers, promotional emails, and VIP invites for the first annual "Lorne Conifer Memorial Benefit" hosted by (yours truly) Michelle Conifer were sent out that week. I made sure the police station saw the flyer plenty of times, that they were rubbed in the fat faces of Mayor Williams, Detective Perry, and all the rest who doubted me and opposed Lorne. Lorne was a good man. They would see. I made sure to invite that prick Kalopoulos; he and his prissy daughter were VIP guests.

"You could show them all at the event, Michelle. You will stand vindicated when they see your radiant virtue. Or…"

I was on a walk. After I made the invites and assembled the planning committee and the rest of the proceedings, I felt like my mind was a little scrambled after scrambling around so much myself. I decided to take a breather. I was always a big reader, but I never cared for the tacky "self-help" genre. That is, until after my husband died and my world got turned upside down. Suddenly, magically, it was helpful. I was reading this one book, *Perspectives of the Strong Heart*, after Lorne's incident. A lot of it was still gibberish, but I extracted a nice lesson, or maybe it was more of a mindset. It suggested every burden or struggle one faces is self-imposed. This is to say that you create your own burdens, and therefore, it is your responsibility to rid yourself of them if they become too cumbersome for your mind. I loved this approach, and I took it to heart. On my walk, I remembered and recited some of the lines I particularly liked. That way, amidst the breeze, the trees, the lush blades of grass, and the faint beckoning of the graceful birds above, my worries melted into and out of my lungs with every breath.

It was so nice to shrug my shoulders and forget all of my worries on my walks—about Detective Perry, about state and federal prosecutors, the private investigators, the prying media, and the dismissive, suspicious community I'd found myself in. None of it defined me. Why was that you may ask? Because I didn't allow it to! For weeks after that, I continued to walk and read and let my mind wander as it unencumbered itself. It was beautiful.

The next day at work, I was called to the dean's office. Everything was oak (the table, the shelves, the chair I sat on), as I'd largely come to expect from sluggish, stable academia.

"Of course, Dr. Conifer..." the dean said. "Personally, I believe you. And yes, you *will* keep your job here for the time being. But until a verdict is reached or someone else is convicted for sure, the university cannot, under any circumstances, come out in official support for your case." He threw his hands up with palms to the sky. "I'm sorry. That's just the way it goes."

"Dr. Goldstein, have you happened to see any of the promotions for Lorne's memorial benefit circulating lately?"

"As a matter of fact, I have." Goldstein's tone lightened a bit.

"How would you like to be a VIP at the benefit? Free drinks, an honorable mention in front of the whole community, and you can meet and hang out with the mayor. No charge, just show up. I'd be pleased to have you."

"Michelle… I'm flattered…"

"Michael told me he would like you to come. He talked about how cool it would be to have you, a published author and the head of a higher ed institution, to honor his father. I'm hosting it, by the way. There's gonna be a lot of good that comes from this, Dr. Goldstein."

He smiled at me, and when I left his office after we firmly shook hands, I knew I had him in my pocket.

I heard the voice on my walk back to my new car: "Lorne is looking up from hell right now and gnashing his clean, white teeth." It was nice to be rid of that station wagon once and for all. It was a relief of sorts.

Chapter 58 – John

I had nothing to lose, and I had to keep my head up—that was the most important thing I'd learned from going through a divorce, having a devil daughter, and bringing a federally illegal empire into existence. You just had to keep moving forward. Now that crackhead Lorne was dead, it was time to go on and try to make the right moves—over and over again. I was invited to Lorne's charity benefit thing. Not only that, I was a VIP guest, and so was Rachel. I was hesitant to tell her, and I was still deciding whether or not she should go. The scene she could make out of spite could undo all of my progress with her.

I'd consider myself an objective guy, and objectively speaking, Rachel had two chief traits that dominated her personality and enabled her to dominate those around her: She knew how to use leverage—she was smart—and secondly, she was *relentless*. She'd gotten that second trait from her mother. I remembered one time when Candice and I were still together (back when I still called her "Candy"), she wanted to go on some trip to Tulum. Every day, she asked me about it, and every day, my answer was an unflinching, "Nah, I think I'll be busy that week." The more she asked, the more powerful her questions became, until she graduated to a "we'll see" from me.

Well, it didn't stop there. Candice decided to call everyone close to me—family, friends, employees, *clients*—and make her case to them. It got to the point where everyone I talked to brought up the trip to Tulum, and not only that, but everyone *urged* me to go with Candice. "Come on!" they would say, "you and your wifey should have some fun!" After some time, she broke me down. I gave the company notice of my week-long absence, and I took Candice on a wallet-busting excursion to Tulum a week later. It was against my better judgment, my plans, and my *will*.

In that way, she was a threat to my manhood, my freedom. Maybe that was why I built up so much resentment toward her during those years. Holy Jesus. I'm sure I did some stuff, too, and she had her usual complaints. But man, if she wanted something, she wasn't going to stop until she got it or you stopped her.

Anyway, that's part of what I saw in Rachel—all the brutish persistence of her mom coupled with my ability around people. A truly hellish combo. In a small way, I kind of felt for Rachel; it must be a burden to know you're so talented and already have so many gifts. She was a true force of nature, and I was proud of her—but also fearful in so many ways.

I had a phone call with my investigator, where I got a much-needed progress report and advice on Lorne's memorial benefit coming up.

"Okay. How is working with Perry goin'?" I mopped my front teeth with my tongue. Damn, I did that whenever I was nervous.

He cleared his throat. "It's fine. Perry's as straight-edge as they come."

"Whaddaya mean by that?"

He *humphed* for a second. "This guy's finding a murderer no matter what. Even if there isn't one."

"Shit... what the hell does that mean for me? Is he doing anything illegal I could get a lawyer on?"

"No." More reassuring. "He's too by-the-book for that. He'll follow the law every step of the way. Proper procedure, this guy. For you? You're fine. You gotta keep laying low and assisting with this investigation. It'll only help your case at this point."

"Okay, okay. So, you don't think I'll... be suspected?"

"Nah, no. Just keep assisting with this case, John. Then you really won't."

"This is a fuckin' mess."

"It sure is."

We hung up. "Yeah," Anders said, "he wasn't lying. I'd say that was all sound advice."

What was I gonna do with Rachel? I still didn't know. I was never haunted by these types of things. Very few problems or people couldn't be outsmarted or, at worst, run away from. But Rachel stuck. She was always there because she had to be. She was like her mom's strong-armed punishment to me, back from rehab and oblivion.

If Rachel could never truly love me back, wouldn't that make her a callous person, unworthy of even her father's love? What if Rachel was too harmed, too scarred already, to be capable of loving anybody? But there I went, talking about love and family like I was some softie; I thought age did soften me up. The less I focused on the business, the more I saw all the crumbled remains of everything in my single-minded wake. Holy Jesus. I couldn't tell if I had too much on my mind or too little. Was I thinking about the right things? Impetuous, unruly, *ruthless* Rachel.

Shit. My mind was on the benefit, which was now in less than a week. But why? Because Rachel. It was all Rachel, all the time in my head. The benefit meant more torment, more decisions to be made on her behalf.

"Just leave Rachel at home," Anders said. "She can't say anything then. No scene. No yelling. No fighting. Just you, the mayor, clients, and a great public appearance."

I sighed for what felt like forever. The time trudged on, then my mind came to a halt. As per usual, Anders was right. My plan was decided, calculated for the benefit—no devilish daughters to interfere, and I could still keep her content enough.

Thanks to Anders, I was able to ease my mind for the rest of that night and return to work.

Chapter 59 – Detective Perry

Something didn't add up. Lorne was a man of questionable moral standards with a lot of competing incentives for him to die. He was a trust fund recipient. He wasn't only a political figure, but a particularly crafty one—largely unsuccessful but persistent as all hell. He was seriously delusional, a liar, a philandering sociopath, a child abuser… but he was willful and very strong in that way. He could get people to listen and follow without much effort, and any man (even one as incompetent as Lorne Conifer) who could do that in this godforsaken world could at least carve out some obscure niche for himself. That was the case with this guy.

Kalopoulos hired a private investigator, and I collaborated closely with him—not too closely, though. It would have seemed odd for Kalopoulos not to have done so in these circumstances, and I studied him and his P. I. I watched what they were willing to share. We scanned all their docs, and I had my guys hound for inconsistency, cracks, slip-ups, mistakes, or anything that might have come across as odd. So far, they were clean.

In times like these, I thought back to the academy, my instructor—the crazy one with the glasses, who we called "Goggles." He'd always blurt out, "The only thing routine about this job is the lack of it!" He'd seen some serious shit, and he wasn't afraid to tell us about it. That's what made it interesting for me, and in a way, he was inspiring to a young cadet who had dreams of serving and protecting.

Once I actually got my newbie ass onto the force, it turned out ol' Goggles had been right. Dead right. Hopelessly right. I moved up and around, was betrayed, was honored, was shown the ropes, and showed the ropes myself. But no two crimes were the same. At the end of every day, after ten-odd years on the force, I couldn't find anything to hang my hat on—a bread-and-butter, a code, or a procedure to really trust in. The officers came and went, the town changed and grew, and as it did, every crime got grayer and grayer.

I'd always dreamed of being the good guy and fighting for what was right. But as an investigator, I saw some mean stuff, and I realized horrible things. I even discovered something that crushed the kid inside me, that destroyed my only reason for becoming a detective in the first place: There were no such things as "good guys." Nope. Life wasn't the comic book I'd always taken it for. It was much messier. It gave me a chronic sickness that made me doubt everything—hell, it even made me doubt myself.

With not much else to believe in, I turned to the badge. Sure, it was cold and spotty, and it got dusty if I left it untouched for too long, but it was tough and steely. I didn't believe in good or bad, but I believed in the law, and it was the law that could outlast all of us with enough time.

I had the holy hammer of justice in my hands, and I wasn't afraid to swing it around until it found a skull to crack.

"Mr. Perry, you should've been there twenty minutes ago with a coffee and a workout done! You're pathetic! Don't make up for your inadequacy and speed up now—that's *not* what you should do! You make me sick, Perry." That was Sergeant McQuinty, my coach and inner drill sergeant. He kind of kept me in line and stayed on me for the little things, which I definitely needed to hear throughout the day. Sgt. McQuinty was a constant voice in my head I'd named.

Mayor Williams was a rich man. But who in politics wasn't surrounded by rich people, if they weren't rich themselves? The gate to his hilled driveway was broad and iron, and his assistant spoke to me through the speaker. He was already expecting me.

"You should've already found the murderer, Perry! You're as lazy as an old dog." I drove up. *Man, why can't all the roads be as smooth as this driveway?*

"Please sit down." Richard Williams had a silk voice. If I didn't know any better, I'd think he slept in an ironed, pressed suit. He seemed to carry himself that way. Just from being in his presence, you could feel the warmth of his tone, as if he really *wanted* you to be there with him. That, of course, was an extraneous detail to the case.

"Mayor Williams, it's a real pleasure. I'm just going to ask you a few questions regarding the murder of

Lorne Conifer, then I can let you get back to running the city."

"Murder?" Mayor Williams sounded shocked in a soft and polite kind of way. Once again, it's important to note this isn't a significant detail to the case. "What made you folks deem it a murder?"

"Well, narcissists don't kill themselves." I laughed at my own joke.

"What about the likelihood of an accident?"

"Given the circumsta—"

"You think you can just go and blab details about the case? This is exactly why you were relocated! You think this is teatime? Huh, Perry?"

I stopped short and began again, "Uh—for now, that information is confidential. Unfortunately, I can't share much more."

"Well..." Mayor Williams chuckled softly, still standing, and looked down at me with big, stern eyes. "I'm gonna need to know what I'm answering questions about, right?"

I looked away for fear he'd see right through my eyes. No, that wasn't possible, but I should've studied more about the relationship between the mayor and the police department. Who was the law here? Of course, I was. But I enforced his right to make decisions, right? I looked down at my badge and back up at the man who could take it away.

"You scared of him or somethin', Perry? You're no better than a pussy cat!"

"Yes, sir, of course." Then, I proceeded to tell him all of the generalities of the case—nothing too specific.

He continued looking at me with big eyes. He didn't flinch, but I thought I saw his jaw flex quickly as he stared. "And who are the suspects right now?" He was just doing his job. He was a calm presence, but he wasn't exactly *calming*. He gave off the impression of a coiled spring, loaded up—a cocked gun, pointed and ready but clean and sleek.

"Sir, it's not within my... I mean, I can't—"
"Am I one?"
"No. You are not."

He stood there with one arm on his mahogany desk and two fingers on his broad chin, thinking away. For such a public figure, he was a very ponderous person. I respected him. He'd done a lot of good for this city, and especially the police force. "Perry, tell me, how many suspects are there again?"

"I'm not at liberty to discuss that at the moment."

"Okay then." The mayor chuckled to himself. It was amazing how small he could make you feel.

"On with it, Perry!" Sgt. McQuinty yelled in my ear.

"What do you... ahem... what *did* you know about Lorne Conifer?"

"Regarding what? His trust fund? His reputation? His family?"

"All the above. If you please."

The mayor wiped his tongue across his teeth. "Well, where do we start?" He scooted his chair back and drew a long breath, made a face, then went into the story. "He's into perceptions. But *you* know that. Always wanted to be seen as a family man. In every conversation, he needed the upper hand. Charming… if you only talked to him for a bit. Me? I could see right through the guy. But—"

"Okay, but what about his trust fund?"

"What about it?" The mayor asked.

"Well, has anybody ever mentioned it to you? You *are*… or were… competing against him, so it had to come up at some point in passing. With an aide or strategist maybe?"

"Yeah," the mayor said, stroking his chin, "a couple times. One of my campaign strategists liked to talk about how he didn't need to go after many donations because so much of his campaign was self-funded. Pretty amazing stuff, really. I'd never seen anything like it, and I know a lot of wealthy folks." The mayor chuckled.

"Right." I nodded, still feeling as if the mayor wasn't giving me everything I needed. He had to know something. I dug deeper. "And what do you know about the people who surrounded him—aides, strategists, managers, cabinet membe—"

"He didn't have a cabinet. He'd never won anything, remember?"

"Right. But could you tell me about his team? What intel did your people bring in as you were competing against him? Anything... out of the ordinary?"

Time seemed to slow down as I waited for his answer. It was weird. He seemed to be thinking a lot about what he was going to say. The whole thing struck me as odd. I felt like rushing him, but that would have taken him aback. Better to simply let him talk.

And then his answer shocked me.

"No, not really. Not that I can think of."

"What do you mean, 'not really?' There was no one on his team that may have wanted his money? His fame? Jealous, maybe?"

The mayor looked at me with large eyes. It was like he was quizzing me and scolding me at the same time. Really uncomfortable. He continued to stare. Mouth with tight lips, brows hugging the tops of his eyes. His stare was impregnable. The politician without the mask. My only conclusion: There was something he didn't want me to know. Something lurking. There was something unspoken in his silent glare. The room fell silent, but my mind lit up with winding possibilities that only complicated the case.

"Not that I could think of."

Politicians were weird, frightening. I took his word for it and continued on with the conversation.

"You have to push further, runt!" Sgt. McQuinty yelled in my ear. "If you gotta try harder, then try harder! If you gotta bend the rules, then bend the rules! It's for the good of the law, Perry. Remember that."

I took McQuinty at his word. I took the mayor at his word. The conversation went on, and I got little out of it. It seemed that all was lost except for the lone suspect. Every lead was dry except for one: Michelle Conifer. I left the mayor's mansion after a weak, politically safe conversation with one face floating in my mind. *Michelle Conifer.*

Chapter 60 – Rachel

I got a text from Michael Conifer last night. Dang, I'd forgotten he even existed, and I thought everyone else had, too. I hadn't seen him at school for like six weeks, then he popped up on my phone out of nowhere. Just like that, he was right back in the mix of my head again. He was a weird one. Sometimes, I felt like he was only those dinky glasses he wore. Ugh. Even thinking of his face made me smell vomit. But he sent me an interesting text, and I knew it meant something because Estelle said, "Oooh," like it was some sort of big reveal or huge enticement. That was all I needed to catch my attention.

The text read like this:

Hey Rachel, sorry about the project and my absence. A lot of crazy things happened one after another, and then, in a tragic accident, my father suddenly passed away. There's a memorial charity event in his name for the whole community next week, and you're a guest of honor if you would want to come. I was wondering if you would be able to make it? Also, I won't be at school for a little longer. Hope you're doing well.

I was high when I got that text—not from my dad's weed, but from some edibles I got from my friend's older brother after doing a favor for him. I liked when I was high because I could be objective about things instead of reacting emotionally like some animal. He didn't seem too broken up about his dad. Maybe he was more like me than I'd thought.

"You should go and *not* tell your father about it. Leave him in the dark and surprise him. Oh, you have everything, Rachy…"

I immediately shot downstairs after getting that text and tried my best to hide my smirk. Skinny John was in his office wing of the house, typing away in the late hours of the night, just like his employees under him. I was going to see what he knew. His neck was craned and hunched, like he was chained to his monitor. I swung around the door frame like a little girl right into the office. It looked like he was possessed—under a spell.

"Have I told you that ever since you stopped going to the gym, you've looked like a skinny little cross-country nerd?" My dad was sensitive about his body, even though he'd gotten those beautiful Swedish genes with the long limbs and slender torso.

He looked up at me with beady eyes. There was no love in them, but I wasn't really taken aback. "I'm working right now, maybe you can abuse me later."

"Aww, big daddy's bein' a wittle baby," Estelle said.

"Oh, come on, Dad. It's just a joke. You know I just get emotional sometimes—don't look at me like that." He sighed, then I did a fake one to match and mocked his exasperation. "Did Lorne Conifer die recently?"

"How do you know who that is?" He paused. "Can you stop walking around so much?"

"He was a boy in my grade's father. I heard rumors. The mayoral candidate, right?"

"Yeah, he did."

I could see he didn't want to give me much. "Is there going to be some kind of… funeral?" His body got even stiffer. I smelled fear.

"Can you smell that, Rachel? It's fear." Why were her instincts so in tune? Dang, I hoped she would never decide to use them against me one day—so on point.

"How would I know that, Rach?"

"Didn't you work with him?"

"I'm not a part of his family, I have no idea."

"How did he die?"

"I don't know."

"Oh. Okay. Doesn't him dying hurt your business, though?"

"Yep, it does. I need to get back to work."

When I turned around toward the shadows of the house, I let them engulf me. I traipsed back upstairs into the dark as a smile crawled across my face.

Chapter 61 – Michael

My mom chose me to speak at the benefit—giving me less than a week to prepare a… speech? Tribute? Obituary? I didn't know what I was supposed to do or say for my slot, and the worst part was my mom didn't seem to either. What role was I going to play? I couldn't figure it out.

"Michael, I am saying this to you as a friend and a confidant: Do *not* give a speech at the benefit. You can let your mom know right now you're not going to do this, and it would give her plenty of heads-up to plan stage time accordingly. Don't be a fool."

It made so much sense to let it go. To drop my pen and have no pressure for the benefit—no opportunity to look like a brazen buffoon, a disappointment to his late father's name. But the more I sat still and dug into my inner well of thoughts and shadows, the more I felt a guilty and painful twang within me. It was something small and strong—an immovable figment—a part of me that only kicked and wanted. Was that unique to me? It wanted to drive me, but for now, it was just a lone, longing twinge—heedless, buried, ghastly.

"But then again, this could be an opportunity to have a platform. To stand up for something and speak to people who matter. But Michael, as always, it is your choice."

"What are you trying to do to me right now?" My tone was flippant. My thoughts were few, but my feelings were many. I needed an answer from Beel.

"You ask that question as if I have malicious intent. Come on, you're better than that." Beel had a funny way of making me forget what I was flustered about while keeping me flustered all the same. I was a bull, and he always had the red towel to pull out in front of me—to make me run angrier and kick up the same dust to irritate my eyes and make me sneeze. What the hell? Then, he came at me again, this time from a totally different angle.

"You should really text Rachel again. Maybe she just didn't see the first one. She needs a nudge, that's all. I think she's in a tough place now, too. You should be understanding. I think you still have a chance."

I don't know why, but after Beel said that, things got redder and I sank down. Everything around me grew heavier and more arduous. I felt like I was moving through Jell-O, and my thoughts slowed down, too, growing increasingly negative. Why couldn't I just think positively? Why couldn't I flip my mindset into happiness right away? People with a lot less than I, in much more unfortunate circumstances, seemed much happier. After all, I was alive, right? At least I knew that. But was that even a good thing? It would make me so much happier if I had happy thoughts.

"Of course you're lucky to be alive!" Beel screamed. "I *need* you. The people in your life need you;

there's a girl out there waiting for you! Michael, you are blessed beyond compare, and that's why you have the strength to reach out to Rachel, to make the speech, and to tie it all together for the benefit and beyond! You can choose to lift yourself out of this. And Michael, only you can do that."

"Lift myself out of what?" I mumbled.

"Just text Rachel again."

"No! No!" I was done being a pawn—used by Beel, my father, and then my mother. I was tired of being desired then thrown away. I was tired of being ripped away from friends by my father. I was tired of being alienated from my own mind by Beel. I was disgusted at the thought of serving my mother's interests, looking clean and good and having her son put on a little show to clear her name. I was done with all of it, sick and fatigued of being tossed around in the waves that I'd never asked to be thrown into in the first place. Did I deserve that? Did I deserve to either get embarrassed or ignored? I walked through dark catacombs—everywhere a dead end or a dead person. It was by the light of an unreliable torch that I saw everything; it illuminated my entire flickering, tiny world that was mainly just rusty drops and pools of mud. I didn't even know if I hated or loved myself.

"Those are just human constructs, Michael. You're getting caught up again."

What was it all even worth? *Nothing*, I concluded, too weak to whisper. Instead, I kept that conclusion in my head, where I kept most things. Was I lonely? Was it as easy as something physiological? Were my gross, pathetic problems all too human? Thinking that made it even worse.

"How about you go on another walk, Michael? Then get back into your room with a clear head… a lil' smooth pen… and speak your truth for the benefit. They need to hear your voice, the stories only *you* can tell." At that point, Beel was nearly pleading with me. What was the point? Beel was selfish, and this was definitely for his own reasons, his own motivations, just like those of a human. I didn't know what Beel was, but I felt as though he was a little more human than he would like to admit.

He thought he was transcendent. I thought he was as low as dirt. I stopped, then I started again, like a broken car, a broken boy. I couldn't get him out of my head, but I could disavow him at every turn. I was sick of my realizations, and I was sickened I'd even realized that.

"I'm going to speak my truth all right, Beel." Then I laughed at myself—or maybe it was at Beel—and it was the first time I'd laughed in a while. After a long walk, I sat down with a loathsome pen and got to writing.

This speech at the benefit would be nothing but the truth. *My* truth. *My time* and my turn. I didn't know what was happening inside my head, but thinking and overthinking made me feel worse. I decided, at long last and after long bouts of pain in my tired mind, to stop thinking and start writing.

Chapter 62 – Michelle

There were so many plans to be made, and I'd hardly gotten through any of them. The more I scrambled, the less I got done. I had the table sets, the chairs, the room, the lighting, the stage, the sound, and so many other things jostling for my attention. If not for that volunteer planning committee, I don't know what I would have done.

"Make sure Detective Perry's a VIP guest and he sits right up front toward the stage. In fact, it may be advantageous for you to give him a speaking role. Make sure Kalopoulos brings Rachel. You need those two together at the party." The voice always gave me great advice, and I wasn't going to give up on it now, especially when I depended on its maneuvers the most—this was a pivotal point for me. It was time for the community to see what I'd put on.

Oh, and Michael had a speech to give, too. I paid it little mind. Why would I have? A timid boy giving a heartfelt, tentative speech was what the people wanted. It would move them. I didn't even have to check on him, really. I figured he was stressed, but so was I.

All of my colleagues were invited—just not as VIPs, for the most part. I talked to Perry, and he said he'd bring his family. Big score. Finally, the stage was set, and the time drew nearer. I was about to be home free, basking in Lorne's memory and bringing honor to his "great" name. Of course, I'd be keeping his last name because he was a great man. I'd let the community know that. I'd be sure to have the event last long but also make it packed. Oh man, what an opportunity, and what a great idea this had been. It was just stressful—very, *very* stressful.

Chapter 63 – Detective Perry

I didn't care how often I repeated myself—I'd never worked on any case quite like this. It was subtle yet had twists and turns. I was dealing with a lot of competent people who had many different interests, and that didn't exactly make my investigation any easier. Motivations are everything in an investigation, and there were too many big players who worked around Lorne who could have had legitimate reasons for seeing him gone.

Even after all this work on the case, I still didn't know much—nothing conclusive as of yet, and no big leads besides Michelle. She was the only one in the house when it happened and would have known Lorne's regular morning routine on the day of the heart attack. Also, the amount of caffeine in his blood was far too high to simply have come from drinking it. There had to be something else, *someone* else. And that someone was Michelle, as of now.

Oh, and that was the other thing: It somehow leaked to the media that there was only one suspect so far for the murder of Lorne Conifer. Worse yet, it was only a matter of time until they found out who the suspect was and why. That would really make her reel—hell, possibly even make her a flight risk. I didn't know what to do. But that was the honest goddamned truth. To hell with it, man. I was gonna get to the bottom of this, regardless of the shifty players.

Another thing that pissed me off was that Kalopoulos sold drugs yet had an assistant, probably many of them. Then there was me—I was out here busting my ass for the state and bringing a criminal to justice, and I didn't have shit for a secretary except for my hand, my laptop, and my trusty memory (which was a little less trustworthy during these chaotic times).

I'd just gotten off the phone with Michelle. On the call, I was sweet and slow. I said "yes" to her invitation and nodded through the phone like a good guest—because that's exactly how she was treating me. She wanted my family at the benefit. I agreed. She wanted me not to "do any work there, for Lorne's sake." I agreed. She wanted me to meet her side of the family and shake hands with all of her friends at the benefit. I agreed.

Of course, all of my agreements were in vain and unofficial. I was an investigator, a detective, an agent of justice. I was not a friend of the family, nor was I a friend of Lorne's.

Chapter 64 – John

Our boardroom had seamless, glass, floor-to-ceiling windows overlooking the courtyard and, on the horizon, the downtown. It was spacious, sleek, and accommodating—perfect for making stuck-up money guys feel right at home.

I was in a shareholders' meeting. Correction—I was being grilled in a shareholders' meeting.

"So, what's our angle with the city now that Conifer is gone?" a keen, inquisitive, old voice asked assumptively. It was an investor. A big one. "Do we have any plans? Any initiatives?"

My brain defaulted. I was already in a fog, and a high-pressure board meeting was not doing me any favors. It wasn't my fault. None of it was. Yet, in the meeting, I felt like prey being stalked. This was new for me. All eyes steadied and zoomed in on me—they were all old, some women, mostly men. I was always the man with the plan, but our plan had been busted on account of some random bullshit. Now, I needed to buy time. I was going to get this location in Colorado even if I had to kill for it. And I was willing to kill.

"We've begun early talks with Mayor Williams on the legislation and grant for the new location. However, the more pro—"

"And how are those going?" It was the same investor who asked the first question. He was an old man, bald on top, gray and white around the edges of his scalp, with thick, horn-rimmed glasses he'd either bought yesterday or forty years ago. He had a comically large nose that suited his overinflated ego. One thing about "money people" is they really knew how to ask questions—they'd been doing it all their lives. Investors were used to asking questions; they were comfortable with it, and the worst part—it gave them the power. The questioner always had the power. They had others falling back on their heels, stammering responses, while the investors sat back and squinted their beady eyes. Yeah, I may have been wealthy myself, but I was an entrepreneur—an executive and builder first and foremost. I didn't like career investors because they didn't have the courage to really step into the arena and put *their* necks on the line. They were just crude gamblers at the racetrack. But me? I was the fuckin' golden jockey.

"Well, we just started on those," I said in my most respectful tone possible, "so it's all still in the preliminary stages with Mayor Williams. Unfortunately, I think he may have caught wind of what we were planning with his challenger, and..." I clicked my tongue against the roof of my mouth, "that may not work well for the near future in this locale... but—*but*—we have options in our outlook. Lots of them still within Colorado."

"And how does this affect the timeline?"

I was pretty intuitive with my body. Being an entrepreneur, I'd trained my emotions and studied my own physiology extensively—my anxieties, my frustrations, my weaknesses. With that said, I was having a nervous reaction to this same stuffy voice with his prying questions and raspy, keen tone.

"Take a breath and take your time," Anders said. "Remember, Johnny: time and space above and before anything else. Just relax."

He was right. But how could I relax right now? I felt as though my skills and track record were being questioned, like I was on trial or some shit. And for what? A freak death—some lousy guy we shouldn't have bet on in the first place ate it, and now, I was stuck holding his shit bag.

"It's going to push us back a bit, but we could still be on track for next winter."

Aggressive sighs and a chorus of exasperated laughs erupted around the boardroom, too many to count. What the hell was this? I'd built this company. I'd built this brand. And now I was being chastised. Demeaned. Ridiculed by people who had never gotten their hands dirty a day in their lives.

Then, something of a low rumble overtook the room. That throaty growl belonged to a man at the head of the table, with a full head of white hair in a clean navy sport coat—the chairman of the board, Darya Mukherjee. The white noise of the scratch and shuffle of the other stiffs in the room emphasized the weight of Mr. Mukherjee's statement. "If we went with Mexico instead, we'd still be ahead of time, and it'd be cheaper—even with transport. But you know this."

His calm, deliberate words were like a snake sinking its fangs into the side of my neck. *Ugh*. So smug, so condescending. And he still found a way to communicate his point like a suggestion, if not a command. It all gave me chills, and not the good kind. Fuck it. Anders could talk me down, but he couldn't perform miracles. And in that glassy, glossy room, with all those hungry eyes heating me up, what I needed was a miracle. Their hands were clasped together like they were praying. But they weren't praying. And if they were, it was for my downfall—they were praying for me to step back or back down. I was going to do no such thing.

"Mr. Mukherjee, with all due respect, that's just not our brand. We're not a faceless conglomerate. We're not a company that produces some product for the cheap. That's never been what we do. So why would we do it now?"

His reply was sharp and quick. "Growth, John. Strong, secular growth so this company can keep its solid reputation with shareholders."

I stormed out of the room as soon as the board meeting ended. What the hell else was I supposed to do—sit there and kowtow to those greedy pigs? I felt like I should've learned this lesson a while ago—sometimes, what you raise and care for won't love you back. It can get diseased, ill, or can even grow up strong and healthy just to punch you in your weak gut—the same gut you busted for over a decade to see it come to life. Those board members—those soulless white sharks—were just like everybody else. They loved you when they could take something, and they stopped loving you as soon as you had nothing left to give.

Was that just life, though? Why did that leave a pit in my empty fucking stomach? It was like I couldn't get even one genuine person to just be my friend because they liked me for who I was: Johnny. Come to think of it, I'd lost all my friends while I was raising the kids who both deeply resented me—my daughter and my company. Life's an ungrateful bitch sometimes. I was all for moving forward, but here and now, I couldn't seem to find where to go.

In the parking lot afterward, while I was standing blankly in my mixed-up rage, I got a call from Michelle Conifer.

"Hi, Michelle?"

"John!" She sounded like she was surprised I'd even picked up.

"Uh-huh."

"Listen, I only have a minute, but for the benefit… it'd be great if you brought Rachel, too. I was just calling to confirm you would because there'll be a seat open for her, and… it's in Lorne's honor, ya know." Then, she sniffled.

Oh god. Well, I couldn't take that kind of guilt on. "Yes, of course, of course," I assured her. Then I hung up as soon as I could. For some reason, I was sweating in that moment more than I had been in the boardroom. That lady was something else. She didn't have much in the way of social graces, but she was smart. Definitely smarter than Lorne. I wondered what their relationship was like when he was still alive; my P.I. didn't get much out of Michelle on that. Then, I wondered why I was wondering anything about that at all. I got in my car, cracked the windows, and drove away.

"Just sit back and listen to the hum of the wind. Maybe play a song you like." Anders was trying to put me in the moment. I guess he was a friend. "Ah, no engine sound—electric. You at least know you're doing one thing right."

Rachel slipped into my mind. There was no way in hell I was going to take her to the benefit. That could get dangerous and disruptive real quick. She was a ticking time bomb out in public with me.

"Don't worry about them, Johnnyboy. They don't deserve you or your ideas. It will all become right in due time."

Anders tried his best to put me at ease, but all his kind words washed away amidst the trouble in my mind.

Chapter 65

Reader, do you ever get the slight yet grandiose inclination that you are somehow… special? Because you just might be. But what would be the way to tell this? How would you verify what is truly special, then measure yourself against it—that frilly, arbitrary standard? There is no verification, reader, except your own.

No? What is stopping you from being your own standard-bearer? It is only with others that the very meaning of life and the acute destruction of it can be shared and experienced. You don't need them, but they very well need you. They need your vision to make them appear. They need your ears for their voices to be heard. They need your nerved skin to give a sensation. They are extensions of your existence, nothing else.

Even I like to have fun sometimes, and there is no time like the present. Occasionally, you need to know when not to listen to me, or anyone else for that matter. Demons are not just figures or people or ideas—they're impulses that live inside you, searching ceaselessly for a way out. You see, that's why it's common—so terribly, wonderfully common—for devils to roam clean streets and for ghastly tinctures of lust to be so easily disseminated for every soul to consume with an immense appetite. Demons live in everyone and everything, and if you don't get them out of your head, then you will be eaten from the inside and trampled from the outside.

There is danger everywhere. But danger, dear reader, defines life; a deadly life is the only one worth living, where walking the line between creation and destruction is the highest, surest form of existence.

Demons are not the exception; they are the rule. Do you think Lorne had demons? Do you think he is the ghost of one now, with subliminal influence beyond the grave? These ponderings may be easy for you to answer, but they are worthy questions all the same.

There are things coming, reader—things you may not understand. You may see things that bring up more questions for you than answers. The memorial benefit is approaching. Its time draws ever nearer as you read these words. This will be an event that may distort your preconceptions and wrap your mind around false pretenses—it may mangle the lurid perception you thought you had. No matter. Because there really is none, reader. It's all a construct.

You will read through things at the benefit you may not be ready for. This is okay, for what challenges you changes you for the better. This is always the case. All I ask, reader, is that you draw your own conclusions about the benefit and its ending. That will be the only way to freedom for you.

Chapter 66 – Rachel

I loved when my dad was flustered. I didn't know why I felt joy about that, but it didn't stop me from savoring every second of his nervous tics and animalistic pacing around the house. But seeing him frustrated only made me want to see it more. One sample was enough to make me want to eat and drink in his exhaustion, his pain. Was I wrong for that? I don't know—was it wrong to cheat on your spouse who did nothing but love you? I didn't think I was in the wrong for wanting to see righteous pain smeared across his twitching face and quivering body. He was definitely having a problem at work. It was also the night before Lorne's charity thing.

When I was high on edibles—the golden gummies I used to replace the weed my dad had taken from me—I kind of saw my dad as a kid. Skinny, tired, helpless, and lonely. He had a lot of money, a lot of respect, and a ton of accolades he'd gathered throughout his entrepreneurial career. He was one of those corny "hustlers" that sold T-shirts in high school and worked his way up from there. He was a schemer of all sorts, a mover and a slimy shaker who could convince anybody of anything—except for me, of course, his god-given kryptonite.

When I floated in the clouds, I could see him from above and through him, *almost* understanding him and his motives. I almost saw him for what he was—selfish but scared. And maybe those two traits were more linked than I thought. But I wasn't going to stop punishing him, bringing him to justice, until I got my mother back and things went back to normal. But I knew they wouldn't. I loved seeing him as a kid because I loved to see him helpless. Estelle said that in giving him what he deserved, I was also being kind to myself, and self-care is in too short of supply these days anyway.

It was all straightforward, really, but most people wouldn't get it. They wouldn't understand what he'd put me through. They wouldn't be able to wrap their heads around the soft spot somewhere deep within me that was still tender. Whatever. It was his loss. *I* was his loss.

I was picking out a dress for the big function the following night. So much of my clothing was casual or understated—I still liked my selection, though. I swiped through the many hangers, one by one. It became mindless after a while. Then, a flash of red lightning struck my eyes. "*That* one," Estelle said. I was totally on the same page; I needed to stand out at the benefit—to make sure a lot of eyeballs would turn and locate me quickly. A fiery red flash among the drab crowd. I would wear a statement, and I was going to make one, too.

Later that night when I walked downstairs, I could almost hear my dad's shot nerves sizzle as I approached him. He had his work clothes on, but at that time of night, they looked disheveled and messy. His face was twisted up and bleached white—that is, when he wasn't touching or rubbing it. This guy could have used a joint, but I wasn't going to help him out.

"You look like you could use a drink, Dad."

Biting his lip, his eyes were crazed.

Estelle didn't care one bit. "Just ask him. Don't be shy, baby." I started to bite my lip, too—kind of like my dad. Why did I feel like I had to be so careful here? I didn't think he suspected anything, and I didn't think it was a very sensitive situation. Regardless, I stayed on high alert. I felt like I was tiptoeing with my words around the wild man, the rich man with a five o'clock shadow and the bitter taste of failure fresh on his white lips. Ugh.

After no reply for a minute, he continued to stand there. I couldn't tell if he was constantly twitching or perfectly still. I'd studied him for a long time, watched him, taken note of his patterns, how he dealt with conversations, what he wanted out of any given situation. I thought I knew all of his default modes. Until now, I thought I'd seen all of his behaviors. How could someone be so blank and frenzied at the same time? I felt a weird shiver travel up my shoulders and neck.

He started walking away. "Don't let him go!" Estelle urged.

"Hey, Dad." I swallowed, but not out of fear. "Do you have any plans tomorrow night?"

That stopped him right in his tracks. Oh god, he was very still then. His whole body rotated around as if he were a statue. His eyes still had that wild look, but they were a bit sadder, startled. He waited a little longer. His eyes patrolled my body, my stance. And when he opened his mouth, his words came out as fast as his eyes when they jerked around me. "No. Not as of now. Why?"

I wasn't going to let his rushed pace back me into a corner.

"Slow him down."

"I was really just wondering... You seem stressed. Is everything all right?"

"I'm not stressed. I'm fine."

"Okay. Well, I just wanna make sure everything's okay. Did something happen at work?"

He grunted, followed by a swift, "No."

"Okay. Well, I'd hate to see you feel like... you were being treated unfairly at work."

"No, you wouldn't." He laughed coldly, exasperated. It was an angry chuckle, the kind that squirts out of your nostrils and mouth because you just can't keep it in your goddamn lungs where it belongs.

"Why do you say that?" I asked him another question. I liked to think of my question storms as more of a technique—a hailstorm, with each pellet leaving behind a tiny cut. The goal was to create a great red river to bask in by the end of it.

He just snorted, then his face darkened.

"Dad, why are you walking away again?"

"You really wanna know why, Rachel?" His voice was raised, and his body was tense. He was a pressure cooker.

"Why?"

Then, he locked eyes with me. It was like he was trying to stare me down. He was just gross sometimes. "Because everything I love hates me back. And what do I do? Huh?"

I breathed so he could hear it. It wasn't strained or aggressive, just a deliberate inhale so he could know I was doing it. Maybe he could feel it himself. As Estelle kept repeating, I "slowed down the pace."

"Listen… I wanted to know what you were doing tomorrow night so that maybe… maybe *we* could hang out."

John froze. He gulped, confused and defeated and skeptical of my kind words. "I'll… have to check my calendar."

"Why? What would you be doing?"

"I don't know," he said with that same exasperated laugh. "Why are you so insistent on tomorrow? We could always do it tonight."

"I just get the impression you're hiding something."

"About what? What would I be hiding?"

I made myself a statue, made sure I didn't flinch or stutter. I felt a tailwind behind me, like I was unstoppable—a goddess channeling the light and power of my mother. He just kinda stared back, bewildered. I spoke with the strength of a warrior poet, "Where will you be tomorrow night?"

Chapter 67 – Lorne

She knew. She knew about the benefit.

Not only that, she knew I was trying to hide it from her. She was so still, so sure, but the worst part was she was fucking right. She was planning something, teasing me about it. I was so sick of the charade, of all of them, everywhere in my life. I just wanted to scream and run away. Or maybe I wanted to eat and consume more and more and never stop filling my bottomless desires. That's what all of this made me want to do. But how could I be in the muck without getting sticky myself?

"Just keep playing it cool. Remember, you're supposed to be forgetting her, ignoring her, shunning her reprehensible behavior. Then, and only then, she won't have power over you, and she'll either realize the sacrifices you've made *or* she won't be worthy of you anyway. Either way, you win."

"I'll have to check my calendar," I said. "Otherwise, I don't know." I shrugged my shoulders, gave her a 'meh' look, and turned to walk away for the last time.

"Hey, wait!" she yelled. "Dad? Dad… fine! You're a dick anyway! The only thing you know how to do is lie. You've never done anything original in your life!"

Then, just like that, the egg was cracked. I kept walking away slowly while she continued to yell at me and stomp. She hit me with every insult, reasonable or otherwise. And with that, I was another step closer—another string cut. She'd come crawling back eventually.

But how did she know about Lorne's memorial?

"It's everywhere in town," Anders said. *Damn, of course.* What the hell was I supposed to do? Motherfuck. I couldn't have her go there, with me, next to me, with all those important people. A couple of our investors would even be there. God, what would they think? Nothing good. Why was I so scared of Rachel? She was a force, a nuisance, because she would do anything. Away from her, I pondered, then I paced some more behind closed doors. At the end of it all, I had one choice. "If you give her this ultimatum, you'll regret it, John. There's a better way of going ab—"

"Agghh!"

"Don't do something stupid, Johnny, come on."

Just shut up right now. If Rachel is willing to mud wrestle, I can, too. She was willing to do anything? So was I. I could play her game and win. Something came over me like a shadow. God, it was a rush.

Downstairs, I found her in the same place. She was thinking. I couldn't imagine her thoughts were about anything but me. I didn't waste any time. "Rachel," I said, more like a command than a question. She perked up like an animal about to get fed. She was grimacing with a twisted face, angered but also soft and, under it all, smiling. "I know you know about the benefit."

"Mm-hmm."

"John, just take a step back." Anders was always the de-escalator. Smart man.

"You know why I don't want to take you."

"No, why?"

"Stop playing games. All you wanna do is hurt me. That's all you've been doing."

"That's actually not true."

"Well, I've been hurt enough."

"What do you mean?"

"Rachel, stop..." Desperation twisted in my gut, and I blurted, "I'll give you all the weed you want if you don't go to the benefit tomorrow."

Her grimace, her twisted, fake contortions in her cheeks, and her beautiful, thin brows morphed all at once into a grinch-like smile. It covered her whole face. She'd just been fed what she wanted, and I had nothing left to give, nothing left to offer in the way of what her bottomless pit of a body craved. I fell into her trap, into her endless wormhole that hungered for me. I didn't have the strength to swear, run, or cry. Or I guess I just didn't want to. I felt kind of frozen at that moment. *Shit*.

"I have all the weed I need, Pops." Then, turning away, she said, "See you tomorrow night," and disappeared. She sauntered back up to her room, the place where she hid and tented her fingers, biding her time.

"Start breathing. Make calls, take action," said Anders. And I should have listened to him.

Chapter 68 – Detective Perry

On the morning of the event, with the setup volunteers there, I scoped out the venue with my guys. Well, we did more than scope it out. This was too good of an opportunity to pass up. Michelle was there. She was very watchful and outwardly friendly. We shook hands vigorously. She wanted to meet all of my guys, who all wanted to be inconspicuous. It was a more intimate meeting than I would have liked, but not more intimate than what I'd planned for.

"Perry! Make yourself at home! Just don't bug the place, ha!" She cracked herself up, and her inflection was a kidding tone. But we both knew she wasn't joking, and I knew she suspected we were up to something. In reality, we were on duty, with a job at hand. Once again, I'd be remiss to deny the law or justice. Sometimes, you just had a good feeling about an investigation, about a decision or an event.

Back at the station, I got to sit down with the chief in his office. This was a high-profile case, so I had all eyes on me. But unfortunately, I wasn't getting the resources I thought this case deserved. It was all in the name of justice, regardless. The chief had a handlebar mustache. I would joke with him and say he belonged in the eighties. He looked like a stereotype among stereotypical cops. All he was missing were some aviators.

He slapped a folder on his desk as I sat down. I combed through it quickly. Finally, he clicked his tongue and opened his mouth. "What's the newest with the profile on Kalopoulos?"

"One development is that, after talking with Mayor Williams, I got the inclination he doesn't like John. I don't think it's personal, but their interests are not aligned, and that's concrete at this point."

"Inclination? What are the facts? What did he say, exactly?" The chief was a thorough man, detailed. That's why he was in his position.

"Why didn't you give him the quote right away? Huh, Perry? Get your head together on the details, or you'll be out of a job soon!" The Sarge was energetic today.

"Here's the exact quote, sir." I slid him a note I transcribed during my talk with the mayor.

"This just doesn't mean much, Perry. There's still nothing definitive about Williams's official disposition here. In fact, *Kalopoulos* is the one who's a lot more likely to have known or taken part. You know this, right?"

I wasn't quite sure what he was talking about. I must have missed something. "Um, yeah. Yeah, I figured that, sir. But why do you think so?"

"What? That Kalopoulos should be a suspect?"

"Yeah."

The chief scoffed. "Lorne wasn't going to win. He knew this. They worked closely, regardless. Lorne was his ticket to a bigger presence in the area—his business has been wanting to establish a building out here for as long as I can remember. He'd be clamoring at the city clerk's and mayor's office all the time—either him or one of his cronies—looking for a permit and a license to sell and distribute here. Mayor Williams's platform was always in direct opposition to John."

"But why would John *kill* Lorne? Even if Lorne was going to lose, why would John have reason to commit that level of crime? He wouldn't have anything to gain, would he?"

"You need to study more, Perry."

"Yes, sir."

The chief scoffed again and said, "John can't have that platform lose publicly again. He just can't. It would set a terrible precedent for his odds in the future and would make his company have to go through underhanded routes to try and penetrate this market."

"Still seems drastic," I said.

"Not for a guy like John."

When we finished our conversation, I thanked him as usual and left. I'd never once considered John. Not him for anything. I didn't think it possible—that is, until the chief told me it was. From then on, I didn't know what to believe. I didn't know who was involved. All I knew was that *someone* was involved in the death of Lorne Conifer, and it was someone inside Lorne's sphere of influence. Who it was? I had to figure that out. How I was going to do it? I didn't quite know.

Motives could be ascribed from all angles. The coroner said it was death by overdose. Caffeine overdose. I had my guys searching for caffeine anhydrous purchases everywhere—online and in retailers both far and wide.

The bottom line: I was going to get to the bottom of this. The benefit could be crucial to finding the source. The benefit could bring up some clues. I was going to keep a keen eye out for anything that could lead me in the right direction. At the memorial benefit, I just knew that many potential leads could come together.

Here was my goal and my hunch: I would arrest Michelle within the week. I would have enough on her to put her in cuffs finally. It would happen, goddammit. Michelle Conifer would be arrested on suspicion of murder in the first degree. It would happen, and I'd get my prize. It would happen, and I'd get my recognition. They would see it in the papers. They would all see it in the papers everywhere—the nationwide scandal that no one could solve but the sharp detective who stayed by the book.

Chapter 69 – Michael

I had the speech prepared. *A platform*. The name itself conjured thoughts of elevation and isolation, all while having a *connection* with the audience. With a platform, the eyes and ears that follow you are like active receptors—if your pollen is potent enough, it will cling to them to then be spread even further. The pollen in my speech was a part of me, a big one that hurt when I got it onto the page.

I guess that was why Ernest Hemingway said there was nothing to writing because all you had to do was "sit down at a typewriter and bleed."

The words of the speech flowed onto the page easily and heavily, but when I saw what the paper contained, what I'd channeled into it, I was appalled and shocked—it had my vital life force on it, imbued within it. I was scared to take pictures of it, fearful of duplicating the energy into a digital world that could spread it so far. But why did I not want my message to spread, to grow? Was that not why I'd written it? I didn't even want to touch it for too long because its force left an imbalance in my hand that felt like a shock—it was both hot and cold and made me immediately close my eyes when I felt that vital sting.

That paper of my written speech gave me something I'd never had before. It was a reflection, a dubious and daring mirror that showed not myself, but my life and the consequences of my red cuts and purple scars. It showed me as a battered boy, and I knew that's what I was. I didn't want to be one—it made me a victim. I didn't want to believe I had these wounds until I had to, until I saw them in front of me and couldn't ignore what I had to face. This was a revelation; I didn't care if it appealed to the eaters and drinkers in the audience because this was my part, my time, and no one else's. I thought it would leave an impression, a hairline crack in their minds, some tether of understanding between their souls and mine. It would be strong, thin, and vital, like a spider's sacred web.

I was in the car with my mom on the way there, shaking. She didn't seem to notice the vibrating tension oozing out of my body, my ghostly face, nor my shaky breaths. She almost seemed elated, not in a confident way, but crazed—determined, fixed, and oblivious. Then, something rose up from within her—an impulse, a nagging thought that bit her and made her react.

"Do you have your speech?"

"Yes. I do."

"She has no idea what you wrote," said Beel, "but she's not gonna like it when she finds out. What are you prepared to do against the backlash, the carnage that ensues?" Another shiver traveled up my back and into my mind and soul.

"How long is it, roughly?"

"You're screwed. You need to make something up. Or just say it's a surprise." Then, Beel laughed, mocking and malicious. "Man, I don't think you can handle this. You could always abort the mission. Nothing wrong with being a coward if you stay unharmed, right?"

"Umm," I hesitated, too preoccupied with the weight on my shoulders to be fielding her picky question. "Uhh… it's not that long. Just generic."

"Oh *god*," Beel groaned. "What the hell does *generic* even mean?"

"Okay. Well, it needs to stay under ten minutes." Thank god she was still fixated and oblivious, not even considering my time on stage as much of a variable at all. "Oh. And don't be afraid to cry. It's better that way, Michael. You need to show how you really feel. It's important."

We arrived at the venue. It was a function hall at an upscale restaurant—a dainty bar at one end, a small makeshift stage and podium, and high ceilings throughout. Everything was clean, and the air smelled faintly of flowers and fruit. It was intimate while still being spacious, and at the entrance was a picture of my late father, smiling with sunglasses next to his precious wife and only son—smart people, loving people, vulnerable people.

"Stand near the picture of your family, get the people filing in to recognize you," Beel said. His remark turned out to be more of a premonition than a command. As I sat in the near-empty room, my mom came up to me after a carefully frantic once-over of the hall.

"Hey Mikey, once the people start coming in, you and I are gonna stand at the front entrance, sort of near the picture of your dad. Make sure you say thank you and smile. Okay?" I think I nodded slowly to her. "Okay, I'll let you know when it's time."

I felt like I dreamed that scene, almost like Beel himself manufactured it in my head—of my mom with her work glasses on, in a rare instance of her hair and makeup done, urging me with all of her will, unblinking. I felt a force within her I never had before—something that was unlocked yet inescapable. For the first time in maybe ever, I felt as though my mom was exerting a strong amount of agency over her environment, laughing, pointing, commanding, watching. *Did my dad die just for my mother to step into his role?* I didn't like this train of thought, but what did that matter at all? When did my feelings have a bearing on anything that happened in my life? There was a slow boil within me, and the steam needed to escape the confines of my body somehow. I wanted people to see it.

I thought of crumpling up my speech—of trashing it, forgetting it, leaving it in the waste bin and in the back of my mind like sludge. But why did I write it in the first place? I stood by Lorne Conifer's giant teeth on the welcome display. They were clean and inviting, aspirational almost. They were polished and perfect. They showed the face of someone who didn't really exist. Those pearls were more of an idea than anything physical. They painted a picture in the viewer's head of civility and straight roads—stability and old oak trees all in a line. And it was a complete lie, a fantasy, a vicious seduction. Those teeth, aside from being spotless and sturdy, were forceful and sharp; they held pain, and they were ready to inflict it at a grim moment's notice.

The people I smiled at and greeted alongside my mom were there to celebrate and mourn—the faceless sheep, there to honor someone they didn't know. In a twisted way, my dad was still winning beyond the grave, still gathering a crowd and eliciting tears and smiles—his own type of art. He painted expressions on people, he played them like instruments, and like a good musician, he practiced and performed religiously.

I looked at my mom. She was wearing the widest grin I'd ever seen on her face. That had to be fake, but I'd never known my mom to be a faker. She had a shit ton of flaws, but she was always principally, faithfully real.

"Why do you think your mother is doing this?" Beel asked with a prodding iron. "Why do you think she's putting this on? Do you think it's out of the kindness of her bottomless heart?"

I watched as more people filed past me into the function hall, toward the bar. Then, with their drinks in hand, they gathered around the vases of expensive flowers like restless hummingbirds.

Chapter 70 – Michelle

Everything seemed to be situated in a decent place. All was working well, and the people seemed happy. The bartender was working double time, but that was okay because I'd paid for the best. It was necessary tonight. Until this point, I'd never felt like I needed to win people over. Tonight was different—this situation was different. As happy as I wanted them to be, the many people who continued to pile into the venue served as numbers and tools. I didn't much care for that approach in any facet of life, but tonight was different. Tonight, I was stricken and attacked by the law, and all I planned to do was defend myself.

The tools were well-dressed and in their pretentious places. The room smelled of fine liquor and vibrant gardens, optimal for physiological comfort as far as humans go. So, when I hit the stage, everything was in place, as I'd planned. Of course, I had some contingency plans, too, because I wasn't a cretin, and I wouldn't be taken for a fool. This situation, this desperate corner I was backed into, called for calculated measures and bold strokes. I was that bold woman to take up Lorne's mantle. Cue the gentle tears. It established trust and familiarity.

"Hello, everyone," I said through the mic to the filled room, just as I'd practiced so many times before. I sniffled with a bashful smile. *Yes, bashful. That was me.* "First off, I just want to thank you all for showing up and supporting my family, our cause, and each other in this time of need. I know I'm relatively new to this community, so you opening up with welcoming arms means the world to me. It truly does. My name is Michelle Conifer, Lorne's wife. My son Michael is sitting right there in the glasses... oh god," I said as the sniffles got louder, and my eyes welled with kaleidoscopic, saline bubbles. "I'm sorry. I really am, this is..."

Then, I started to full-blown cry in the middle of my opening. I'd planned on crying, but I didn't expect it to be this loud or this hard. Every tear felt heavy and magnified by the two hundred sweeping eyes. I just went with it, mainly because I had to, like some force had sucked me into an inconvenient emotion. They all watched me and hung on to every snivel and croaked word. The stillness was shattering—not even a cough from the audience could be heard. It made my thoughts race and my mouth slow up even more.

The voice mumbled something that broke through to my ears as I froze there in the silence. "The boy, the man, the *charity*, Michelle. Don't wander from the charity. Your parents are watching. Where is Detective Perry? How many people are in the audience? No one can blame you, not even Lorne. Let the tears flow on the biggest stage and allow them to become an ocean that engulfs their hearts indifferently. They're commiserating right now. This is good."

"Anyways, I love you all for coming out here and showing your love. You guys are doing a great thing by being here and seeing all of your enthusiastic faces is a healing presence for me and my family. For our first speaker of the night, I'd like to introduce Doctor Barbara Byers-Muthe, founder of the Byers-Muthe Cancer Foundation. She runs one of the leading cancer foundations in Colorado and is a recipient of half…" As I spoke, I found a calm center to cling to until I finally handed the stage off for the first time to Barbara. The applause started to rattle in. Then, somehow, people began to stand, still clapping.

They gave *me*, Michelle Conifer, a standing ovation.

With all the heaping trouble I'd been through the past few years, I was vindicated. I was stronger. *Where is Detective Perry?* I thought as I stepped down and traipsed toward the seat alongside Michael, my parents, Lorne's parents, and his sister.

I glanced over at one of the VIP tables, where Perry should have been sitting. I got a little more worked up when I saw his vacant chair next to the mayor, who was now intently listening to Barbara. It was a good thing she was a captivating speaker; otherwise, these people would have thought I was some maniac, staring and fixating on something imaginary that kept fluttering around the room. Finally, I looked over toward the bar on the far side of the function hall. There he was. The detective had on a chintzy sport coat and beaten leather shoes. Perry had one cocktail in each hand he carried back from the glitzy wall of glasses and lights that acted as the backdrop for the bartender.

"He's frustrated, Michelle. He's numbing his sorrows and confusion. How could his only suspect garner such tempestuous applause? He has no answer. Your mom looks good and healthy tonight. Be thankful."

I focused on Barbara and sat back in my chair. I may have even been smiling.

"Don't smile too broadly, Michelle. Wow, Barbara is in great shape. Why are Michael's shoulders so tense? You could use a cigarette after this. Just one. There's someone approaching you."

Before I could hold my breath, there was a tap on my shoulder. It was my mom, whispering with a small half smile. "Michelle, there's someone here to see you."

I looked up, and there he was again, this time intimately close, extending his arm down to me.

"Hey, Mrs. Conifer," he started. "That was a great speech." When he talked, it was like he was the only one in the entire room. The shuffling and clinking and Barbara's strong voice were drowned out when Perry spoke down to me in my chair, a soft look of sympathy smeared on his face.

"He sees the progress, the reaction. It's all working for you. You were right." *Was the voice in my head trying to flatter me?*

"Oh, thank you. Really, that means a lot. I think Lorne's watching over us right now… he's making this go right."

"That's amazing. Listen, any chance I could talk to you for a quick second?"

I figured he was about to apologize for prying for so long. *What else and why else would he want to pull me aside?* I thought it was safe. "Of course."

"Hi," the detective said with a smile, "you must be Michelle's parents."

"Dad, Mom, this is Detective Perry. He's been helping out a lot lately." They looked pleased and confused.

I went with him to the annex, drink in hand, but I had yet to take a sip. He didn't take a drink either. It was quieter out there, and he had an easy way about him. I was more comfortable with the fact that I was infallible that night, above accusation and disdain, standing on top of the community's pity for me, a widow and a single, educated mother.

"You've really done a good job here. This will be a great thing for the community with all the money coming in. And also, you're bringing people together. Lorne would have loved this."

"He still does."

"What do you mean?"

"He does love it, just not from earth."

He nodded like he'd just heard a foreign language. "Do you have any spiritual views, Mrs. Conifer?"

"Please, just call me Michelle."

"Of course."

"Well, I believe that all life is sacred. And essential."

"That's amazing."

"I'm sorry I cried so much up there. I just still can't believe Lorne is gone from us. And I can't believe you'd suspect me of—oh god!" It was important to remember that sobbing made me vulnerable. Humans could trust you more, and even someone like Detective Perry wasn't immune to biology.

"Hey, hey, hey..." He made a face and reached for my shoulder. He placed his hand there. It was a light, sympathetic touch.

"Please don't touch me!"

"I'm so sorry."

"I'm going back to my seat now."

"Wait, please... yeah, um, you're a professor at Briggiton, right?" Suddenly, he was like a little kid, stumbling forward, hunched, desperate. I made him so. I shrank him. I owned him tonight.

"Adjunct, yeah."

"Okay. Wait, wait, wait. Hold on, please, just one more second."

"I need to get back to my family. Maybe you could do the same thing right about now. At least your kids have a father," I snapped.

He was stone-faced. Something about my comments hollowed his eyes. From an angle, under a certain light, he looked like a single-minded shark that already had death in its black pupils. "Is it true that Briggiton University has stores of caffeine anhydrous in its research lab—on a shelf in Closet A of its noncontrolled compounds and chemicals?"

I did nothing. I thought nothing. I simply walked back to my chair to sit with the lead table, mourn Lorne's death, and celebrate his life with the rest of the family. I felt nothing except a dryness in my mouth. The cocktail still in my hand was of no use. Nothing was of any use. Barbara was still on stage, but I heard nothing. I didn't dare look back—back toward…

"Is something wrong, Michelle? What did he say to you?" Everybody at the table was looking at me, including Michael. He didn't have his glasses on for some reason.

"He wants to look more handsome and grown-up for the crowd," the voice said.

"It was nothing, Mom. He just…"

"And with that, I'd like to reintroduce Michelle back up to the stage. Thank you so much, everybody. The generosity tonight is truly remarkable. You're all amazing!" Applause erupted, then more heads turned my way. The whole crowd knew where I was sitting, and somehow, the overwhelming sympathy from earlier seemed to harden into scrutiny. Everyone, staring and hollow, wore the same stone face Perry had used on me a moment ago. I went to the stage because I was obligated to do so. I was called, and therefore, I had to go up there.

Perry wasn't giving in, but this wasn't over yet.

Chapter 71

It was the perfect time. I was around all these fake people—people with no thoughts. They were more like thought vampires, sucking the intelligence out of those around them. Disgusting and pathetic. I found it funny how the emptiest among us were the most judgmental, but that's where we were.

We sat with the mayor and a few other stiff people with pliable minds. It was empty people who influenced other empty people—that was it. It was also empty people who usually controlled things and other people, exactly like my dad did. Their world was the outside world, plain and simple. Once they saw a ledge, they would grab it and climb—climb for all it was worth like the monkeys they were. That night, I would expose my father as a ledge. Anyway, he needed to lose more in order to rebuild himself fully from the ground up—right now, he was just a disgusting swine. Maybe he'd even cry for my mother back. We'd have to see.

Michael's mom traipsed back onto the stage. I had to clap for her because everybody else did.

"She looks frumpy," said Estelle. "Also, why is Mayor Williams smiling so heavily? He looks like he's just won a contest, not attending a memorial."

If the mayor was younger, he might have actually been kind of attractive. He was still pretty broad under that suit. The woman started talking pithily, then my dad got up—probably to head for the bar. Perfect.

I heard muffled cries that were barely audible to me, yet everybody else seemed to be tuned in and attentive, so I mirrored them, but only because I wanted to. "He was a strong man, someone who was sensitive enough to pick up on emotions, and he had..." *Sniffle, sniffle, small sob.* "He had all of the tools necessary to deal with people. Lorne served in the Navy for four years, where he was then honorably discharged after continuing to struggle with Lyme disease, a battle he'd fought for nearly all his life... There were too many 'Lorneisms' to count—Lorneisms being beautiful sayings that came from him during the..." *sniffle, sniffle, croak,* "during the simple times of life. Even when I was frowning or crying, he'd say my face was like art. I'll never forget the way he made me feel, and I know so many others feel the same way."

"I can just tell this nerdy hag was abused." I wasn't expecting that from Estelle. She was a loose cannon, but she also shot pretty straight, and this would have been huge had she been right. I didn't know what to make of that, so I just let it pass. Instead, I got up and walked over to Williams unsuspectingly, like I was on my way to the ladies' room.

I crept behind him then approached his ear. I was too close to him to turn back now, especially because once he heard me, I was locked onto the mayor's eyes—big, dark, and accusatory. It was clear I was going to tell him something, maybe something important. And I *was* going to—I had to. I had the medicine on the tip of my tongue, sitting and swishing, ready to be spat out to the right ears.

***

I told Rachel to say the words she soon uttered. Why? Why do you think, reader? Because problems are the default. What are "problems" but the building blocks of life itself? Don't look at me as an adversary! Better yet, help me. Or don't. But either way, there will be pain you'll wish would go away, and as soon as it does, you'll inflict some yourself.

You're a vessel, not a terminal, reader, and you're my vessel. Denying it is foolish.

***

Mayor Williams looked at me, disturbed, annoyed, intrigued, and—most of all—genuinely spooked. I'd spoken my truth. It needed to get out, and it finally fell upon the receptive ears of a suit who could do something about it. The rest of the table didn't hear me, but they looked at me, and they watched as I walked away while the mayor agonizingly contemplated what I'd just whispered to him.

In the bathroom mirror, I saw a face done up that didn't have to be. It was natural, a little splotchy in some parts, and there was a freckle I didn't care for. But it was a pretty face. The older I got, the more I grew into a not-so-miniature version of my Mediterranean birth giver, the dark-skinned duchess, the sultry go—

A wave welled up inside me, and I closed down everything just to stop it. It was a tsunami, and I had too much makeup on to let it out at this function. At least Estelle was there to calm my nerves, to quell the memories of her, the feelings they evoked.

"You did the right thing, Rachel. The future can be yours now because, deep down, you know you were right to take action. Now just focus on what that scrumptious, meaty mayor is gonna do about it."

And what did I tell Mayor Williams? What were the words whispered to warrant such a look toward my father? Well, the simple answer is I took fear and made it real. I analyzed and embodied my father—his pain, his future, and what would hurt him most. I took that, balled it up, and threw it into the universe's gaping jaws.

In other words, I told Mayor Williams that John Kalopoulos, my father, was the one who killed Lorne Conifer.

He seemed shocked, and it made me feel so, so good. His reaction was like a perfect painting. His face was like art at my simple words.

***

Remember this: You don't know what you would like to see. Michelle is about to break down, and the sickening thing is that you're rooting for it; you want to see that unfold in your mind and watch the problem expound itself. It is something transcendent, beautiful, and sickening within you that impels you to root for chaos—like a sports-crazed child. You root for me. You are just as ghoulish as I. You barely even differ from me, reader. I am just infinitely more powerful than you, and you are subject to my whims.

Watch as I tactfully weave this scene into a nightmare. Tremble before the confluence of the veil and the divine, a ghastly marriage of two unlike worlds that only I can set into motion.

Chapter 72

I was called to the stage but dreaded being associated with my cringeworthy mother. I rose from my chair, and all the loathsome faces turned my way. Why was my mother so insistent on bowing down to the toxic and battered memory of my late father, the monster? She looked at Lorne through rose-colored glasses—stained and tattered. As a captor, she was so obedient. But me—I was not... or less so. I was still a child, a ragdoll, a victim.

Who was my mother to deny that to a whole community, to the world? What was the truth if there was such a thing? And did my pain exist to a point where I could verify it? Did it exist even if I couldn't project it onto others—to this star-studded, bubbly crowd? Did it matter? Was my pain a pawn? Could I turn it into something worthwhile? Or was it a detestable human construct, something to give to victims like a sedative? The word "pain" was like opium to the masses, searing a victim complex on the soul of the wretched, brown world.

"Reader, are you reading this? Are you seeing into him? He's as fallible and impure as dirt!"

Beel was wrong. He was dead wrong. I was the heart and soul of my own world. I was a king if I said I was. I could meld and shape as I pleased—my own soul and psyche, the antidote to the whims of vicious externals.

Lightning crept through my veins. The grief of a torn nation clashed with the heights of the greatest triumph. And the rage inside gave me strength. The storm inside me was unexplainable, and it gave me chaos and confidence. Confidence.

I walked to the stage, and the audience seemed plastic and still and lifeless. I was conscious of everything around me without being bound to it. I only needed myself. In front of me were the biggest decision-makers, the doubters, the well-wishers, the spidery opinion-spewers, and the rest of the crowd—but they were only distractions from my mission and my catharsis, while also being vital pawns in a game only I knew how to play.

"Michael, you're playing a dangerous game. I'd just take inventory of yourself before you do anything reckless."

I situated the whole of my essence before the microphone that overlooked the crowd of even more "microphones"—some tall, some light, but all of them ready to mindlessly perpetuate the ripple of my unholy crusade—all of them ready to blare my message of my father once and for all.

"My mother is waving, let me out!" I sneered at Beel's final, feeble attempt to scramble my mind—that most vital bastion I'd tempered on my own through lonesome trials of fire. He wanted to discredit me, to make me think he was me and that, really, I was possessed by something not of this world. But he was a liar and a thief, and I'd already fortified myself enough to have vanquished him.

With fists gripped tightly around my sacred scripture, I caught a glimpse of my mother, front row and off to the side, smiling statically and stonily—she was unmovable in her brick wall posture and plastered-on smile.

The beast pleaded and wailed like I'd never heard before, and it was all nonsense such as, "I don't know what you're doing but give me my body back!" and "Curse you, Beel! Curse you!" I chuckled. *As if a real human sixteen-year-old would ever talk like that.* Beel would foil me no further. I would choose to have him serve as a guide only—he taught me to overcome myself while also being the one who was overcome himself.

"Hi, everyone," I said. "My name is Michael Conifer…"

I continued my speech's introduction, just as I'd practiced so fervently and for so long before this bright moment. The lights cascaded over my face like a handful of close, embracing suns.

What were these tethers being undone, being ripped apart to free me? It felt good. It felt liberating. I had millions of eyeballs—cameras, sensors, beams, lasers, nets, and lenses—directed at me. They descended on me, yet I rose above them and their mechanistic scrutiny. They were fake propagators of exactly what they captured and *nothing* else—not thinkers nor creators nor inventors—reprehensible receptors, cowering before the one who dared to utter a new word. I was the variable in the equation no one had factored in, the one who'd returned scarred and strong from the gaping pits of wan hopes yonder.

I was done with my personal intro, so I started to unleash that which so corroded my heart. It was both compulsive and planned, caked in the dirtiest and lowest of desires; yet it aimed to express the highest triumphs of the soul over the depravities of the earth.

Someone was going down tonight.

***

I wasn't in my body. I was somewhere else.

I heard my voice, but it was Beel who commanded the speech, talking to the crowd and thinking his own thoughts inside of *my* head. I had no parallel or precedent to compare this to. I was panicking because there was nothing else to do. I was possessed and dispossessed, drowning in a sharp, coherent grave. This wasn't nonsense or insanity—this was something else entirely. Nonsense was lazy delirium, and insanity was a gross miscalculation of reality. This, to my chagrin and hatred, was neither of those wretched things. I was displaced by the monster in my head.

He won, reader. And everybody saw him win. Their ears were flooded with Beel's very will. I continued to speak, begrudgingly… and zealously?

I saw my mom stir with an animalistic panic crawling all over her body, but I continued to tell what my heart knew and what Beel wanted to project. "My dad—he was... an abuser. He only desired accolades and applause—and he never *once* paid attention when it was the least bit inconvenient for him. I feel myself..." I sniffled as the memories crept in—dark pictures of towering figures, winged vampires, blood like vapor in the air, stiffening my lungs, sinking my body slowly into the grave. The crowd disappeared. I had only my words that were forced to spill from me—they were me. And I hated those words. I hated it. What had been done to me—I couldn't forgive.

I felt like I was ridding myself of toxins, but was that really good for the audience? Did it even matter? "My father, Lorne..." I sniffled, trying to get the hard ball of sludge to pass from my throat. And all the while, *the eyes*—they stared. The ceaseless receptors were unfiltered, unscrupulous. All these countless eyes—blue, green, mostly brown—wanted to do was take the energy I doled out, save it, label it, then use it as a stone for my tomb or a stair to climb.

There were no servants. There were no heroes. There were no leaders in the mob I looked down upon. Whatever they would do with these bleeding words, I didn't know. Was I up there in front of the many eyes because I had to be? No. I could have declined, I could have stopped, I could have refused the speech altogether. But I didn't. Something forceful compelled me forward.

I walked in something like a dream. I rose higher while my body sank; it stayed down on the stage while I left my body and told the truth—about me, about my father, about my life.

I told it all in front of the audience, and Beel's voice slowly quieted to a whisper until I couldn't hear him any longer, only the crowd's applause.

I scanned the crowd and saw many faces. I saw Rachel. She stared at me. There was something in her eyes like satisfaction, catharsis, and maybe admiration. She smiled and winked at me, and that was all the applause I needed.

I found my mother. She shook her head slowly, staring into the distance with eyes like fading stars, waiting for their inevitable return to the blank oblivion of space.

Among the rampant reactions from the crowd, I saw Detective Perry leave. Just before he left, though, there was a look on his face—like triumph. He felt he won, and maybe he did. With the power and content of my speech, maybe it would give him reason enough to arrest his primary suspect, my mother. Where I would be left after that, I didn't know. I would probably go live with my grandparents, who were in the Denver area. That would have to do for me, the wanderer. But starting anew would be enough because after every clap and cheer from the audience, I knew *I* was enough. I knew I no longer needed applause to feel triumphant, even though finally having it gave me prickles of pleasure everywhere. I would be fine. I would speak from then on with a strong tongue. With a tougher constitution, I would look at the world through steely eyes.

But I would never lose my laughter. In fact, I would regain it after this whole ordeal. And I would reclaim my whole life. And I owe it all to the act of facing myself. Facing my own monster. The one that made himself at home in my head would, from then on, be used to my advantage. I would not be without trouble or struggle, but I would be stronger. I would be better, and I would know how to improve even more.

I faced my monster. In front of the crowd, in front of the town, the detective, my mother, and the rest.

There was nothing I couldn't handle.

Chapter 73

And what have we learned from this story, reader? It is that there are monsters in all of us, and they seek to become us every single day. But the monster of destruction is also the monster of creation. Choose wisely, and you will see. Choose foolishly, and you will also see—me. I will always be there with you. Alongside you, I will stride—ahead, above, and below.

I am you, reader. I am who you are. If you are reading this, I have engulfed you already.

I constructed this whole story out of a desire to make you see yourself. I wanted you to make Michael's realization; I want you to have his arc. Conquer your monster and get on with your life. Amidst the pain, there is hope. Among the snakes of suffering lie a brighter horizon.

Exactly how Michael scanned the audience and what he saw is how the characters ended up. Rachel saw a strength in the truth Michael told, and what is true always wins, reader. In Michael's truth he told on the stage, Rachel saw what was possible in her own father—catharsis and forgiveness. It took a long time, but their relationship mended over many realizations later. Understanding, reader, is the key to the sky, unlocking potential from within to then soar beyond your monsters.

I hope you've understood me better after reading this. I hope you have gotten better acquainted with me, the monster in your head. I want you to suffer and succeed. Those two things are linked, not disparate. Suffering and success.

And what am I left with at the end of this story, you may ask? Well, I am the monster. I will always be fine. The monster will live on. Chaos will always lurk and reign and gnash its teeth at the world of order. Your world teeters on a cacophony of quivering strings. But you? You *can* be steadfast, reader. You can be strong in the face of chaos. I've given you all the tools.

Thank you for finally becoming my friend.

About the Author

Nick Oliveri treasures the unique potential behind every person's story and values sharing those tales with the world. Skilled at crafting sentences that bring his characters and their narratives to life, he is passionate about the beauty the written word has to offer.

Nick is a former startup co-founder dedicated to the onset of the circular economy. Born in Ukraine but having grown up in Massachusetts, Nick currently resides in San Jose, CA, and loves wine, hockey, surfing, philosophy, art, and of course, reading and writing.

Nick has more novels in the works, so keep an eye out for his future writings.

Other Works By Nick Oliveri

The Conjurer

Her

A Boy Just Like Me

Life's a Rip-off: A Book of Poetry

A Genocide Too Small

CPSIA information can be obtained
at www.ICGtesting.com
Printed in the USA
LVHW101612190323
741978LV00001B/7